LONG TIME
GONE

Books by Mary Connealy

The
CIMARRON
Legacy
BOOK TWO

LONG TIME GONE

MARY CONNEALY

BETHANYHOUSE

a division of Baker Publishing Group
Minneapolis, Minnesota

Published by Bethany House Publishers
11400 Hampshire Avenue South
Bloomington, Minnesota 55438
www.bethanyhouse.com

Bethany House Publishers is a division of
Baker Publishing Group, Grand Rapids, Michigan

Printed in the United States of America

Library of Congress Cataloging-in-Publication Data
Names: Connealy, Mary, author.
Title: Long time gone / Mary Connealy.
Description: Minneapolis, Minnesota : Bethany House, a division of Baker
    Publishing Group, [2017] | Series: The Cimarron Legacy ; Book 2
Identifiers: LCCN 2016036495| ISBN 9780764230080 (cloth) | ISBN 9780764211829
    (trade paper)
Subjects: | GSAFD: Love stories. | Christian fiction.
Classification: LCC PS3603.O544 L66 2017 | DDC 813/.6—dc23
LC record available at https://lccn.loc.gov/2016036495

Scripture quotations are from the King James Version of the Bible.

Cover design by Dan Pitts
Cover photography by Mike Habermann Photography, LLC

Author is represented by Natasha Kern Literary Agency.

17 18 19 20 21 22 23   7 6 5 4 3 2 1

Long Time Gone is dedicated to my grandson, Luke. He has the best smile and the sweetest heart of any little two-year-old boy in the world.

1

Abandoning his sister to save his brother, Justin Boden felt as gutshot as Cole.

He left Heath Kincaid behind to find his little sister, Sadie, feeling as though he were tearing himself in half to make that choice. But he had only minutes to get his big brother home to stop the bleeding and tend his wound. Still, leaving her behind went against everything he knew about caring for his family.

"No." Cole's words were slurred. "Sadie." He drooped forward until he almost lay on his horse's neck.

Justin gritted his teeth. The outlaw who had gotten a bullet into Cole was tied over his saddle, its reins tied to Cole's horse. But Sadie was missing. So Justin had to ask if there was more than one villain chasing them.

Justin grabbed the reins out of Cole's hands and turned up the trail. Leading two horses, one with his wounded brother, trailed by one with the unconscious outlaw, forced Justin forward—the trail was too narrow to look back.

Cole didn't have long. If the gutshot was a bad one, it might already be too late.

Sadie was missing, and if the man they'd taken prisoner wasn't alone, killers might be on her trail—or have her even now. Even King Solomon would have a hard time deciding what to do about this.

Turning his back on Sadie was like cleaving himself in two. But he did it and then pushed hard up the trail for home. Only a few more minutes and he could get Cole inside. If he'd been gutshot—and that was what it looked like—they couldn't save him.

It nearly drove Justin mad to think of it.

The trail twisted and turned. It bent so it went alongside the mountain, then headed up a while until it got so steep it was impossible to climb, then it wound off sideways again to another spot they could climb. It was narrower and steeper with every step until on some of the sideways stretches, one of Justin's booted feet was in a stirrup dangling over a dead drop, while on the other side he could have reached out a hand and brushed the mountainside.

He came to a place the trail had caved off. He sure hoped his horse knew how to walk on tiptoes.

Justin prayed for all he was worth as he passed the narrow spot.

One more steep stretch and finally he skylined himself at the top of the mountain. A gale of wind hit him and warned of cold weather coming in. Northern New Mexico in November could be wretchedly cold or it could be pleasant. It was picking this moment to be nasty. He hung silhouetted against the clouds, then dropped down. He was stunned to see the ranch house right at the bottom of the hill. Oh, he knew the hill all right, covered with heavy woods, steep enough to make a mountain goat faint, but he'd never thought of it as hiding a trail. In his lifetime he'd never used it nor seen Pa use it.

Far below in the ranch yard, someone charged out on horseback and galloped for Skull Gulch. Two men had ridden with him besides his family. He'd sent them ahead fast with orders to run for the doctor.

Justin descended quickly, buffeted by a bitter wind that had been blocked on the uphill side of the trail. This downhill side was as steep as the uphill and just as heavily wooded. Justin followed a badly overgrown trail.

John Hightree, the Cimarron Ranch foreman, ran out of the barn. John had been with the ranch since before Justin's birth, and Justin trusted the man with his life.

Justin yelled, "I need help with Cole, and someone bring this varmint we caught inside and leave him tied up." Justin didn't have time now to give their prisoner another thought.

Rosita, their housekeeper, who'd grown up on the CR, stepped out of the house, took everything in at a glance, and got very serious. Considering the amount of blood, that didn't make her a genius.

Justin jumped down and rushed to Cole. His men were at his side, easing Cole off the horse. Together they carried him inside to Ma and Pa's bedroom on the ground floor and stretched him out on the bed.

Blood was everywhere. Too much of it for a man to survive.

Justin was a man of action. He fought for his brother's life by doing something. Moving fast. He had clung hard to the notion that if they could just get Cole home, quit shaking him up, stop the bleeding, and get a doctor's care, he'd make it.

Justin made things happen with the strength of his back. If he laid his hands on something and used every ounce of his muscle, it'd move. Now he wondered if any amount of hard work would save Cole.

Rosita hurried into the room with a basin of steaming water and cloths tucked under her arm. Justin stepped aside for her; it was either that or get run down.

"I sent for the doctor," John said.

"Justin, I need your hands." Rosita ordering him around. And Justin was supposed to be the boss.

"Where is Sadie?" Rosita was focused completely on Cole, but she had noticed everything. "Why is *mi niña* not with you? Where's Heath?"

"Heath is bringing Sadie." Justin needed to go for Sadie. But it was taking both his and Rosita's hands to care for Cole. And he had an unconscious man in the kitchen with information that could stop a murder.

And he couldn't send someone else to help Heath and Sadie, because he needed John and he didn't know who else he dared trust.

Rosita unfastened a belt Cole had rigged tight around his waist, trying to keep his lifeblood inside.

Two of the hired men came in carrying their prisoner.

For a while it was a fur ball. Helping Rosita tend Cole. Shouting orders to his men to make sure the man was secure. Worrying about Cole. Near frantic about Sadie.

Rosita's orders were louder than Justin's and cut through the rest of the din.

She uncovered the gunshot, gasped, and her lips moved in a quiet prayer as she dipped her cloth in the basin of steaming water. She began washing, and Cole shouted in pain. Justin knew he was completely knocked out, because Cole could take a lot without so much as a groan. This cry of pain would never have escaped had Cole been awake. Rosita hesitated, frowning, her brow furrowed with worry, but she went right back to her doctoring. Justin hoped she didn't do more harm with the scalding water. But in a situation like this, Justin trusted her more than he trusted himself.

The prisoner stirred and groaned, then started struggling against the ropes that bound him.

John had helped carry the outlaw in and now he kept him under control.

Justin couldn't stand the distraction. "There's a solid lock on the cellar door in the kitchen, John. And that trapdoor in the floor is the only way in and out of there."

"Good idea. I'll take him down."

All they needed was for the man to revive, get loose, and bring chaos to the place while all their attention had to be on Cole.

John boosted the man to his feet and dragged him away.

Taut minutes passed as they battled to stop Cole's bleeding.

"He's taken care of, boss." John came in. "I'll stand guard over the desperado."

Justin nodded as John went out again.

Rosita's care of Cole was painstaking. She snapped out orders, and Justin did as he was told as fast as he could move. It was as if he could hear the ticking of the clock—time running out on Cole's life.

Justin remembered so many times Rosita and Ma had cared for all the injuries that stemmed from the harsh conditions of a New Mexico ranch. When it was Justin or Cole or Sadie, the tender care often ended with a kiss and a cookie. Justin knew this was far too serious to end as pleasantly.

"I am not going to fix a tight bandage because the doctor will soon come. I want him to be able to get to the wound without hurting Cole further. But we have to keep pressure on."

"There was another man who rode ahead of me with Alonzo. It's Ramone."

Rosita's head came up. "Ramone? The man who killed your grandfather Chastain all those years ago?"

Justin nodded. "It might not be as we think. I'll tell you everything later."

Rosita washed her blood-soaked hands in the basin and dried

them on a cloth Justin had brought. Then she turned back to Cole just as his eyes blinked open.

"Cole's awake."

"Where's Sadie?" Cole's voice, weak and so soft it was hard to hear, but his thoughts were clear.

Justin's gut twisted. "Heath's got her." Justin had a feeling that was the absolute truth. And of course he wanted Heath to get her, yet he didn't want him to *keep* her.

"Go, for heaven's sake. Get out of here and go help."

A clatter at the back of the house drew Justin's attention and diverted Cole's. He wished it'd be Heath with Sadie.

Wished it, prayed it, but feared it was not. This day was just too deeply stacked with trouble.

Doc Garner burst into the room, and right behind him . . .

Justin almost groaned out loud. He'd hoped for the sweet, wise, skillfully trained Sister Margaret. Instead his stack of trouble just got higher.

2

Angie DuPree rushed into the room and stumbled right into the doctor's back.

She nearly pitched him facedown on top of a bleeding man.

Strong arms caught her so fast she wondered if someone had been waiting for her to get into trouble. The doctor spared her one annoyed glance, then rushed around the bed and bent over the patient.

The doctor reached for the bandaged wound as she realized it was Justin lying there. Horror swept through her and then the hands that set her on her feet drew her attention. She glanced sideways.

Justin.

Her eyes flicked back and forth. It was definitely Justin who had her wrapped in his arms. She'd felt them before.

So it was Cole who was hurt.

Covered up like this, though—unconscious or nearly so— with all of his personality and his way of dress hidden, she was shocked at how much Cole resembled Justin. Both of them tall with dark brown hair. Their eyes matched too, a blue as dark as the starlit sky. But Cole had shorter hair and in the normal course of things was tidier and better dressed. But right now he was a mess.

"Aunt Margaret hurt her ankle and Miss Maria came out with us, but she said another man is hurt?" Angie said weakly.

Justin nodded. "That's Ramone. I'm glad you could come and . . . help."

Angie suspected he tried to disguise the doubt in his voice, but since she had her own serious doubts, she heard what he didn't say.

She looked back at Cole, and a wave of dizziness almost staggered her. Some of it was the sight of so much blood, though she also had a strange blast of what felt like relief that it wasn't Justin lying there. And then she was disgusted at such a thought. Cole being hurt was just as terrible. She was here to help and who the patient was didn't come into it.

Some of the dizziness, of course, might be because she had no idea what to do, so she was scared to death. But Aunt Margaret had tripped over a misplaced schoolbook this morning and was limping badly enough she needed medical care herself. She'd sent Angie out here, and one of the other two ladies from the orphanage, Miss Maria, came along and had been sent to another house to tend another man. The doctor said he needed youth and speed and that a lack of knowledge wouldn't matter.

Well, if Angie could stay upright, he'd get all of those. Youth, speed, and ignorance.

Lucky man.

"Thank you, Justin." He let her go. She felt wobbly again but covered it up as best she could and rushed to stand next to Dr. Garner. Aunt Margaret said to obey him, lend him a hand. She squared her shoulders, prayed hard, let her head clear, and waited.

Rosita, the Bodens' housekeeper, stepped aside. Angie knew her, too. She'd met the whole family and most of the other folks who lived and worked on the Cimarron Ranch. They came to church every Sunday morning as she did. Aunt Margaret had talked about them a lot, as well. The Bodens supported the mission generously. And Aunt Margaret loved Sadie Boden. In fact, Angie suspected she loved Sadie more than she loved her.

Which Angie richly deserved, though Aunt Margaret was nothing but kind.

"Miss DuPree," the doctor snapped.

"Yes, sir." Angie had no problem with sharply given orders and raised voices. It reminded her of her mother.

"Get across the bed from me. I'll need your hands over there." When she was in place, he handed his doctor bag across Cole to her. "We talked about what I might need from my doctor bag."

There was a bedside table so she set the bag down, opened it, and waited.

Already working, the doctor glanced at Justin. "The shot is through and through. I won't have to dig a bullet out. Tell me what happened."

Justin spoke of an ambush, a gunfight. There was an outlaw imprisoned in the cellar. She followed Justin quite well until the doctor told her what to grab out of his bag. She lost the trail of the story at that point.

Her contribution to the chaos was a fumbling business because she was unfamiliar with the tools and supplies Doc Garner requested. She doggedly worked on.

The doctor powdered Cole's gunshot, then put a folded piece of gauze over his belly.

"I need to roll him to his side and work on his back. I'll need your strength here, Justin."

Almost instantly, Angie found herself being pushed just a bit and squeezed between Justin and the table. The doctor and Justin lifted Cole with such gentle strength that Angie felt tears blur her vision. She'd never seen men so gentle.

"Miss DuPree, hold the bandage right here." The doctor grabbed her hand and placed it on the thick pad covering the wound. "You press hard on the front of his stomach and don't let this dressing slip while we put the carbolic acid on the exit wound."

The doctor waited until she reached her arms in and had a firm hold on the bandage. Then Dr. Garner tended Cole's back.

"Now hold this compress on his back while I bind them both in place. Justin, keep him steady on his side until I'm done. I'll pass the gauze under him and you catch it and bring it up his front."

"It's a gutshot, Doc." Justin's voice had a terrible grief in it.

"I don't think the bullet hit a vital organ. He'd already be dead if it had. He's lost a lot of blood, and that'll leave him weak for a while, but he's got a decent chance of making it. There's always fever—there's no avoiding that—but if it doesn't turn septic, he'll survive. Cole's a strong man and you've done a good job of tending him. The bleeding probably washed out everything from inside. I hope, anyway. Now we wait, get him to drink water as often as we can, and pray."

The doctor wrapped the bandage. In the stillness of his efforts to keep the bandages snug, Angie caught on to the rhythm of the doctor tucking the strips under Cole's body, then Justin bringing the bandage up to where the doctor could get at it again. She became aware of Justin so close beside her. He had obviously been through a long, hard day, yet he smelled clean, like the outdoors and horses and something else she'd never smelled before. If strength could have a smell, she'd say it was that. He'd rolled up his sleeves to his elbows, and the effort to hold Cole on his side and lift so the doctor could pass the gauze under him caused corded muscles to bulge on his forearms.

She'd been close to her husband, of course, in wifely ways.

But she'd never been near a man like this. Working at his side, watching him do his best in a loving way.

"That's it. I'm done. Ease him onto his back." The doctor fussed more with the bandage, straightening it until he was satisfied. "Get Cole some of that water."

Justin stepped away, then came back quickly with a tin cup.

She saw the love Justin had for his brother. It seemed so at odds with how she'd always thought of family, despite Aunt Margaret's kindness. Aunt Margaret was Angie's father's sister. And her mother had always disparaged Aunt Margaret's manners as coarse and common, her religion boring and foolish.

And when everything her ma had forced Angie into went wrong and Ma had died, leaving her to a disastrous fate, Aunt Margaret had saved her and taught Angie a lesson about love she wouldn't soon forget.

"Angie." The doctor again snapped out orders. "Go fetch more warm water. We need to bathe the blood away. And ask Rosita for a clean nightshirt for Cole. She could make some broth, too. He needs water most of all, but if Cole wakes up, we should try to get some food into him."

Angie hurried to obey, keeping the list in her head. Not that it mattered, for she was sure the doctor would remind her of anything she forgot.

Angie rushed to the kitchen and was filling a basin just as the back door opened.

Sadie and Heath came in.

"How's Cole?" Sadie, Cole's sister, looked frantically around.

"The doctor is with him in the bedroom just down the hall."

"Thank you." Sadie hurried away with Heath right after her.

Angie followed with hot water.

She stepped into the room as Justin shouted, "Sadie!" His voice was loud enough to wake the owls in the woods at high noon, let alone a merely unconscious man. Cole's eyes flickered open and he smiled at Sadie as if her coming inside was terribly important. Justin hoisted Sadie in the air and hugged her.

The sight stopped Angie so suddenly the water sloshed and nearly spilled. She'd never seen such a display of true affection from a man before. Cole couldn't get up and hug her, but his eyes gleamed with pleasure.

Justin set her back down with a broad smile and shook Heath's hand, then slapped him on the back hard enough a smaller man might've just been knocked straight to the floor.

Heath held up well and started talking to Justin fast and quiet. Angie couldn't understand what he said, except that a man had attacked them and was now dead. Her attention was turned as Sadie sat down on the side of the bed and took Cole's hands.

"How are you?"

"Just fine. The doctor patched me up."

Something flickered across Sadie's face, the expression equivalent of calling her brother a liar. Sadie looked at the doctor as if talking to Cole were a complete waste of time. "Where was he shot? Did he need stitches? How long will he be in bed? What do we need to do to care for him?"

The doctor started talking, and Sadie listened to him as if his words were being carved in stone with a finger of fire.

Angie was in the middle of the two chattering pairs. The doctor and Sadie, hovering over Cole, Heath, and Justin. She was struck by a moment of feeling an outsider. She didn't belong here in the midst of this family time.

Squaring her shoulders, she ignored her foolish hurt feelings, because of course they all needed to talk to each other. She set the basin on the bedside table. Besides, she was used to not belonging.

Then she remembered the broth and a few other things the doctor had asked for. Grateful for an excuse, she left the room.

Rosita was nearly running when she stepped into the hall, heading for the bedroom.

From the hallway, Angie heard Rosita say *"Mi niña!"* in a voice that rang with pure joy.

Angie went on into the kitchen. It was well-stocked, and she had a few very modest cooking skills. Thank the good Lord that included boiling a hunk of meat in water. It wasn't hard to find the makings for a nice beef broth. She kept busy in the kitchen.

Alone.

Chance Boden's eyes flickered open to the sight of his wife Veronica, his precious Ronnie, on her knees clinging to his hand, her face buried against their joined fingers. He flexed his fingers to caress her beautiful blond hair. At the movement, her head came up, and her snapping blue eyes went wide with surprise, then with joy.

"Chance, you're awake!" She launched herself to her feet and threw her arms around his neck.

Only then did he realize he was lying in bed. He tried to hug her back and found he couldn't move. Not an inch. His fingers were free, he could turn his head, but every bit of him was bound like a hog-tied calf at branding time.

"What's going on?" He was a man who lived in a hard land. He awoke every morning ready for trouble. He moved faster than he could think. And right now, not being able to move made him feel like danger was coming at him like a stampede.

Or no . . . his head cleared more. Not a stampede, an avalanche.

"How long?" An avalanche had come down on his head. The rest of his men had survived, he remembered that much. He remembered Heath Kincaid, his hired man, tending his leg with uncommon skill. Then Chance hesitated. Did he remember or had someone told him that? He was in Denver. Sent to a special doctor. His leg broken with the bone sticking out of the skin. They always amputated with injuries like that.

Ronnie lifted her head from his chest, new tears, but hope like spring lightning in her expression.

"You've had a fever for so l-long." Her voice broke. Then her chin lifted and her jaw went firm. She swiped at her eyes with her sleeves. "But now—now—" She quickly stood and rushed to the door of a small room. Chance had no memory of coming here and yet he knew where he was.

"Nurse, my husband is awake. Is the doctor here?"

Chance thought of his leg and the terrible break. He tried to look down, but he was bound securely. His stomach twisted, for he knew if he could see, the blankets would be flat where there should be a leg.

Ronnie, his precious Veronica. His wife for twenty-five years now. She spun away from the door and was at his side instantly.

He should be grateful to have survived, yet he couldn't stop the words. "My leg. Is it . . . ?"

Kissing him with wild pleasure, she smiled. "Your leg is going to be fine."

"Fine? But they had to amputate—"

Fingers, strong, callused yet still delicate, pressed against his lips. "The doctor was able to save your leg. It was so badly broken from the avalanche that it was a near thing, but the doctor—well, he had to keep you still." Her eyes flashed with mock anger. She jabbed one finger at his nose. "You don't have a still bone in your body, Chance Boden."

The doctor swung the door open. "He's awake? The fever broke?"

Chance had never seen this man before in his life.

The man, white shirt-sleeves rolled up, hair disheveled and

overlong as if he didn't have a spare half hour ever to get it cut, went straight to Chance's leg. "I'm going to take the leeches off now."

Chance jumped, except only his head and fingers moved. "Leeches? What is going on? Why am I tied down?"

Ronnie blocked his view of the doctor hard at work. She brushed his hair back off his forehead.

Chance was suddenly aware that he could smell himself. "How long have I been tied here?"

Ronnie kissed him again, which distracted him. "You've been more asleep than awake for two weeks now. Your fever has come down and gone back up so many times I've lost count."

"Six times." The doctor's fingers were on Chance's leg, and it was with a whoosh of relief that Chance felt the touch. He also felt pain like his leg was caught in a bear trap. It hurt enough that Chance noticed it as separate from his all-around misery.

"Six times what?" Chance clamped is jaw shut to keep from hollering in pain.

"Your fever came up and went down six times. Today is the sixth, but you never woke up before, and the wound in your leg was red and infected." The doctor lifted his hand and held it high. He was catching light coming in through the window.

Chance realized the man was holding a fat, black leech. "What kind of doctor are you?"

"The finest doctor alive." Ronnie pressed her cheek to his.

"Someone tell me what's going on."

Bending back over Chance's leg, the doctor said, "You were already feverish when your wife brought you here from the train. I stitched up the wound, working on the muscles, but I couldn't close the skin because that would trap the silk threads inside you and you'd never heal. So I sewed up muscle, and we couldn't put a plaster cast on your leg because the wound needed tending. It was absolutely essential we keep you from moving that leg, so we tied you down to the point you couldn't so much as twitch."

The doctor straightened, looked over Ronnie's shoulder, and smiled. "It's my own method for broken bones of this sort. I must say it was a stroke of luck you got your leg broken when you did, because I've just begun using some new techniques."

"Luck?" Chance wondered if the doctor was completely sane.

"Your fever was a bad one at first and the wound around the leg, wide open like that, showed some infection, which prompted me to get the leeches."

Chance felt prompted to reach for his gun.

"Then after nearly a week, your fever broke and I was able to remove the stitches in the muscles. I had to abrade the skin of the open wound and stitch that, then up came your fever again. You slept some natural sleep after that, and we got broth and quite a bit of water down your throat. Kept you alive so I could try more things on your leg."

Chance was being experimented on. Well, since his leg was still there, it was probably right to have no objections.

The doctor held up another leech and studied it with absolute delight.

Shuddering, Chance said, "It's been two weeks?"

"Yes." Ronnie took up the story. "The second week, another set of stitches had healed and your fever was more general. It'd break and then come up again."

"Six times in all. It's all in my records."

"Did I introduce Dr. Radcliffe, Chance?"

He shook his head. "Is there any possible way to loosen these straps?"

The doctor set the leech aside as if he'd quit playing with a pet. "I'll remove the stitches today. It's time, but I want to watch the unstitched wound overnight. Tomorrow I'll put a plaster cast on your leg. When that hardens, it'll be possible for you to move. But until the wound healed you had to stay still, and now, until the plaster hardens, you can see that every move is sure to jostle unknit bones. The healing would need to begin all over again."

The doctor stood and patted Ronnie on the arm. She got out of his way as if that signal had come before, many times. Sounding far less dotty now, the doctor adjusted his round steel-rimmed glasses and said, "You are going to be well, Mr. Boden. I have saved your leg. It's my brilliance, but the doctor who sent you here, the young man who tended your leg right after the accident, and the vigilance and devotion of your wife, who has not left your side for two weeks, all combined to delay your journey to meet St. Peter."

The doctor turned back to Chance's leg. Ronnie smiled as tears of joy filled her eyes. And his wife was not a crying woman.

If she was happy, he reckoned he was, too. But he wanted to be untied and he needed a bath. He wondered how long it would be before the doctor let him dunk himself in the river to clean up.

3

Cole was going to live.

Justin was a while believing it, but finally he did.

And then, as if he hadn't had enough shocks for one day, he had to stand there and listen to Sadie announce she was marrying Heath Kincaid. The parson showed up as if Sadie had sent a telegram through the air asking him to come out.

They were married at Cole's bedside.

Justin witnessed the vows. They hit him hard, as if he'd never heard them before, and he had a few times—but not for a little sister. *"In sickness and in health, for richer or poorer, as long as we both shall live."* These were fierce promises to make. The vows were eternal. Heath and Sadie—smiling all the while—swore before God to keep them.

His baby sister. He remembered Sadie vaguely as a baby. Justin was three when she was born. She'd been the most delicate, pretty little thing. Everything in him had known this was someone he was bound by God to protect.

Then she'd gotten older and become a torment, and he'd been too big to fight back against the little imp. Cole had been known to say the same thing about Justin.

With his throat tight, confused about whether to fight the wedding or celebrate it, he instead stood silently.

Heath had saved Pa's life in an avalanche. And he'd taken a bullet for Sadie, even if it was just a scratch. And he'd just caught the man who'd brought a lot of trouble to the Bodens' door.

Heath was a top hand, smart, loyal, honest, and fearless as a grizzly bear. A good Christian man. Of course, Justin was fine with his sister marrying the coyote.

But Sadie was too young to get married, and good as he was, Heath wasn't good enough for her. Justin had yet to meet anyone who was.

He wished Ma and Pa were here. They'd be the ones asking questions and guarding Sadie. But they weren't here, and much as Justin didn't like it, he had no say over what an adult woman—sister or not—did when it came to choosing a husband.

But he saw Sadie's happiness, and Heath had brought her home safe when Justin abandoned her to save Cole. So Justin welcomed Heath to the family with some grace.

As if he had any choice in the matter.

Finally, the sheriff came and pestered Justin until he left his sister alone with her new husband, and his brother alone with Doc Garner and his pretty, clumsy little nurse, Angie.

Justin knew Angie way better than he should. He'd met her the day she came to town, stepped off the train, and collapsed in his arms. He'd never forgotten how she'd felt and was overly aware of her ever since.

He went to question their prisoner. Justin had locked him in the cellar, and it'd been quite a while. Maybe the varmint would be ready to talk.

"Bring him up." Sheriff Joe Dunn was giving orders.

Justin had taken more orders today than he had in his whole life. Ma and Pa were exceptions to that, who'd always bossed him around. But as a rule he was a man to take charge and proud of that, because someone had to run this ranch, especially now with Pa being hurt.

Justin was ready to have a long, brutal talk with this prisoner, who was in on the shooting of Cole and most likely all the recent troubles that had beset the Boden family.

After he dragged the man up from the cellar, Justin saw Sadie and Heath eating in the kitchen. He badgered Heath to come and talk to their prisoner. Finally Justin had to face facts.

Heath and Sadie were much too busy.

Their prisoner had been untied when they put him in the cellar. There was only one way out of there—a sturdy trapdoor in the kitchen floor, and it was solidly locked. Justin probably should have asked the sheriff to put this outlaw in shackles, but a real cranky part of Justin hoped the low-down back-shooting vermin tried to escape. It would be Justin's great pleasure to stop him.

They walked with him to Pa's office, and there was no escape attempt. Instead he sat down, crossed his arms, and looked between Justin and the sheriff. "What are you folks up to? I haven't got a dollar to steal, and my horse is a broken-down old nag. If you're thieves, you're picking on the wrong man."

"You shot my brother today, nearly killed him. You can polish up your lies while you spend the rest of your life burning in Yuma."

The man's eyes shifted as if looking for a way out, but then he steadied himself and instead of running he fought his expression into lines of indignation. Leaning forward in his seat, he said, "You attacked me, mister. I wasn't doin' nuthin' wrong, just riding along—"

"You're wasting time," Justin cut him off. The man had been given too much time to concoct his lies. "Who are you working for?"

Justin wasn't waiting for Sheriff Dunn to ask a question. "Who hired you to kill Chance Boden?"

The man jerked his head back like Justin had slapped him. "I ain't got no idea in the world what you're talkin' about."

"No one has been on that trail for years. I'd never heard of it, and I live ten minutes from there, and you expect me to believe you were just riding along."

"I expect you to believe the truth!" The man sounded weak. Justin glanced at Joe, a man nearly as old as Pa. He'd been the lawman in Skull Gulch for as long as Justin could remember. He was relieved to see distrust in the lawman's eyes.

"What's your name?" Joe finally asked a question. He was better at this than Justin was. Start at the beginning. It made sense.

"Folks call me Arizona Watts. I'm just passin' through. I never shot nobody."

"So you have no job, no acquaintances in the area."

"Nope, don't know a soul. A man's allowed to wander."

Heath's voice came from behind them. "I was with Dantalion when he died."

Justin didn't let the surprise voice distract him. He was looking right at Watts and saw the color drain from his face at the mention of Dantalion.

"He told me he was trying to catch up with you, Watts. He was dying, and he wasn't hiding a thing from me."

"No! I've never heard of the man."

Sheriff Joe said, "A dying man's word carries a lot of weight with me." He narrowed his eyes at the prisoner. "And I know Heath and the Bodens mighty well, and I don't know you a lick. Are you going to tell me what you were up to and who you're working with? Or should I just lock you up until the circuit judge comes by?"

Justin knew Heath was lying, trying to trick Watts into a confession. Heath had given a quick rundown of all that had happened when he went back for Sadie. Dantalion took his secrets to the grave.

"Dantalion had one thousand dollars in gold in his pockets and a letter saying he was getting paid that much for attacking the Bodens." Heath watched the man like a cat watched a cornered mouse. "How much was he paying you?"

"A thousand dollars? That lying cheat. He told me he'd give me twenty-five for every Boden I killed." Watts's mouth clamped shut so fast they all heard the snap.

"That enough to keep him locked up for good, Sheriff?"

"More than enough." Joe looked at Watts. The old sheriff had slowed down, and his belly was round. He had thick white hair and eyebrows so bushy he oughta comb them. But he was a wise man and tough enough to keep peace in Skull Gulch for the last thirty years. Pa claimed him as a good friend.

"Near as I can tell, Watts," Sheriff Joe said, "you haven't killed anyone yet. But not for lack of trying. In New Mexico Territory, attempted murder is enough to lock you up for the rest of your life or even hang you if the jury's in a foul mood. But if we could have a name, we might look for the man behind this crime and go easy on you. You knew Dantalion, is that right?"

Watts looked up, sullen and angry, and all he said was, "No jail will hold me, and it won't be because I have to break out. I'll walk right out the front door, and you'll apologize as I go."

He said it with such assurance that Justin felt a chill run down his spine. There weren't many people with the power this man claimed.

The sheriff's eyes narrowed again as he studied the man. He asked him a few more questions, but Watts sank into complete silence and wouldn't be budged.

A quiet movement from behind him made Justin turn to see Heath was gone. But he'd come through. That Kincaid was a mighty handy man to have around.

Justin was going to have to get used to the idea of him, especially since the man was now his brother.

4

Justin stood at the back door and watched in the falling dusk
as the sheriff rode away with their prisoner. Snow gusted, the
temperature had been dropping all day, and it looked like one
of New Mexico's deep freezes was coming in. He never knew
how long that might hang on.

The exchange with the outlaw had left him frustrated and
worried. And he wasn't a man who liked the feeling, either. He
hoped they were clear of the trouble. And he suspected they
were, at least for a time, yet it wasn't over. And with the two men
possibly taken care of, if there were only two, they should be
safe—at least until their unknown enemy reorganized. Someone
had given Dantalion that thousand dollars in gold.

Even believing they had time to get to the bottom of this,
Justin, standing in the back door, let his eyes slide from place
to place, everywhere a man could hide and aim a gun. He felt
the presence of a dry-gulcher hiding in the deep shadows as if
murderous eyes were crawling over his skin.

"The doctor says—"

Justin yelped and whirled around.

Angie.

And she'd just witnessed him make a fool of himself, which set his temper on edge. Through clenched teeth he asked, "What did the doctor say?"

"I'm sorry to startle you." A smile flickered on her lips and was gone. The little brat was doing her best not to laugh in his face. With his back to the outside, Justin felt he was still under a gun, so he stepped inside and slammed the door. High time . . . all the warmth had been sucked out of the kitchen.

He needed to calm down.

In a moment of rare desire to explain himself, he said, "I was looking at all the spots a man could hide out and take a shot at me. I didn't expect anyone to come up from behind."

All amusement was gone from her eyes. Her hair was in disarray, a mass of pretty blond curls. She pushed the curls off her face. Her hazel eyes sparked with worry, and Justin knew the worry was for him and for all the Bodens, not for herself, dragged into the middle of some strange mysterious conflict.

Justin prompted her, "The doctor?"

Now she looked startled as if she'd forgotten all about what she needed to tell him. "The doctor wants me to sleep with you."

"What?" It was more a shout than a spoken question.

She slapped both hands over her mouth, and her cheeks flamed so bright he half expected her hair to catch fire. From behind her hands she said, "I mean, he wants me to spend the night with you."

Justin was losing the ability to breathe.

This time she covered her eyes. Finally she managed to drop her hands and face him. "That is, to *sit with Cole*. He, uh . . . the doctor and I are both going to stay so someone is with Cole at all times." She turned away, probably wishing her cheeks weren't quite so pink.

Justin was so grateful to be distracted from the trouble they faced he could have hugged her.

Except that would be stupid.

With a visible effort she peeked over her shoulder, then faced him. Her voice dropped to a whisper. "I don't think there's a very good chance Sadie and Heath will want to take a turn sitting with him."

Justin was afraid he was blushing too, and that was so ridiculous it helped him get ahold of himself. "Well, that's fine then. I—we appreciate your help, Angie. Sincerely." He cleared his throat and forced himself to change the subject. "So, have you had some supper? Let me find Rosita."

He had to walk straight for her because she was between him and the rest of the house. She seemed to forget exactly where she was and watched without moving.

He came right up to her, almost nose to nose, and he found it so pleasant to stand this close that it took too long to ask, "Can I get through?"

She flinched and jumped backward. It gave him some satisfaction. He'd been off-balance ever since she'd startled him. But since she'd started blushing and whispering, he felt a lot more like the one in control of the conversation.

Justin didn't holler for Rosita, because he saw a pot of something pushed back on the stove. Rosita had been in and out of the sickroom, running and working as fast as she could ever since they'd brought Cole home. He had no idea where she was right now, but he wasn't going to pester her to serve food.

"Let me fill you a plate." Justin headed for the stove. When he got there, he looked back, jabbed a finger at the kitchen table. "Go ahead and sit down."

She gave him a look so odd, like maybe she was watching a longhorn bull dish up supper. But she didn't say what was the matter; instead she sat down hard. He was glad she'd been close to a chair.

He turned to the stove and was quick getting her a hearty

serving of Rosita's delicious chicken stew. When Rosita was upset she cooked, and it looked like she'd outdone herself today. The stew was thick with her hand-cut noodles and smelled warm and meaty. Rosita couldn't make a bad meal, but this was one of his favorites.

There was a plate heaped high with biscuits sitting beside the stove. Besides that, in the kitchen window perched a layer cake with white frosting and two pieces gone. It appeared that Sadie and Heath had already eaten. Beside the cake, two pumpkin pies were sitting on a wide windowsill, along with two golden-brown loaves of bread ready for breakfast, and huckleberry jelly that looked freshly made. A ball of butter was right next to it.

Rosita had as bad a day as the rest of them, and Justin was struck by how much he loved the sweet lady who'd been like a member of the family for his whole life. And his next thought was how much he missed Pa and Ma.

Shaking off the sad thoughts, he focused on how hungry he was. Maybe Angie was, too. She was still mighty thin, her cheeks hollow, her dress showing wrists that were skin and bones. But compared to when she'd first come to town, she looked mighty healthy.

And here she was, right in the middle of it all when she had no part in this trouble. He filled another plate and brought food over for the both of them. He got them each a knife, fork, and spoon, then set the biscuits between them and sat down.

"Thank you." She blinked her wide hazel eyes and gave him a look full of wonder. And never had a simple thank-you sounded so heartfelt. Since he couldn't figure out quite why, unless she was desperately hungry, he decided to ignore it and warn her that she was taking her life in her hands every second spent around the Bodens.

"I'm not sure you know what's going on around here, but if you spend time on the ranch, you need to be on your guard."

"I know you arrested someone."

"Yep, the man the sheriff just took to jail. He calls himself Arizona Watts."

Nodding, Angie asked, "Did you know Maria came out with the doctor?"

Justin paused. "Yes, I think you told me that. It's been a long day."

"We were told that Maria's brother, Ramone, is here and not well. Was Ramone with Watts? Did Ramone hurt Cole? I saw your prisoner for a second, but that's not Ramone, is it?"

Angie went back to eating in a way that reminded Justin of just how weak she'd been from hunger and thirst when she'd stepped off the train in Skull Gulch. He recalled the weight of her in his arms and how she'd barely found the strength to whisper "Aunt Margaret." She'd come from Omaha to live with her aunt, Sister Margaret, at the Safe Haven Orphanage.

Justin wished Rosita was here to see Angie gobbling down the meal. Their housekeeper would've been pleased to watch someone enjoying her cooking this much.

"Nope. In fact, we think Ramone's in danger, too. We think the folks who have been harassing our ranch wanted to find a way to blame their crime on him. Maybe plant some evidence and then kill Ramone so he couldn't defend himself. Ramone and Maria grew up around here, but Ramone went to Mexico a long time ago. He was suspected of killing my grandfather. The man who built this house."

"Ramone was suspected of murder?" Angie pressed a hand to her chest. "Poor Maria. I could tell when she talked to Sadie it was painful for her. She defended her brother, but what she spoke of led you to him, is that right?"

Justin felt the need to tell her the gist of the story. "About a month ago someone set off an avalanche that nearly killed my pa. He and Ma have been in Denver with a doctor, who had a special treatment for a badly broken leg. He's going to be all right, although healing from a wound that serious is a slow business. They'll be gone all winter. We thought the avalanche was an accident until Heath began to suspect someone was behind it. While we investigated it, someone took a shot at us—Cole, Sadie, Heath, and me. Heath was shot saving our lives."

Doc Garner stepped into the kitchen and broke off Justin's storytelling. Since his goal had been to warn Angie there was danger around, he figured he'd said enough for now.

"I smelled the food, Justin." The doctor had a smile that made a body start healing up before any medicine was given.

Angie took two more fast bites and her plate was clean. She gave the pumpkin pie a look of longing, then pushed her chair back and rose. "I'll sit with Cole, Doctor. You come on in and eat."

She hurried out of the room. When she was gone, Justin felt like he could still see her, like a man still had a shining light burned into his eyes if he looked too long at the sun.

A hard slap on his back brought him out of the daze left from watching her.

Doc shoved back Angie's dishes and sat down. He'd already filled his own plate from the stove, which made Justin wonder just how long he'd been staring.

"You know, that young lady acted like she would dearly love a piece of pie, Justin. Why don't you take one in to her, and one for yourself, too? No reason you can't eat while you're sitting at Cole's bedside."

"That sounds like a fine idea. She seemed hungry still."

Justin had two plates with pie and two forks and was out of the room fast. He thought he heard the doctor chuckling, though he didn't bother going back to see what was so funny.

5

Angie wrung a cloth out and pressed it to Cole's head. He didn't have a fever so he didn't really need cool cloths. But she was here and it seemed like the thing to do.

She'd just centered the cloth on his forehead when Justin came in with two slices of that delicious-looking pie. Angie hadn't had pumpkin pie for years. When her father was alive, it'd been part of many holiday meals, but things had turned bad after he died. And Mother, worried about money, had let the servants go, and heaven knew Mother didn't know how to bake a pie.

Angie was on the far side of the bed, and she watched Justin come around and offer her the dessert. It was all she could do not to start crying.

"Thank you."

She'd never seen a man serve food before. She'd never really seen a man enter the kitchen. After her father died and her mother descended into useless bitterness at their reduced circumstances, Angie had done her best to cook for them. But there was no one to teach her, so what little food they had was simple. She often wondered if Mother would have let them both starve.

"Sit down for a bit. Have your pie. Cole is . . ." Justin's word faded as he looked at his brother. He cleared his throat, and she realized he hadn't quit talking on purpose. His voice had broken, as if he might be fighting tears.

There was no sign of such a thing, and she looked closely at his dark-blue eyes, so she was sure.

He loved his brother.

Angie found herself fighting tears, too. She stepped back to give Justin the privacy a strong man must need when dealing with such powerful emotions.

Sitting in the corner, she took a bite of pie.

Finally, Justin, with his back to her, said, "The doctor thinks he's going to be all right if a fever doesn't catch him. I've always heard a gunshot like this, in the stomach, is deadly. But Doc says this is far enough to the side it missed hitting anything important. He said getting shot in the liver or bowels or kidneys is what can't be fixed and leads to death."

Then Justin's shoulders squared and he turned and gave Angie a hard look that made his eyes glitter. "He's going to make it because I won't settle for anything else."

She wondered if he expected her to argue, because he looked ready to fight anyone who disagreed with him.

She had no desire to disagree. "Dr. Garner said his carbolic acid is very useful to fight off infections. He also cleaned the wound. Your Rosita did a very good job, although the doctor was afraid of threads from Cole's shirt being lodged in the wound. He said when a bullet passes through fabric like that, it can happen. And a thread, or anything with dirt on it, can start an infection."

She thought of the long, meticulous job the doctor had done, how much blood there was, the moments of Cole's wakefulness and how much pain he was in, and how bravely he bore it.

Her husband had never had a brave, long-suffering moment in his life. And that was the last thought she was going to have about her marriage—for the rest of her life, if she could possibly arrange it.

"You said Heath was shot?"

Justin swallowed, then nodded. "A while back, by a man on top of that big mesa. Did you notice it when you rode in?"

"Skull Mesa. I've heard of it. The town is named for the place."

"We heard an old Pueblo story about a woman kept by Don Bautista de Val, who used to be a partner in this ranch. He was a nasty old man according to my ma, who knew him a bit when she was a child. Don de Val was long gone by the time I was born. He had two children, Maria and Ramone, with his Pueblo mistress. That's why Maria chose to tend him while you came here with the doctor. Finding the connection between them led us to Ramone."

"I was with Sadie when Maria claimed Ramone as her brother."

"Ramone worked at the ranch back in my grandfather's time without saying a word about being the Don's son. When Grandfather Chastain, my mother's pa, was killed, Ramone disappeared and was known to have run for Mexico. He was suspected in the killing."

"Maria believes in her brother's innocence. She knew where he was and told us. If she thought he was guilty, don't you think she'd have protected him?"

"We found him early this morning. He was in terrible shape, living in an old wreck of a house with little food, afraid to come out except at night because he knew he'd left here under a cloud of suspicion. We were bringing him home this morning when two men attacked us on the trail. That's when Cole was shot. We managed to capture one man, while the other threw himself off a cliff rather than be taken prisoner."

Angie gasped. "He killed himself?"

"Not deliberately. He was running into what looked like

heavy woods. He dove off the trail through the trees and didn't see the cliff. The man's last words threatened that more trouble was coming, that he wasn't acting alone. If you stay around here long, it's possible you could come under their guns, Angie."

Justin frowned at her, worry in his eyes. "I don't want to risk anyone else's life."

"Send everyone away, Justin." The new voice, deep and shaky, drew Angie's attention, and Justin leapt out of his chair. Cole was awake.

"How can we send *everyone* away, Cole? How? Are you saying we should abandon the ranch?"

Cole tossed his head fretfully, and the damp cloth slid away. Justin caught it and wet it again with cool water. He returned it with too much gentleness for such a rugged western man.

"I don't know. But how can we stay?"

Justin knew something was wrong, because Cole didn't have a lot of backup in him. He'd rather stand and face a fight than turn tail and run. And he figured the men at the ranch felt the same. Still puzzling over it, Justin adjusted the cloth on Cole's head, and heat came through the rag almost instantly.

"You're running a fever." Justin's voice was sharp. "Angie, get the doctor."

She was out of her chair and calling for the doctor before Justin quit giving the order. There would be time to wonder about threats to the ranch later. Right now, caring for Cole and seeing him get well was all that mattered.

The ensuing battle for Cole's life drove every other thought from Justin's mind. Attempted murder, conspiracy, hired men with mysterious plans, cowhands who might be betrayers. Justin didn't have time for any of it.

Sadie and Heath seemed to give up any idea of a honeymoon, even to the point of giving up private moments. They worked along with everyone else, bathing Cole with cool cloths, getting water down his throat, coaxing him to drink the willow-bark tea the doctor recommended for fever and the broth Rosita and Angie kept warm on the stove.

Rosita went nearly mad tempting Cole with the best sickroom food she could find. Mulled eggs and mashed fruit. Warm milk, rich with sugar and cinnamon, poured over bread. Angie watched and learned from her. It was clear Rosita loved Cole like her own child, as she did all the Bodens, and she seemed determined to hold him on this side of the Pearly Gates with the weapons of gentleness, good food, and relentless prayer. She worked day and night to lure him into sufficient wakefulness that he could swallow.

The doctor pretty much lived at the Cimarron Ranch. His steady presence had two very separate effects. Justin was glad the man was there and caring for Cole, but his constant vigilance seemed to announce to the world just how desperately ill Cole was. Doc Garner was summoned away for other patients a few times and had to go, but otherwise he was like a new member of the family. Angie was there all the time, helping the doctor when he was there and following the orders he left when he couldn't be. Sadie and Heath were on hand too, so Cole was never alone, day or night.

Justin slept in short patches, haunted by dreams of his brother's death that jerked him awake. He never sank into deep, restful sleep. His mind was too filled with how badly this could end.

He rose in the dark on the fifth day of Cole's struggle. The silence in the house nearly rang in Justin's ears. More so than usual. The night was pitch black. As he did multiple times each night, Justin threw back the covers, pulled on pants and a shirt over his woolen underwear, and hurried down to check on his brother.

As Justin padded down the stairs, he thought of plenty to worry about. Cole wasn't drinking enough water, wasn't eating enough food. He rarely woke, and when he did, he was out of his head, raving and tossing around until they all hoped he'd slump back into unconsciousness to avoid hurting himself.

Today the fever raged higher than ever. Cole had lost weight, and his cheeks were hollow. Deep shadows made his eyes seem sunken and bruised until he looked like he'd lost a fistfight.

Every time Justin went into that room he expected the worst.

Now he watched his hands shake as he reached for the door-knob, but he couldn't stand to wait until he gathered his nerve. He shoved the door open, half expecting to see his brother had died.

Angie slept, sitting in a chair, her head cradled in her folded arms, resting on the mattress. Cole's hand rested in her madly cur¹ing hair. His eyes open, studying Angie as if she were his own personal guardian angel.

Then Cole's gaze shifted. He focused on Justin and smiled. Really fully smiled.

"Cole!"

Angie's head shot up, terror etched on her face as if she feared the worst, too. And then all the terror melted away and she smiled, the biggest smile Justin had seen since she moved to Skull Gulch a few weeks back. Her life before, back in Omaha, had been a grim business, or so it seemed.

"The fever broke." Cole sounded weak, yet he was making sense and his eyes were bright with his usual intelligence. His hair was soaking wet, lines of sweat trickling down his face. He'd been flushed from the fever for days. Now the hectic color had returned to a much more normal shade.

Angie stood. "It happened a while ago. Cole got some water down. We talked a bit and I—I guess I fell asleep. Drink some more water, please."

She had a cup and pitcher close to hand. Cole was lying flat, so Justin came up, slid one arm under Cole's shoulders, and raised his head. He drank the full cup and asked for more.

With a delighted smile, Angie poured. Cole finished about half of it.

"I'm going to stir the coals in the kitchen stove and heat a bowl of broth for you. While it warms I can start breakfast. We need to rebuild your strength." Angie rushed around the bed, past Justin and out toward the kitchen.

Justin lowered Cole to the bed. "You've given us a long worrisome week, big brother. It's about time you left off being sickly."

Cole flinched as he settled back onto the bed. He reached for the bandage at his waist. "If you call this getting better, I'm glad I slept through a week of it."

Justin wanted to do something to make Cole more comfortable. He wanted it so bad that it stopped him. If he was too nice, Cole would know just how sick he'd been.

"Tell me what I've missed." Cole trying to take charge, even from a sickbed while he was flat on his back.

Justin talked about the letter Heath had found on Dantalion. "Someone paid him."

"There's a conspiracy against us, and they don't seem to care who they kill, so they must be gunning for all of us. Is the man you hauled to jail saying anything?"

"Nope. He must've given us a phony name too because we can't figure out who he is. Sheriff Dunn is looking through wanted posters. Heath got him to as good as confess, though. So that's enough to hold him, just not enough to find out who hired him."

They discussed the troubles until the food came. Justin couldn't believe how nice it was to talk to his brother again. He'd talked things over with Heath and Sadie, and they'd come up with few answers. Cole wasn't much help, at least not right now. Even so, it felt good.

Justin decided then and there he was going to stop threatening to punch Cole every time he got irritated. The two of them had been squabbling since they were boys. Justin thought it might be time to set that aside.

But needling Cole was one of his favorite things. Maybe he should cut back slowly instead of just stopping all at once.

The night sky was being pushed back to the cold light of dawn. It was bright enough they'd doused the lantern when Heath came in. He took one look at Cole and smiled.

"Good to see you awake, Cole." Heath came close, his blue eyes flashed until Justin could swear lightning struck from behind them. Justin, Cole, and Heath discussed their troubles some more.

It was fully dawn when Sadie came in, saw Cole awake and talking, and burst into tears.

That was Justin's chance to break up their talk. He squared his shoulders and blew out a breath. With his brother on the mend now, finally Justin could think about something besides hanging on to Cole's life for all he was worth. "I've never questioned Ramone like I should. And Miss Maria is there with him and Alonzo, though he's been working as much as he can."

Alonzo was the ranch ramrod, second in charge only to John Hightree, the foreman. But Alonzo's pa, Ramone, was in great need.

"You want company?" Heath pulled Sadie into his arms. She mopped her eyes and held on tight for a few seconds, but soon enough she went to fussing over Cole again.

"I do," Justin said, "but I'm wondering if you're the one for the job. I think he might relax more if I brought one of the women instead."

"I'll go." Sadie looked back at Cole as if she were scared to leave, scared to do anything that might put Cole back to sleep.

"That'd be fine, but let me ask Rosita first. She speaks Mexican real well. I want someone there to catch anything that passes between the family—anything, I mean, that's meant to leave me out. And she remembers things from the old days. I'd like her to hear what Ramone has to say."

"Rosita is in the kitchen." Angie came in with a bowl of broth. "Sadie, if you don't mind feeding Cole, I'll see to breakfast so Rosita can go along with Justin."

Justin walked with Angie back to the kitchen. She had a mysterious upward tilt to her lips, and Justin couldn't help but ask, "What's making you smile?"

"I'm just so relieved and happy that Cole's getting better." She smiled again. "I am so tired—we all are. But none of that mattered when his fever was so high. Now I feel like I could melt into a heap on the floor and just sleep for days."

"I feel it, too. Even when I slept I was tormented with nightmares, mainly about planning my brother's funeral." Justin shook his head. "I should've known Cole was too ornery to die. I should have trusted him."

They shared another smile, one of the most harmonious moments since they'd met. Then they reached the kitchen to find Rosita sliding a large beef roast into the oven. She was singing a hymn quietly to herself, just as happy as the rest of them.

"Rosita, I need some help."

She turned, looking about ten years younger than she had last night. "Whatever you need."

He couldn't resist walking right up to her and hugging her long and hard. "There, I needed a hug. Now I can go back to being a pest like always."

Rosita gave him a teasing slap on his arm.

"I want to go talk to Ramone."

The smile faded, but she kept the sparkle in her eyes. "And you want me to . . . make him a tray of food?"

Justin shook his head. "You're not getting off that easily. I want you to come with me. Ramone, Alonzo, and Maria are all staying in Alonzo's cabin. I want to ask them more about everything, and I want a woman with me, hoping that will soften my questioning some. And you speak their language well enough they can't discuss answers right in front of me before they give me an answer that might not be the full truth."

Rosita reached for the ties in back of her apron.

"I'll take over in the kitchen, Rosita," Angie offered. "Sadie and Heath are watching over Cole. I'll get breakfast to them."

"Umm . . . a simple breakfast." Rosita stopped untying and gave Justin a nervous glance.

He wasn't sure why.

"Yes, very simple. And I'll cook it slow so nothing burns."

"Thank you, little señorita." Rosita lay a strong, callused

hand on Angie's cheek. Angie had made food earlier, but it was only broth.

Angie smiled back with genuine gratitude. Justin saw how she soaked up kindness like it was water and she'd been living in a desert for years.

Justin ran upstairs to dress proper and get his winter coat. He came back down to find Rosita in a heavy shawl, a woolen bonnet on her head, ready to head out. She had a plate in hand with a cloth covering something.

"Biscuits. Let's begin in a sociable way. You can always change tactics."

"Sounds wise. Let's try to keep this friendly." As soon as they walked a few feet from the house, Justin glanced behind him and said, "What was that about cooking slow?"

Rosita gave him a knowing smile. "Our pretty Angie isn't an experienced cook. She says Sister Margaret is working with her. And now I am, but the ways of a cast-iron stove are strange to her. She seems to have done only simple cooking in her life and has no real training."

"A woman who can't cook? I don't know if I've ever heard of that before." Justin glanced back again, more in fear this time than worry he'd be overheard.

Before he could think of another question to ask, they reached the ramrod's cabin. Justin knocked on the door. He was struck by how much time had passed since the attack—a full week. And with Cole so sick, Justin barely thought about what all needed to be done to ensure their safety.

Now it slapped at him like whipping oak branches.

Alonzo opened the door, saw them, and a wary look crossed his face. Justin wondered what it meant and immediately found himself on edge.

"Come on in, boss."

7

"Ramone, you got that scar on your face the day Grandfather Chastain was killed, didn't you?"

Justin sat in a chair at Alonzo's small table, across from Ramone. He did his best not to stare at Ramone's ravaged face. Not because of how it looked. This was the West so he'd seen battered men before, and it didn't bother him overly. It was a hard life. Scars were often a sign of a man who'd survived rugged times. He took many scars to be marks of courage and strength. But this was different. This scar was a reminder of how Justin's grandfather had died.

It was a brutal scar. It started at the hairline, cut down through Ramone's left eye, his face, his chin. The skin was puckered and thickened along the slash. Ramone had a scraggly beard, yet the scar was deep enough that it was visible through the facial hair.

Ramone had a white socket where his eye should be, and it'd been left to heal without any stitches or any medical care at all. It was a horrible thing.

Rosita was talking quietly with Maria, who worked at the stove. The aroma from the room was spicy. Justin smelled the hot peppers so well liked by the Mexican folks. He could eat a few of them, but Alonzo always wanted his food loaded with the bits of crunchy fire. That must be how Maria was preparing breakfast, as the air was so thick with the peppers that Justin's eyes burned.

Alonzo sat at the head of the table with the men. He was a young spitting image of his pa, except unscarred and un-battered by life.

"*Sí*, your grandpapa . . ." Ramone's voice, low and unsteady, faltered. It was heavily accented too, no surprise for a man who'd spent the last thirty years in a land where folks spoke another language. But Ramone had been born in Skull Gulch and spoke English well for the first twenty years of his life. He might falter some, but he got by well enough.

His one seeing eye flashed with fear, but he cleared his throat and continued, ". . . your grandpapa fought off two of the three *hombres* who came at us with their guns already drawn, and the third, Dantalion, their leader, killed Señor Chastain."

Hearing of it brought back the exploding guns as someone had shot Cole from cover and did his best to kill more. Justin had been blaming Arizona Watts, and he was most likely guilty. It sounded like Dantalion had hired him. On the other hand, Dantalion could have just as well done it himself.

Ramone went on, "When Dantalion shot Señor Chastain and slashed me, he knelt on my chest with his knife at my throat and said I'd be blamed for my boss's death, and be-cause he was a powerful man, people would believe him. I'd hang for murder. He said if I ran, I'd live. I was lying there on the ground, in terrible pain, blood everywhere, and I knew he was right. It would have been the honorable thing to stay and face the charges and speak the truth, only that wasn't a choice he gave me. He'd kill me right there where I lay if I didn't agree to leave the country. If I came back and accused him, I'd hang. It was like speaking to el Diablo himself."

Ramone shuddered visibly. "I ran and did not stop until I reached Mexico City."

As he spoke, Justin studied him. The scar reached his lip on the left side of his face and curled his lip in what looked like a sneer. Or maybe it was a sneer, but there was no courage or arrogance behind it, only cowardice and a trace of viciousness, reminding him of a cornered rat.

Yes, Justin understood Ramone's reaction to run. Dantalion seemed like the kind who'd destroy a man without a second thought. But Ramone had other choices. He could have written a letter to tell the truth to the Bodens. He could have left, then circled back and faced up to what he'd witnessed, and trusted Ma and Pa to listen. The ugly wound on his face would have been a powerful piece of evidence in Ramone's favor.

Instead, he'd turned coward and ran and made no effort for thirty years to set things right, all the while knowing Dantalion, a killer, was on the loose.

"I spent my life with my father, Don Bautista de Val, until he died."

The old Spanish Don had been a partner to Justin's grandfather for years. The two of them were given a vast Spanish land grant. Then the United States of America gained the whole area from Mexico in the Treaty of Guadalupe Hidalgo to end the Mexican-American War. To retain ownership of the grant, de Val had to become an America citizen, something that didn't suit him. So he left it all behind and moved to Mexico City to live out his remaining years. His wife and children went with him, of course, while he abandoned his mistress in Skull Gulch, including Maria and Ramone, the two children he'd had with her.

"Then after my padre's death, his wife, who'd borne him children at the same time as my mother, cast me out." Ramone's face twisted in a way that made his scar all the more ugly, the sneer all the more pronounced.

"Don de Val was not discreet with his unfaithfulness, and his señora always despised me, and who could blame her?" Anger seethed behind Ramone's calm words. It appeared that Ramone could blame her, and did.

"I came back to *mi padre*'s ranch and holed up in the old hacienda, or what was left of it. I was defeated. Cast out. I had nothing. An ugly man with nothing left to live for. I came home to die."

"No, Padre." Alonzo reached across the corner of the table and rested his strong hand on his father's trembling arm. "You have family who love you."

"You love a man who's lived his life in fear. I have shamed our family and failed all of you."

Alonzo's hand tightened and he looked determined to convince his father there was a future still.

Before he could speak, Justin went on. He had to find out more about his grandfather's shooting. "Do you know anything about Dantalion?"

Shaking his head, Ramone said, "No, nada. I had never seen him or heard of him before he attacked us, nor since."

"What about Grandfather? He was worrying about his daughter, my ma, needing an American husband to hold on to the land grant. He talked about the governor. Do you think Dantalion worked for the governor?"

"It may be possible. I don't think your grandpapa believed that. Rather, Dantalion was using his connections, without the governor's knowledge, to gain wealth. Señor Chastain believed the governor was a decent man but not vigilant to his duties. Dantalion was working for others, doing bad deeds in the governor's name."

Justin couldn't stand the thought of getting nothing from Ramone. He had to know more. Then he thought of that warning note they'd found on top of the canyon wall, where someone had set off the avalanche that nearly killed Pa. The note had matched word for word one left with Grandfather after he was shot. It read, *This is a warning. Clear out of this land you stole from Mexico.*

"What about the note they found in Grandfather's pocket?"

A furrow tugged at Ramone's brow. He shifted his eyes from side to side, then looked at Maria. "*Donde está la nota? Quiero la nota.*"

"*No veo nada,*" Maria replied in Spanish.

A confused frown crossed Ramone's face that struck Justin as phony. Then, staring at the tabletop, Ramone asked, "What note?"

Justin knew a lie when he heard one. Which told him something he hadn't known when he first came in here. Ramone knew all about the note.

"He just asked Maria if she had seen the note. He wants it." Rosita spoke up, her voice vibrating with anger.

"I just want to see it, nothing more." Ramone looked sullen, his words to Maria taking on a harsh tone.

"Ramone, you speak deceit." Rosita, usually quiet, spoke as if a whip cracked in her voice. "No one knew about that note but family. John and I were told, but Chance and Veronica made the decision to tell no one. But I can tell from how you speak that you know of this note."

"Only what Señor Justin has told me today."

"The Bodens didn't investigate that note or its threat because they hoped the trouble was over when you ran. They were willing to accept you as the killer, even though Veronica especially didn't want to believe it. Perhaps you saw it as avenging yourself on a man who'd prospered while your grandfather lost his holding. Or perhaps you were furious because Frank denied your wish to court Veronica. When you ran, it seemed as good as a confession. But you say you are innocent of that crime, and we believe you. Now you sit here and lie to us and deny knowledge of something that, just from listening, I can tell you knew of. You lie to the family who rescued you from hunger, danger, and loneliness. You sit here well-fed, a roof over your head, with a doctor treating you, and repay the Bodens' kindness with lies. You return evil for good, Ramone. You do not seem like an evil man, but now I must wonder."

Rosita stood in outraged offense before Ramone. With his head lowered as he stared at his hands folded on the table, looking very much like a man in prayer, moments passed in the loudest silence Justin had ever heard.

Justin glanced at Rosita. He'd have confessed to just about anything if she was glaring at him like that. The fact that Ramone didn't crumple meant he was very brave or very scared. What he knew might well be something he couldn't bear to face.

And considering what had already been done to him by Dantalion's hand, being afraid was a very reasonable choice.

If you were a coward. And Ramone was.

He had run before. Justin understood why, though it was still wrong. Doing the right thing, no matter the danger, was right. Yes, powerful men were always dangerous, but Justin would have faced the trouble no matter the danger. Any real man would.

And it was at that moment that Justin figured out something that he should have realized right from the beginning. Ramone was too weak to plan this, but he was also too weak to stand firm if someone threatened him, or bribed him, or both.

With due consideration about just how to handle this, Justin said quietly but with absolute conviction, "Ramone, I want you off this property, now."

Justin thought of when they'd found Ramone, and he'd held them under his guns. Alonzo had taken the Bodens' side over his own father.

With misgivings, Justin felt it was right to say, "Alonzo, you are a man I consider my friend, and you're a hard worker and a skilled cowhand. You are welcome to stay here. But your father must leave." Justin turned to Maria. "I appreciate your help, but it's time for you to go, too."

His voice echoed with anger and betrayal. He'd been overly stern. He could apologize and say it more politely, but the message would be the same. *Get off my land.*

Maria gasped, obviously shocked that she was being asked to leave. But she would have left anyway with Ramone leaving. He shouldn't have spoken so rudely to her.

"I'm sorry, Maria." Justin dragged his black Stetson off and ran his hand deep into his hair, then resettled the hat. "It's been a hard spell and I have no cause to take it out on you." He looked up, hoping she knew he was sincere. She had something she wasn't saying. But instead of looking shifty, like a liar, she looked scared. Even so, she didn't say anything.

Justin promised himself then and there he'd find Maria later when she wasn't under the watchful eyes of her brother and ask her a few more questions.

"It is fine, Justin. I would head for town now anyway. I am needed at the orphanage, and if Ramone needs further care, I will see to it in town. Can we borrow a horse? I have one I rode out, but Ramone will need a way to town. I will keep the horse in the stable in town until someone from the CR comes for it."

"That's fine."

"And I have enough money set aside that you can find a place in Skull Gulch to live, Papa." Alonzo patted his father on the back.

"Let's go, Ramone." Maria began to pack.

Justin hadn't really meant to stand over them and watch them leave, as if he didn't trust them on his land. Although right now, he didn't. But they gathered what few things they had so quickly, they left ahead of him.

Alonzo followed, then waited at the door for Justin. Now

Justin was getting shown off of Alonzo's property, at least out of this house.

He reckoned he deserved that.

Justin followed Rosita into the house in time to meet Cole coming into the kitchen with Heath tagging along behind. Rosita went toward her room, taking off her shawl.

When he saw Justin, Heath said, "I'm going to climb down and have a look at Dantalion's body. You want to come along? We can leave the women to tend Cole."

Cole looked frustrated that he didn't get to go. He held his side, every move careful, not even close to being up to the trip.

"We'll go right after I'm sure Ramone is gone," Justin said. "And for heaven's sake, don't tell Sadie we're going."

"Where are you going you can't tell me about?" Sadie came in, and her smile had an edge. She knew when her brother was trying to get away with something.

"Morning, Sadie."

She'd never give up until she badgered it out of them, so Justin gave in gracefully. "Heath and I are going to climb down that cliff where Dantalion fell. We want to see if we can find out any more about him, search him and such."

"His horse ran off," Heath said. "Maybe we can round it up. It might've settled in to graze and not left the area. There could be saddlebags, even a brand might tell us something. We need to know who hired him."

"Slim chance of catching his horse now. Why didn't you hunt for it right away?" Cole asked.

"Because we were too busy trying to keep you alive." Sadie propped her fists on her hips, but she couldn't maintain the angry pose. She quickly went back to fussing over Cole.

Heath sidled up close to Sadie, too close in Justin's opinion. He admitted he was having a hard time getting used to his sister being married.

Her overly familiar husband rested his hand on the small of her back and said, "We thought you might want to stay and care for Cole. We also knew you'd be mighty tempted to come along on our climb. If you want to go, you can. But a body that's been dead a week is sure to be a gruesome sight. I would spare you that."

Sadie turned from Cole and looked deep into Heath's eyes, as if trying to see inside his head and read his thoughts. She must've liked what she saw. "I'll stay here. Thank you for letting me decide instead of thinking you know what's best and sneaking off."

"You're welcome, Sadie girl." He smiled and put his hand against her cheek, gentle-like. "I like having you along."

Justin was torn between knocking Heath's hands off his sister and taking notes. He'd never had much luck with woman, but then he'd been mighty busy on the ranch and hadn't missed them. Much.

Angie picked that moment to come in. She went straight to the stove and ladled up a steaming bowl of broth and brought it over to Cole as if she were cradling life and death. Right behind her was Rosita, who took up a vigil beside Sadie. Cole was now surrounded by women fussing over him. It seemed a man had to get shot to get some female attention around here.

And since that was such a stupid thing to think, Justin decided it was a good time to head out.

"Ronnie, Cole's been shot." Chance Boden looked up as his beautiful Veronica entered his hospital room. She was so wonderful, he thanked God every day that she was his wife.

She was the strongest woman he'd ever known, but she staggered as she turned to him. All the color fading from her cheeks.

"Is he all right?" Ronnie rushed the few steps to his bedside and sat beside him as if her knees were giving out. She didn't grab for the letter, which told him just how frightened she was.

"I've read it twice while waiting for you to come back. Sadie tells me he's fine, but she also said it happened a week ago. It took this long for her to tell us." Chance frowned and studied his leg, encased in plaster and strapped down to the bed so he couldn't move it. He'd been in bed almost constantly since he got hurt, and the idleness was driving him mad. And that was *before* his son was shot.

"Our son, our son. Ronnie, what if—?" Chance stopped talking before he shamed himself by crying. He thought of the boy he'd brought out west with him. Born to him and his first wife. Cole was tall and dark like him, though Chance's hair was shot through with gray these days. Cole with his city manners and his intelligent blue eyes. A look-alike for Justin, his son with Ronnie. But their two boys acted and dressed so differently there was no mixing them up.

"I have to get back there."

"I know what that means." She talked over the top of him. Her golden hazel eyes flashed with temper. "They waited to write until they were sure he would live. Our son has been at death's door for a week and they didn't tell us."

Chance handed the letter to her. He still had John's to read. "Sadie got married, too. She wants to come visit."

"What!" Ronnie snatched it from him.

"Did you really think that was the thing to tell you first?" Chance admitted to himself that both had been shocks. But knowing Cole had spent the last week fighting for his life nearly made him forget the *other* news in Sadie's letter.

"Who in heaven's name did she marry?" Ronnie scanned the long letter quickly.

"Heath Kincaid."

Ronnie looked up, her eyes bright with wonder. "The cowhand who saved your life?"

Chance grinned. "He seems like a fine young man. I was impressed with him even before he acted so courageously that day."

"He's a handsome young man, too. I don't know him well, but I noticed he had a nice smile."

Chance shook his head. "Stop noticing handsome young men, wife."

Ronnie gave him a hug. Then her good cheer faltered altogether. "She got married and we weren't there." With a deep sigh, she said quietly as if she spoke only to herself, "I would have loved to see my baby girl get married."

Chance held out an arm. She came to him, and they held each other. "So would I, my love. But we will be home soon and see their marriage, if not their wedding. And the life they make in a marriage is the most important thing."

"I know." Ronnie sniffled, then swiped at her eyes. "Now tell me more."

"Here, read these pages." Chance nodded at the letter Ronnie held. "Let's find out what John has to say. He enclosed his own letter. I'm hoping I get a better explanation from him."

"Although he waited until now to write, too."

John Hightree was Chance's foreman and old friend. He was a man to talk straight and not worry too much if he hurt anyone's feelings. That was one of the things Chance liked best about him.

While Chance read a much more graphic description of Cole's gutshot and what had happened to the men who'd done the shooting, Ronnie read Sadie's letter.

John also mentioned that all three of his children had moved home. That gave Chance a deep sense of satisfaction. It was his fondest wish that his children would appreciate the legacy that came with the Cimarron Ranch. He didn't have much time to enjoy it, though, because of other troubles from home, including Heath being shot and the discovery that the avalanche that nearly killed Chance was no accident.

A chill of dread rushed down Chance's spine as he read that the rockslide had been deliberate. Whoever had done that was now threatening his children. Then Chance read a twist in John's letter that hit like a lightning strike. "Ronnie! Shove something in front of the door!" As soon as he said it, he realized there was nothing to shove. "Stick a chair under the knob."

Ronnie gave him a sharp look, then grabbed one of only two chairs in the room and rushed to the door. She jammed the high back of the rickety wooden chair into place, then turned back.

"I want an explanation." Her voice was hard, no-nonsense. Ronnie was a beautiful woman, well-dressed, fine-boned, and delicate-looking with her blond hair and wide hazel eyes. But Chance had learned long ago that her looks disguised the fact that she was as tough as the New Mexico Territory itself. There was no one he'd rather have beside him in a fight.

Chance waved the pages of John's long letter at her. "He says someone's hunting trouble around our children."

"Who is it?" Veronica's voice rose with anger.

"They don't know, but John thinks whoever's behind it has long arms. He says the avalanche was no accident, and we have to consider that we might be in danger. It reached all the way back to when your pa was shot. He insists it might reach all the way to Denver right now."

Chance saw fire flash in Ronnie's eyes as all her fighting instincts rushed to the fore—if there were any that weren't there already. She'd never been satisfied that her pa's killer had escaped punishment.

Her pa, Frank Chastain, being shot had brought about Chance's wedding to Veronica. Chance knew he'd have gotten her to marry him sooner or later. But Frank's dying wish was that his daughter marry Chance. The CR was at risk from powerful men looking to steal the old land grant, and they were doing it based on Frank being born in Canada, then living as a fur trapper in America, then taking Mexican citizenship to qualify for the land grant, then turning back to American once the United States got a big chunk of the Southwest from Mexico.

Frank, who'd changed countries twice already without a qualm, didn't hesitate for a moment to become an American. But there were still men who coveted the land and saw Frank's as easy pickins. There was nothing easy about Frank, and he'd given his life to save the CR for his daughter. Chance had willingly taken up that fight, and now it looked like they had a new fight on their hands. Well, Chance chafed to be part of it.

With a dark look at the shaky door, Ronnie asked, "John really thinks we might be in danger here?"

"He said there's a list of names and we're both on it."

"A list?"

"A list of names that a man was hired to kill, and it includes all our family's names."

Ronnie nodded. "I need a gun." Her first instinct was to fight for her family.

How could a man love a woman more every day when he already loved her with all his heart?

"You can't stay in the parson's house anymore." Ronnie had been walking to a nearby house alone every night to stay with a parson and his wife, who had generously opened their home to her.

The hospital was in a quiet, peaceful neighborhood, a small

building with just a few rooms where patients stayed. Most people healed at home.

There was no way to defend the modest building. "There'll be no more lonely walks. My bed's narrow, but not so narrow you can't stay here with me."

"I miss you in the night, Chance. I'll be glad to stay here."

That was solved, but keeping Ronnie close didn't stop someone from coming into the hospital, gunning for them both.

Chance's hands fisted, and he spoke through gritted teeth. "I'm lying here like a worthless pile of trash. No gun. No way to stand up without a lot of help. No way to protect you."

"Or yourself." Ronnie's eyes flashed. "We need to send for the sheriff. He can go with me to buy two guns."

"And you'll sleep here with me. You're not safe out alone. You might take danger to the parson and his wife." Chance didn't argue about the two guns. He saw no reason to keep someone as accurate and fierce as his wife unarmed. "I need to see the doctor. I've been patient long enough. I need to get out of here."

"No!" Ronnie jabbed her index finger right at his nose. She had agreed to everything he'd said . . . until now. She stopped him cold with her glare. "You've got to let your leg heal for at least six weeks. He said he'd take off the heavy cast and put on a lighter one and let you get up on crutches after that. If you get up too soon, you could still lose your leg, or worse yet, get an infection and die."

"So I lie here, coddling myself while you're in danger and my children face gunmen alone?" Chance fought a brutal desire to rip the plaster off his leg with his bare hands.

"Not alone. They have each other and, thanks to you, they're all under the same roof. And John's there, and Rosita. She's a warrior at heart. Now Sadie has a husband fighting with them. They're safer at the CR than they would be split up."

The Cimarron Legacy.

Chance had demanded they respect all that had been sacrificed to build their ranch. How many times had he told the story of Grandfather Frank giving his life for the land that sustained them all? And now that demand might just save their lives.

Until he could move better, Chance had to be satisfied with that and focus his attention on protecting Ronnie. And he had to take steps fast to keep them safe. Danger could be coming even now.

And then there was a click.

He and Ronnie turned to watch the doorknob slowly turn.

"I brought my climbing gear, but I don't think we'll need it."
Heath dismounted and untied a pack he'd stowed behind the
saddle on his beautiful buckskin stallion. The pack sagged with
weight and clanked like it was loaded with chains.

Justin swung off his horse, hitched his collar close against
the frigid wind, and found a stretch of grass in between the
scrub brush on the side of the trail away from the hidden cliff.
He rigged a halter and staked out his mount to eat while he
climbed down a mountain to look at a corpse Heath had already searched.

It was a complete waste of time. He'd like to yell at Heath
for such a harebrained idea, except Justin was sure the whole
idea had been his.

"Lean out carefully. The trees lining this trail look strong,
but they aren't, and there's a cliff only a few feet beyond 'em."
They both leaned down. Justin was surprised by how quick the
land dropped away.

When they pulled back, both on their hands and knees, Heath
looked at Justin and smiled. "Did I tell you how Sadie saved
my life?"

"No." Justin glanced over sharply as they got to their feet. "I reckon we've been so busy playing nursemaid to Cole, I've only listened to the details that might help us figure out who's behind all this."

"After we caught up to Cole and realized Sadie was missing, when you went on and I went back, I rode straight up on Dantalion and didn't see him until he had me covered with his six-shooter."

Justin could see it on this heavily wooded, curving trail. He knew there was almost no way to beat a man with a drawn gun.

"We were standing there, and Dantalion had me figured for dead so he was talking, gloating. I was worried to death because Sadie wasn't with him and I was afraid he had her, then he said something that made me sure he didn't. I was looking for one split second of distraction to give myself a chance. And I wasn't finding anything.

"Then out of nowhere a rock smashes into the backside of Dantalion's horse. The horse reared, and I got my gun drawn and took a shot. The horses were all fighting us and then Dantalion fell. I couldn't get a bead on him anymore. That's when Sadie comes charging out of the woods with a fist-sized rock in one hand and her other arm loaded with more. Charging an armed outlaw with nothing but rocks to save my worthless hide."

Heath shook his head and spoke quietly, almost to himself, "How could I not love a woman like that?"

He fell silent for a moment as Justin thought of his sister. All his instincts were to protect her and make her life easy, but Sadie was a fighter and it was high time he admitted it.

"I got three bullets into Dantalion. He was dying, bleeding out." Heath pointed at the trail where bloodstains had dried and turned black, but they were unmistakable.

"I started questioning him and, considering Cole had been

shot, I wasn't feeling too merciful. Sadie was trying to convince him to get right with God."

With a chuckle, Justin said, "That sounds like my Sadie."

"She's my Sadie now, but you can call her yours if you want." Heath's blue eyes flashed with mischief. Justin didn't bother to punch him.

Heath went on. "I got a few nasty comments out of Dantalion and searched him and found those papers I showed you. Then real sudden-like he goes from lying on his back on the trail to a desperate attempt to escape. And if ever a man was desperate, I reckon it was him. He charged at the woods, and I went after him and fell right behind him. But I grabbed a tree and held on. Sadie was right there, shouting she'd get a rope from the horse and save me."

Justin smiled. "She's tougher than I give her credit for."

"Yep." The look on Heath's face told Justin that was exactly the point he was supposed to understand.

Since Justin didn't like anyone telling him he needed to act better than he already did, he decided it was time to get back to work. "So, are we wasting time climbing down there?" Justin wasn't looking forward to getting close to an aging carcass.

"Yep, but I suppose we'd better go anyway." Heath sounded about as excited as Justin felt. "I should have gone hunting for his horse right after I got Sadie home, but I was too busy marrying her."

Justin growled, "Let's get going."

Heath grinned. Justin had to admit he liked his new brother.

"It's a lot easier climbing if you can start from the top." Heath grabbed a rope off his saddle horn and tied it to a sturdy tree. "I've put knots every few feet on the rope so we can just skedaddle down."

Since Justin didn't know much about climbing, he took Heath's word for it.

"I'll go first. You make sure the rope is holding and we aren't pulling this tree that's clinging to the edge of a cliff right out by the roots."

"I hope it doesn't decide to wait to tear loose until you're down and I'm dangling from it."

"Me too. How would I get back up?" Heath grinned again and then was gone.

Justin leaned forward and saw Heath scramble down the rope like a big squirrel. The tree didn't budge, but they both knew it wouldn't. The thing had clung to this mountainside for many years.

The rocks the outlaw had landed on were brutally jagged. Dantalion hadn't stood a chance. Of course, if the bullets had struck where Heath said they did, he was dead either way. No man . . . Justin paused. No *normal* man liked killing. It was a sickening thing to shoot a man. Or Justin might say he guessed it was, because he'd never shot anyone in his life. He was glad for Heath's sake that Dantalion's wild escape attempt had finished him. It might help Heath not carry it so heavy on his soul.

Justin swung over the edge and climbed down hand over hand. With the knots it was only a little harder than going down a ladder, and the way up wouldn't be much worse. When he hit the ground, he had to set each foot down carefully. The ground was so broken, there wasn't a level place anywhere.

Heath had picked his way to Dantalion's side and knelt. Justin was relieved to see the cold had kept the body in decent condition. Even the vultures had left the body alone. Mostly.

Heath started digging in pockets while Justin, crouched across the body from Heath, did the same. They found nothing until Heath dragged a small notebook out of Dantalion's boot.

"I missed this." He shoved the small book in the breast pocket of his shirt. "I looked in his boot for weapons but didn't notice this notebook."

"Let's be real thorough. He might have other hideout spots."

As it turned out, they found nothing else. Justin finally stood and looked down at the man. "I've never seen him before."

"Me neither. Not until I came up on him on the trail."

"The man we took prisoner I recognized. He was a layabout I'd seen in Skull Gulch, a newcomer who'd been around only a few weeks. I don't understand," Justin said, shaking his head. "What in the world could this man have against the Bodens?"

Heath studied the body a few moments longer, thinking. Then he pulled the notebook out of his pocket and flipped it open. "Lots of notes." Heath turned the notebook so Justin could see. "The handwriting is so small and cramped it'll take a while to figure it out."

He turned one page after another with the faint rustle of crisp paper. Justin couldn't see what he was looking at and had to fight down an impatient request to grab it and do the looking himself.

Heath suddenly curved the little book and ran his thumb along the edge to flutter through the pages. The quick, careless way he did it told Justin the pages were most likely blank.

He reached the end of the book and froze, staring at the last page. "What does this mean?"

Heath's eyes flashed hot and sharp as lightning. Before Justin could demand to see what was bothering him, Heath shoved the book into Justin's hands.

Justin spread the back page wide and read it. "Chance Boden. Pa's name, with a line drawn through it."

"And then"—Heath reached over and tapped the top of the page—"in tiny print at an angle it says 'missed.'"

The two of them looked up at each other.

Quietly, with menace, Heath said, "And the next name is Veronica."

Justin's jaw got so tense it looked near to breaking. "He had plans for Ma, too."

"And after that, Sadie."

The way he said it, Justin wondered if Dantalion wasn't lucky he was already dead. Although, considering his likely destination in the afterlife, probably not.

Justin nodded. "And out beside her name the word *bait*. What did he have planned?"

"And was it still in the thinking stage?" Heath asked. "Or has he set something in motion?"

"If he did, she might be in danger right now."

Justin thought of Cole, so hurt he wouldn't be able to protect anyone for weeks. John was a tough man, but they hadn't sent him in to stand guard. He was working, not staying around the house.

"I've even eased off on posting a sentry." Justin wanted to kick himself.

"Sadie's there, and she's mighty tough."

"No, she's not."

That tricked a smile out of Heath. "You're thinking of your delicate baby sister, not the woman ready to face a gunman with an armful of rocks."

"I have to admit it's hard for me to think of her as a woman who would do that."

"Read who's next." Heath had memorized the whole list in the seconds he'd seen it.

"I'm next."

"Yep, then Cole, and there's a question mark beside his name." Heath started moving, heading for the rope. "He made that mark after we were waylaid. He knew Cole was wounded."

"We already knew that, didn't we? You're on here, too." Justin pulled the book closer. "The ink is different on your name."

Heath had rounded the body and passed Justin. He grabbed the rope, then looked back over his shoulder. "Different how?"

"The ink's thicker, like maybe he used a different sorta fountain pen. I wonder if you were added later."

"Well, he didn't add it after the wedding, since he was good and dead by then. Now I'm another barrier between him and the CR if his goal was to clear out the legal owners and heirs so he could move in and stake his claim. But Dantalion was dead before we got married."

"He might've seen the lay of the land between you and my sister and known you were going to be a big problem. Killing you stops a wedding, but even without a wedding, killing you gets rid of a man sweet on a woman and willing to fight for her.

"Whichever one of them was shooting from on top of Skull Mesa saw you protecting Sadie. He'd know you were willing to side with us. If Sadie got married, that's one more Boden who'd need to get out of the way."

"You think this is a list of all the people he's out to kill?" Heath asked.

"A hired gun, that's what it looks like. And since he had another man with him, I'm guessing he got the job and then found someone else to do the dirty work. The question mark proves he knew Cole was shot. And he whipped this book out and wrote in it before he rode after us." Justin paused, then added, "Dantalion seemed willing to shoot or hurt whoever he could get at, going all the way back to Grandfather. But what about Sadie? Why is the word *bait* by her name? He must've planned to take her and use her to draw us out and kill us."

"I don't reckon I know for sure what the plan is, but I can promise you one thing."

"What's that?"

"His purpose in putting that word by her name is pure evil. She's in danger."

With a jerk of his chin in agreement, Justin snapped the book shut. "Let's get back to the ranch. Heath, you need to take

Sadie and get out of here. Whatever this is, it's big. A thousand dollars in gold in Dantalion's pocket, that's someone with a lot of money. And when Dantalion hired a man to help him, it turned into a conspiracy. There are more people involved, and Dantalion's death doesn't put an end to any of it."

"I'm not leaving you here shorthanded. That's a coward's way."

"Take Sadie and go see Ma and Pa. I know Sadie wrote asking permission, and I reckon she'll hear back that they want her to come for a visit. Get her far away from here. It'll be one less person I have to worry about protecting. Anyway, if their goal is to kill us all, they might give up if Sadie's beyond their reach."

Never had Justin seen a man so torn by indecision. "They've always done their damage dry-gulching. Lying in wait, back-shooters every one of them. Now that I know, I can take steps. But they don't want to shoot Sadie. They want to steal her away, and that makes me sick to think what they could be planning for her. I want her out of here."

"All right, let's get back," Heath said. "We can talk about it more if your pa gives her permission to come." He looked down at the dead man. "By rights we should haul his body up and give him a proper burial. I'd as soon leave him to the vultures."

"What if there are wanted posters on him?" Justin felt his fists clench, useless, as Dantalion wouldn't feel the beating he deserved. "Maybe we can find out who he's working for. We might be able to get to the bottom of things faster if we haul his carcass in to the sheriff."

"I reckon that's a fair reason to take him." Heath sounded disgruntled. "About the only one."

"How fast can we get him to the top?"

Disgusted but resigned, Heath replied, "About as fast as I can climb up there, and I'm a mighty fast climber. Tie the rope around him under his arms and then take a good grip on it. Don't start climbing yet. I'm going to untie it from that tree and hitch the lasso to my saddle. We'll let my horse pull you both up."

"I'd rather leave him to the worms," Justin said. "A fitting end for a man such as him."

Nodding, Heath said, "Plotting against an innocent young woman makes him rotten enough he might taste too bad even for worms. Now get him hitched up."

Heath scampered up the rope so fast, Justin had to hustle to get Dantalion strapped tight before the rope was ready to start hauling.

The door stopped, blocked by the chair, and then the knob rattled.

"Mr. Boden?" A man's voice was followed by a hard knock on the door. "Are you all right?"

Chance looked at Ronnie, and they both heaved a sigh of relief.

Ronnie rushed to the door. "Just a minute, Dr. Radcliffe."

Chance wanted to help. He wanted to stand between Ronnie and that door. Even though he knew the doctor's voice well after these last few weeks.

Instead, Ronnie unblocked the door, and the doctor came in frowning. "What are you doing with that chair, Mrs. Boden? What's going on here?" His eyes darted between Ronnie and Chance. The eyes then widened, and the doctor blushed. "Uh, you really shouldn't . . . your leg needs . . . that is, if you'd like, I could come back, uh, later . . ."

It took Chance a few moments to figure out what the stammering was about. Then he knew. A married couple. Behind a locked door.

"It's not that," he said. As if Chance had any hope of romance with his leg in pain every time he moved.

The doctor blushed even deeper. Chance hurried to get to a reasonable subject. "We need your help, Doc, and it's serious. A letter came today . . ." The doctor said he didn't want to hear the details, so Chance skipped ahead and got right to the point. "It was no accident I was hurt, Doc. Whoever attacked me might strike again, up here in Denver. I need to get out of this hospital and find a place where we can protect ourselves." And there Chance lay, flat on his back. Talking about taking action when he couldn't even move.

"Not with your leg. It needs more time to heal."

"I'll be very careful with my leg, I promise. I want to be walking right when this is over with, and I know the care you've taken of me and how blessed I am to have your skill and the Lord's healing working through your hands. But you don't want a gunman to come into this hospital. Those who tried to kill me sent a rockslide down on my head, and a group of my hired men rode with me. They didn't care who else died. If my enemies come here, they may shoot anyone who gets in their way."

The doctor's frown turned downright grim. "You're right. You do need to get out of here."

"Is it possible for me to go home?"

"You mean to your ranch?"

"Yes, I could take the train all the way to New Mexico Territory. That's an easy ride coming up."

Ronnie interrupted, "Chance, you were unconscious for most of it. You don't know what kind of ride it was."

Chance pressed on. "I don't know much about fancy train cars, but maybe I could find one to borrow or rent. I could have a bed and be careful the whole time. Once I get back home, I can—"

"I'm afraid that isn't possible." Dr. Radcliffe was adamant. "A train is a modern marvel, but every turn of those wheels shakes the train and it's constant. You'll be bounced along for hours and hours. While it's not a rough ride, it might shake apart a newly knitted bone and completely undo the healing of your leg. It just needs a few more weeks. You sure you can't stay put?"

"What, stay here and wait for a killer to find me? It's not safe here, and I'm putting my wife in mortal danger. You too if you happened to be in the hospital when an assault comes. And what kind of danger will I bring down on the patients in here with me?"

"Well, you can't take the train." As he mulled the situation over, the doctor plucked at the whiskers near his bottom lip, as if coaxing out an idea.

Ronnie said, "There must be somewhere safe here in Denver."

"I'm sure there is, but where?" The doctor was skinny and short, wore a threadbare suit with a stained white shirt. Chance got the impression the man wasn't poor, despite his manner of dressing. He was just absentminded about his appearance, probably because he was consumed with trying to save lives.

"Moving you could be done if we're gentle. We could spirit you away from the hospital. I can think of a way to handle that. Then we'd have to make sure we aren't followed."

Chance liked the way Dr. Radcliffe said "we" as if he were part of this now.

"We could lay thick blankets in a wagon so the ride would be less dangerous for you, and we'd need to find somewhere close. Let me think."

There was a long silence. Chance looked at Ronnie, and the two of them turned back to stare at the doctor, awaiting his answer.

Finally the doctor's chin lifted. He left off his beard-stroking. His eyes took on a bright gleam and he smiled. "I know just the place."

"I got a letter from Ma! She and Pa say we can come!" Sadie looked a little dizzy with excitement.

Justin was hoping her excitement would just sweep her right out the door all the way to Denver.

"Heath," Angie said with a bright smile, "that means you get to meet Sadie's parents."

Justin really needed to catch Angie up with what was going on around here. "Heath has been working on the CR since before Pa was hurt. In fact, Heath saved Pa's leg—maybe even his life."

"Th-then why does he need to go to Denver?"

"I don't." Heath gave Sadie and her happiness a nervous glance.

"Because he hasn't met them as their son-in-law yet." Justin spoke over top of Heath.

Sadie's smile faded, but her shoulders rose and her chin raised higher. Justin was struck by how much she looked like Ma. Right down to the grit.

"If we're needed here, we stay. Ma's letter said a few other things. She's upset we didn't tell her about Cole right away. She had heard that Heath was shot, and I'd never told her that. Oh my, she had quite a lot to say. Now that I consider it, waiting to go until she calms down isn't that bad of an idea."

"I'll take you to Denver sometime, Sadie. And we need to go visit my family in Rawhide. We'll see your folks. And then on our way back we'll get off the train in Colorado City, ride to see my family, then come on back here."

"That will be fine."

"You're going to Denver now." Justin broke into their reasonable little talk.

"Just because you found her name—"

"You're both going." Justin cut Heath off. "With Dantalion gone and winter setting in, it's a good time. They can't regroup until spring."

Heath snorted. Mighty rude.

"Why aren't you two sitting with Cole?" Justin wished he'd

had more time to talk sense into Heath. Why the man felt it necessary to tell Sadie every single thought in his head was a mystery.

"Mel is here." Sadie mentioned Melanie, the daughter of their nearest ranching neighbor, Jack Blake, and a lifelong friend of the family. "Found my name where?"

"In a note—"

"We hauled Dantalion's body up the cliff." Justin cut Heath off, trying to stop him from telling Sadie everything. "We left his body hidden in the woods. If one of our cowhands is a traitor, I don't want them to know he's dead. We'll take him to the sheriff as soon as we can."

"I'll leave so you can discuss this without an outsider listening in." Justin heard pain in Angie's voice. "In fact, now that Mel is here, I should get back to the orphanage. I'm in the way here . . ." Her voice broke then, and she quit talking altogether and turned to leave the room.

Justin grabbed her. He wasn't going to add hurting her feelings to the day's troubles. Not when she'd worked so hard with them to save Cole.

He turned her to face him. "I'm being a half-wit, I know that. Heath and I found out something I don't think Sadie should know."

"Sadie? But Heath will tell her the minute—"

"I'd hoped"—Justin was having trouble letting anyone finish a thought—"I could talk him out of it, but he's determined."

"Sadie girl, your big brother and I found a notebook." Heath spoke so quietly, Justin could barely hear him.

Justin fumbled in his pocket and walked over to hand a little packet of papers to Sadie, opening it as he went. "Your name, with the word *bait* beside it."

Sadie stared at the paper a long while, then swallowed hard. "And you think Heath and I should leave? That I should go see

Pa and Ma in Denver so I'll be safe?" Her voice rose with every word. "Even though Heath and I would have to abandon you and Cole when there's danger all around?"

"That's not—"

"Yes, that's exactly what he wants." Heath talked over top of Justin this time. "And I told him we aren't going."

"We're not going anywhere, Justin." Sadie took Heath's side completely.

"No, I can see you're not. All right, we'll hire more cowhands, do a better job of posting sentries. We know the danger and we'll be on guard."

"Only you can't hire a bunch of tough men to ride for you because you don't know who to trust. You already know someone at this ranch has betrayed you. And our prisoner in town was a man hanging around in Skull Gulch. Right where you'd go to hire more men. Maybe men are waiting in town right now, hoping they can hire on."

"We need to ferret out who we can't trust," Justin said. "And I've got an idea how to do it."

"Whoever it was planned to report to Dantalion most likely. Now that he's dead, your traitor has no one to tell his tales to."

Sadie asked, "Can't you at least trust John and Alonzo?"

Heath and Justin exchanged a long look.

Sadie nodded. "I would trust John with my very life. And we have good reason to believe we can trust Alonzo." She said to Angie, "The day Cole was shot, we found Alonzo's father holed up in an old house, the house Maria was telling us about that night I came to the orphanage. Alonzo's father had a gun drawn and aimed at us because he thought we meant him harm. Alonzo helped calm things down and convinced his father to put his pistol away. If Alonzo had bad intentions toward the Bodens, that would have been his chance to do terrible damage. And he was with us when someone opened fire on us."

"Maybe," Justin said, "but he and his pa had gone ahead. They weren't under fire."

Sadie gave a sigh. "As much as we want to believe Alonzo isn't the source of the trouble, we still don't want to tell him what we are up to. Even if he's loyal to us, careless talk might spread the word without any betrayal intended. And that includes your talk, Angie. Be careful not to mention this to anyone, not even casually."

"Keeping my thoughts to myself is a habit I've developed to an art."

"What does that mean?" Justin asked.

She shook her head at him and waved away the question.

Heath took up the story. "We need to figure out who at the ranch told Dantalion where your pa would be the morning of the avalanche. And those outlaws held off the attack until we were on the way home from de Val's hacienda. Someone gave them the word we were headed that way. We'd be dead if we hadn't turned off the main trail and ridden up that nightmarish shortcut."

"The only ones who knew," Heath went on, "were your cowhands. Just as they were the only ones who knew your pa was headed into the path of their avalanche. One of them passed word on to Dantalion on mighty short notice."

Justin nodded. "And whoever informed him might be planning something else and have it ready for the next time we're vulnerable. Our backstabbing hired hand might ride out to find Dantalion, not knowing he's dead. If we lay a false trail, we could watch and see who the turncoat is. You noticed I left Dantalion in the woods, didn't you, Heath?"

Heath's head lifted slowly. Bright blue eyes flashed. "I did, but I thought it was because you didn't want to upset the ladies."

"It had occurred to me that no one knows he's dead but us."

With a tight smile, Heath said, "We have to act fast. Whichever of your cowpokes was tipping off Dantalion may already have tried to contact him."

"This time the ones setting a trap are going to be us Bodens." Justin took the notebook and pressed it into Sadie's hands. "See if you can read the early parts of this. We haven't had time to do more than take a glance, and it's small, tight handwriting. We'll drop Dantalion off in town and make sure the sheriff keeps things quiet. Then we'll set a trap for the rat who's betraying us while he's on our payroll, and once it snaps shut, we'll see if he starts squealing."

10

Justin and Heath slipped into the woods to pick up their man. Angie watched with Sadie standing at her side until raised voices sounded from Cole's room.

Angie gave Sadie an alarmed look, and the two of them rushed toward their patient.

"If you make one more move . . . !" Mel shouted.

"I've had it with being in this bed."

"And I've had it with trying to convince a stubborn ox to act like a sensible adult man."

"You can't come into my house and insult me."

"Sure I can. I've been doing it for years."

"I want you out of this house right now."

"If you move again, I'll throw a lasso over you and hog-tie you to that bed!"

Angie whispered to Sadie as they hurried along, "She talks to the children like that, though usually not at the top of her lungs."

"Sister Margaret did mention she's not a natural teacher," Sadie whispered back.

"You're all treating me like I'm a child," Cole shouted angrily.

"No," Mel snapped, "we're treating you like you're a badly injured man who needs to give himself time to heal. Anyone with a shred of brains would know that and stop acting like a child."

"She's never actually roped one of the children," Angie said. She paused before adding, "That I know of."

"I'm healed up enough to help protect this ranch."

"You make one wrong move and tear open that bullet wound and you'll be fighting for your life again. And even if you don't kill yourself, you still won't be of any help."

Angie approached the door with Sadie only a step behind.

Mel sat on the edge of the bed with both hands pinning Cole's shoulders down as he struggled to get up. Which couldn't be good for him.

"If you think I'm so fragile, stop being rough with me." He wrenched sideways, gave a loud and—Angie thought—rather phony moan of pain, then grabbed Mel by the waist and tossed her back.

She dove forward but missed him as he rolled to his feet. She landed flat on her face on the bed. Without pause she crawled on her hands and knees toward Cole on the far side. He grabbed a chair as if he planned to use it to drive her back. Maybe add a whip.

"What is going on here?" Sadie roared over the chaos.

Cole froze, the chair lifted up, its legs pointed at Mel.

Mel's head turned hard. She missed bracing her hand on the bed and fell headfirst to the floor. She landed with a hard thud at Cole's feet.

Looking down, Cole asked, "Are you all right?" He set the chair aside, careful not to set it on Mel. It looked to Angie like he was grateful to put the heavy thing down.

Mel dragged herself up so that her head popped up over the mattress. She'd had her brown hair in a braid when she arrived, but now long curls bounced wildly over her eyes and hung halfway down her back. She shoved the curls back from her face and, when they fell right back, blew at them with a tired puff of her lips. "Your brother is the worst patient who ever lived."

"Your old friend Melanie—"

"It's Mel!" This was a correction Angie had already heard several times. Nobody but nobody called Mel Blake, Melanie. Angie had no idea why the woman was so adamant about it.

Cole smirked as he looked down at her. "You are the worst *nurse* who ever lived."

Sadie blinked. Angie wondered what she'd do, whose side she'd take, but then Sadie started laughing. The laughter grew and then Cole broke into laughter, too.

Mel rolled her eyes heavenward, then turned to glare at Cole.

He looked down and laughed harder. "You're a bigger mess than I am, and I've been shot."

Mel chuckled at the comparison.

Angie smiled, but privately she thought they'd both lost their minds. "Cole," she said calmly, "I respect your wish to help, but could you please just rest a few more days? While I think you're close to being up and around, don't forget you were fighting for your life up until only two days ago. We were so terribly worried about you. If you can't stay in bed and rest for yourself, could you do it for us?"

Cole's laughter died. He looked impatient enough to gnaw a hole in the wall to escape his confinement. That gave Angie an idea. "Justin and Heath brought in a notebook you should see. There's a lot of tiny, cramped handwriting at the beginning of it. Could you go through it, see what it says? You could do it lying down, and it really would be a great help. It's a job that has to be done."

Sadie came up beside Angie. "She's right, we need to read it. And there's the other papers Heath brought. Justin read through them, and they seemed to be nothing but notes about money, but someone needs to go through all of it carefully. You understand money, and you've got keen enough eyesight to decipher the handwriting."

Eyes narrowed, Cole said, "You think I'm going to sit around and read notes and do busy work while someone's trying to kill my family?"

"Let me get it. I think when you see the last page you'll decide it's a lot more than busy work." Sadie hurried from the room.

Angie wondered just how she'd gotten into the middle of this family crisis. She hadn't meant to. But she'd been needed, even with all the Bodens here, to take a turn sitting with Cole so he was never alone. She hoped she'd acquitted herself well with her questionable nursing skills. He hadn't died on her watch, so she thought she could claim it a success. She ought to go back to the orphanage while everyone was still breathing.

Sadie came back at a run and nearly skidded to a stop, the little notebook in hand. "Please, Cole, will you get back in bed?"

Angie had seen Sadie spitting mad, and she'd seen her worried sick, exhausted from the long hours at Cole's bedside, and she'd seen her sweet and gentle with her new husband. But through it all, Sadie had always been straightforward. She said what she meant so that those around her knew exactly how she felt. When Angie thought of the years she'd spent keeping every thought and emotion hidden from her husband, a man who knew how to spot a weakness and use it against her, it was as refreshing as rain in the desert.

But right now Sadie looked sly, even sneaky. She waved the book at Cole and said, "I'm not going to show you what's in here unless you agree to rest."

Even her sneakiness was right out front, which probably meant it wasn't sneaky at all. She was blackmailing her big brother.

"What is it about that notebook that has you so up in arms?" He still stood on the far side of the bed.

"Under the covers, big brother, or I walk out of here with this, and you know you're too weak to catch me. You'd better believe me when I say you're going to want to read it. Among other things, it's got Pa's name in it with a line drawn through it, then in tiny print the word *missed*. There's something in here about you and me, too."

Cole came around the bed, and Sadie ran out of the room. Cole reached for his side and winced in pain, and then with his face dark like a coming thundercloud, his eyes flashing with impatience, he shouted, "All right, I'm getting in bed."

"Angie," Sadie called, her voice coming from a distance, "let me know when he's all tucked in like a good little boy."

That started Cole glowering, his fists clenched.

Angie said quietly, "The note about Sadie worried Justin enough he tried to get them to leave the ranch, but Heath and Sadie won't abandon you when the trouble is so close."

Cole quit fuming as furrows of concern appeared on his brow. He nodded at Angie. She wasn't sure why Cole was fighting with Mel and why he seemed to clash with Justin until she was afraid—even with Cole laid up—the two brothers might come to blows. It wasn't unusual for him to snarl at Sadie, and she snipped at him right back. And he seemed to delight in insulting Heath, but usually that just made Heath smile.

When she dealt with him, he seemed like a perfectly reasonable man. Very intelligent. Polite almost to a fault. She could tell he had city manners, and she knew he'd gone back east to college and lived in Boston for a time.

Why didn't they all just talk to him in rational ways? It worked just fine for her.

He climbed into bed and pulled his covers up. Mel smoothed them, and he glared at her until she stopped.

She grinned and said, "I need to head for town. The children need me."

Mel headed out just as Angie raised her voice, "He's resting now, Sadie." More quietly to Cole she said, "I'm afraid Sadie is in terrible danger."

The change in Cole's expression was deadly.

"You have to rest right now and regain your strength. With Dantalion dead, those who are after your family may need time to reorganize. But there's no doubt in Justin's mind that they will attack again. So use this time to heal. Please."

Sadie returned with her book and went straight to Cole. She handed it to him, then sat down on his bed and flipped it to the back. "Let's start here."

Angie saw his eyes focus, then narrow.

Rosita chose that moment to come in, and Sadie said, "Rosita, look at this."

Angie left to get dinner. She already knew that notebook was a portent of menace coming straight at the Bodens. She wished Justin and Heath would come back. And she wished this time she wouldn't fill the kitchen with smoke.

11

"We need to get back." Heath swung up on his horse.

The body had been turned over to Doc Garner.

Sheriff Joe was thumbing through his pile of wanted posters.

The town's undertaker was building a coffin. Dantalion was going to be buried quickly and quietly.

Justin felt itchy, like he'd left a new calf alone in the path of a wolf pack. Or in this case, he'd left his wounded brother and his baby sister and the rest of the folks at the CR in the path of outlaws bent on killing. But they had to make one more stop.

"I need to talk to Maria. She's back at the orphanage. I've got some questions I want to ask her."

Heath looked down the trail toward home, and Justin knew he was thinking about Sadie being vulnerable. He almost told him to go. Justin would talk to Maria and come along in a few minutes. Then again, it wasn't wise for anyone from the CR to ride alone, not right now.

Maria had stopped herself from talking when Justin questioned Ramone. Now she was away from her family, and Justin hoped she'd tell him what was going on.

"Let's go, then." Heath reined his horse toward Safe Haven Orphanage.

Just moments later, they dismounted, hitched their horses, and went inside. The school was unusually quiet, but in the distance they heard a low murmur of voices.

Justin figured it out when he smelled something delicious. "It's high noon—mealtime. I hope it doesn't take all three women to feed the children. With Angie helping the doctor at our place, Mel out there for a visit, and Sister Margaret with a sprained ankle, they'll be shorthanded."

"I'll wait by the horses. No sense disrupting things more than necessary."

Justin walked toward the back of the building while the front door opened and closed with Heath going back outside. Justin peeked into the small dining area to see twenty or so children eating with enthusiasm. He swept his eyes around the room and saw Sister Margaret smile and begin to rise.

"I was hoping to have a word with Maria." Each of the three ladies sat at a different table with the younger children. Each table sat six. There were four tables, and the fourth one had older children sitting together without an adult. All the children looked clean and well-fed, and their table manners were probably better than Justin's.

"Miss Maria, would you be able to talk with me for a few minutes?" He could see she was very busy.

One of the older girls stood. "I'll sit at your table, Miss Maria."

"Thank you, Stephanie." Maria gave Justin a worried look. Considering all that had been going on with her brother, this was a worrisome business.

Justin wondered if there was more. Someone had definitely been informing Dantalion about the goings-on at the CR. If it was Alonzo, who better than his aunt—a relationship neither Alonzo nor Maria had admitted to publicly—to pass on messages?

Miss Maria came quickly. She was wearing a plain brown dress. She wasn't in a nun's habit as were Sister Margaret and Sister Louisa. Though she'd devoted her life to the orphanage, Justin knew Maria had never become a nun. Considering she lived like one and dressed nearly like one, he wondered why she hadn't taken the veil.

Her hair was the deep black of her Spanish and Pueblo heritage, though now it was shot through with gray. She wore it pulled back in a tidy bun at the base of her skull. Maria came close before she lifted her eyes to Justin's. They were black as coal, intelligent eyes, dour eyes. Justin knew Maria had always carried the weight of depressed spirits, but being a solemn woman was far from being a conspirator with murderous intentions. Even so, she might know things Justin didn't.

This woman had talked with Sadie often back when she'd worked here. Maybe Sadie had said things in passing that Maria had told her partners in crime.

With regret, Justin decided he wasn't leaving here without answers. He didn't like upsetting Miss Maria, but until this thing was settled, Justin was going to upset a lot of people. And that wouldn't stop him from asking his questions.

He stepped out of the dining room and gestured toward the front of the building.

Maria led the way down the short hall. Justin knew there were private rooms where Angie had been when he'd brought her home.

His first meeting with Angie was when she'd stepped off a train and collapsed in his arms. She'd been barely able to speak the words "Aunt Margaret." Justin had only known one Margaret in Skull Gulch, so he carried her to the orphanage and left that skinny little handful of fragile woman behind. It seemed as if he'd been worrying about her overly ever since, but most likely that was because he'd had a hand in saving her. That was the kind of thing that created a bond between folks.

"My main reason for coming here is . . ." The dining room door opened then and several children came out, walking toward Justin and Maria. They had to pass them to get upstairs to their rooms. The door opened again.

There was to be no more chance for a quiet talk, not here. And Justin didn't want the children to overhear. With Maria still clutching his arm, he tugged her toward the front door. They stepped outside. The Safe Haven Orphanage was set away from the town's main businesses. Heath adjusted the leather on his saddle, standing between their horses at the hitching post.

Justin felt Maria withdraw. Her hand, still holding his arm, slipped away. Justin knew the ladies from the orphanage very well and he had all his life. But apparently Heath was too much of a newcomer to trust. Or maybe Maria saw the people moving around town and didn't want to be seen talking to him.

Justin wouldn't get any answers here.

"Let us talk alone for a few minutes, Heath. We're going to walk around the back of the building."

Heath's eyes were sharp, and he no doubt saw Maria's tension. "Go on. Take all the time you need." He turned back to his saddle as if adjusting the saddle correctly was a matter of life and death and could not be delayed.

Walking around the building, Justin took Maria's hand and slipped it through his crooked elbow as it had been before.

"I need to know how often you saw Ramone before we found him. What did you say to him?"

Maria didn't react to that—not strongly, not like she was being accused of betrayal and conspiracy to commit murder.

They finally reached the back of the building. There was a large yard with a seesaw and a swing. The children played outside most days, but the wind was sharp today. Justin was used to the harsh conditions, and Maria had lived here all her life, yet she hadn't bothered to grab a shawl when they came out. They wouldn't be able to talk long in the wind.

"I could tell that you had things to say but weren't willing to speak in front of your brother. I'm hoping that without him here, you'll be willing to help me."

Maria stopped in her tracks and folded her arms across her chest. She stared at her feet awhile, then glanced up, her expression heavy with fear. "Ask your questions. If you don't like the answers, you can just throw me in jail."

So maybe he did upset her with his first question. Her unfair accusations were frustrating, and Justin's temper snapped. "I am not throwing you in jail."

"Why wouldn't you if you think I conspired to harm your father and shoot your brother?"

Justin had to admit that was a fair question. "I would if I thought you did that, but I don't. I just need to find out if maybe you trusted someone and your trust was misplaced."

Miss Maria, sixty years old if she was a day, raised her head and faced him bravely, as if she expected a beating. Her chin trembled, and her eyes glittered with unshed tears. "So I am either a criminal or a fool, is that it?"

"Please, stop. You're overreacting." She really was, and Justin had to ask himself why. He suspected it was because she knew something and her loyalty was badly split.

She said something in Mexican that Justin didn't understand, but her tone rang with hopelessness. "I love Sadie and have always respected your family. Now I do something that may cost me my life."

"No, Maria, please. We can protect you." He bent lower to meet her eyes. "I promise—"

A rifle shot rang out, the bullet exploding the wood right beside Justin's head a second after he bent low.

"*No, alto!*" she screamed. "*No mas! No muerte.*" She hurled herself in front of Justin just as he tried to grab her and shove her behind him. He had to get her inside. The impact of a second bullet sent Maria staggering against him so hard he slammed into the orphanage wall. The gun fired again and again. Maria's body jerked each time; the bullets were hitting her. They fell sideways to the ground, as if she were tackling him to save his life. Justin rolled to put his body between her and the barrage of bullets.

As Justin dragged out his six-gun and braced to take the next bullet, gunshots came from another direction. He saw Heath run out from behind the building, gun drawn, shooting at their assailant. The hidden gunman broke off the attack.

Justin had his pistol in hand and leapt to his feet. Hoofbeats thundered away.

"I'll get the horses!" Heath dashed out of sight. Justin took one step to follow and fell flat on his face. He looked back to see Maria had a tight grip on his pant leg. He reached down to tear loose the grip, then stopped as he realized what it was.

A death grip.

He got free, then crawled toward Maria just as Heath went galloping past the orphanage. Justin could imagine him rushing after that gunman alone. Dying alone.

"Heath!" Justin roared. "Come back!"

Heath pulled up hard on his buckskin and wheeled the horse around. He looked at Justin's shirt, then at Maria.

Justin noticed for the first time that inside his open coat, his shirt was soaked in blood. "I'm not hit. That back-shooting coyote got Maria. This is her blood."

Justin turned to Maria. A pool of blood was growing under her. She'd been shot in the back. He knew those bullets had been meant for him. Heath didn't dare go charging off alone.

Justin swore an oath to God that he'd find whoever did this and see him hanged.

He'd heard the shooter ride off, yet Justin felt exposed. How could he know if the man might come back? How could he know if there was only one coward out there in the trees?

Justin swept Maria up into his arms and rushed through the back door of the orphanage. The kitchen and dining room were in this part of the building, and to his relief the room was empty. He hated exposing the orphans to such a horrible sight as their teacher dying in a hail of bullets. Add in Justin's fury and the chance he might say something ugly that these children would remember all their lives and he was grateful they were gone.

When Heath charged in through the back door, he nearly tripped over them. Doc Garner was out at the CR. He wasn't staying there all the time anymore, but he rode out often. Justin had passed him on the trail to town. Waiting for Heath to come back, Justin rolled Maria over to see that three bullets had hit her. The back of her brown dress was drenched with blood. They made up a tidy cluster of shots in the middle of her back. Whoever was behind this filthy crime had a fine aim.

He recalled the first shot that had barely missed his head. After that one, the man aimed at a bigger target, his chest. And Maria had given her life to save him.

Sister Margaret came hobbling into the back room, leaning hard on a cane. "I heard gunshots." She stumbled to a stop, and her eyes went wide with horror. Then she moved again and dropped to her knees beside her old friend. "No, Maria, no. Please, God, no . . ."

Justin, seeing where the bullets had struck Maria, didn't bother sending Heath for the doctor. The wounds were the kind that no amount of doctoring could heal.

"Let me see to her." Heath came up beside Justin and urged him aside, rolling up his sleeves. Justin remembered that Heath had treated Pa until Doc Garner could get there.

As Justin moved aside he heard a whisper. Maria lay facedown on the floor. Heath cut the back of her dress open with one slash of his razor-sharp knife.

Leaning close, Justin said, "Hang on, Maria. We're doing all we can."

She breathed painfully in and out. "*Meh . . . hee ko.*"

Justin put his ear to Maria's lips. "What did you say?"

"*Viva Meh-hee-ko,*" she said faintly.

Justin wasn't sure he heard it right. "What is she saying?"

Heath shook his head. "I don't know."

Justin glanced at Heath, who was pressing strips of Maria's dress into the awful circle of bleeding wounds.

Heath looked away from Maria to Justin, then Sister Margaret. "There's nothing I can do. There's nothing anyone can do."

Sister Margaret rested a hand on the back of Maria's head, her lips moving in prayer.

A long breath came that went on and on, exhaling every bit of air in Maria's lungs, and there was no strength left to fill them again. With the last bit of air, she said, "*Tener cuidado.*"

"Sister Margaret, do you know what she meant to say? *Meh hee ko?*"

"Mexico, pronounced in the Spanish way."

Of course, that was how Mexicans pronounced the word. "And what's *viva?*" Justin asked.

"She's saying 'Long Live México,'" Sister Margaret said.

"But why speak those words with your dying breath?"

"*Long Live México* are the words of a revolution."

Justin looked between Sister Margaret and Heath. "What revolution?"

Shaking her head, Sister Margaret replied, "There is no revolution that I know of, though we are taught those words when we study the Texas war for independence from Mexico. Texans said, 'Remember the Alamo,' and the Mexican army and those loyal to it said, 'Viva México.'"

It made sense now. He remembered hearing the phrase back in school. "And what else did she say? *Tener cuidado?*"

Sister Margaret shook her head again. "I didn't hear it. That phrase means nothing to me. Are you sure you heard it right?"

"*Cuidado*—isn't that what they call Juarez? Cuidado Juarez? Juarez is right across the border from El Paso. It's about the closest Mexican town to us." Justin wasn't sure of anything anymore.

"She's gone," Heath said. He seemed to have lost all his strength. His head bowed low for a long minute. Finally he gently pulled up the edges of her cut dress out of respect and modesty. He rose from his knees and went to the kitchen sink to wash his hands, moving slowly, as if the weight of the world rode on his shoulders.

It made Justin look down to see his shirt, his arms, and his pants covered with blood. The clothes were beyond cleaning, although Justin suspected he'd never be able to wear them again regardless, not without thinking how his actions had led to the death of Miss Maria.

Justin glanced back at Heath and saw him moving like an eighty-year-old man. He wondered what it cost someone with healing skills to lose a patient this way, to lose a woman to a violent attack. He knew what he felt. A wretched, soul-deep guilt.

"They were gunning for me." Justin looked down at the lady, who had worked for so long with Sadie. His sister was going to be devastated. "I took her behind the orphanage so we could speak privately. I asked her about Ramone. I wanted to know when she'd first spoken to him. I didn't even get a chance to ask her anything."

Sister Margaret said, "She has always been a woman of low spirits. I worried about that many times. If anything, she's too easily pushed around by the children."

"She just reunited with her brother for the first time in years, and she was frightened because I was suspicious of him. And she jumped to the conclusion that I was suspicious of her. Now, because I had to ask my questions, she's dead."

Heath came back, wiping his hands and arms on a kitchen towel. "And whatever she knows, whatever made her say 'Viva México,' died with her. We can ask Rosita about that other phrase."

He threw the towel on a nearby table with a burst of anger, then seemed to get ahold of himself again. Unrolling his sleeves, he said, "I don't think you can be absolutely sure that gunman was shooting at you. He might have been trying to silence a woman who knew too many secrets."

"About what?" Justin was mystified.

Heath's jaw went tight as he looked down at Maria's still form. "About a revolution."

12

Heath went for the sheriff. When Joe Dunn came, he was solemn to the point of tears at what had happened to Maria. And he had no idea what Maria might have meant by "Viva México," or if she might have been talking about Juarez.

"Doesn't seem to be any trouble at the moment between America and Mexico, none I've noticed here in town anyway. How can there be a revolution when the two peoples are getting along fine?"

Justin said, "But are there folks willing to kill to stir up trouble with the goal of starting a revolution?"

Sister Margaret brought a blanket over, which they used to cover Maria's body. Justin carried her to the town's undertaker. He'd just been there earlier today with Dantalion's body. He wasn't pleased to be such a regular customer.

Justin and Heath told the sheriff all that had happened. When the sheriff ran out of questions, Justin said, "Time to head home."

Heath nodded without replying. They left the jail, and after a few quiet paces he reached up and patted Justin's shoulder.

"I feel terrible about Maria. I feel like the worst kind of sinner to be glad none of those bullets hit you."

Justin remembered the way Heath had come charging around the orphanage building, gun blazing. "I don't think he'd've quit shooting if not for you, Heath. He only broke off when you opened fire. You saved my life."

Heath nodded. "You Bodens really can't write a list long enough to give me credit for all I've done for you."

That quirked a smile out of Justin, one quickly suppressed.

Then Heath said somberly, "Rosita said something about . . ." He rubbed his head as if trying to shake loose the memory. Heath looked worn clean out, and Justin had to admit he felt the same. He realized they hadn't eaten since breakfast and it would be dinnertime when they got home.

"About what?" They reached the orphanage, where their horses stood tied to the hitching post. The critters hadn't eaten since breakfast either. Mounting up, Justin noticed two large bowls on the ground in front of the horses. A few grains of oats remained.

Margaret had seen to their horses, God bless her.

"I'm trying to remember . . ." Finally Heath gave up and shrugged. "I can't say her words exactly, but the impression I got was that under the peaceful surface, many people—or maybe just a few—want this land back as part of Mexico."

Justin tried to remember as well, not sure he'd even been there when Heath heard Rosita's opinion. "We'll ask her about it when we get home. And see if she knows what *tener cuidado* means. And we'll see if she actually knows any people with those attitudes." Justin thought of his questioning Miss Maria and what it had led to. He'd stop kicking up questions if he wasn't fighting for his family's life.

Heath nodded. "Let's get home. I don't like that we've been gone for so long. And I don't want to be on the trail after dark.

Keep your eyes and ears and nose open. And keep low. No sense making a good target for anyone."

They set a quick pace. They'd made it about halfway home, when Heath said, "Mel headed out this morning and is back working at the orphanage. It's time to send Angie home—you know that, right? Cole doesn't need anyone sitting with him anymore. He mightn't be at full strength, but no one needs to watch over him. We know for a fact the orphanage isn't safe, either."

Justin had an image bright in his head of Angie at the orphanage, bullets flying, her dying under the gun of a dry-gulcher. He should keep her at the CR. He frowned at Heath, who grinned back at him.

"And one of the two women leaving is making you upset. I wonder which one?"

Justin wasn't about to admit that Mel hadn't even occurred to him. It was that delicate, sweet, beautiful, citified Angie who was in his thoughts. Which was stupid because Mel was one of the finest women he knew, and she'd make the perfect rancher's wife, while everything about Angie told Justin she'd be better off back in a city. She looked like she belonged in refined clothes with an equally refined husband. And Justin wasn't that. In fact, she'd be a perfect wife for Cole. And just thinking that made something burn in his gut that he'd never felt before.

Jealousy.

Justin didn't want to think about it. "Just keep up. See if you can get some speed out of that puny horse of yours."

Of course, Heath's buckskin was one of the prettiest critters Justin had ever seen. Big, strong, well-trained, and quick as lightning. But needling Heath was a good way to end this conversation.

"See if you can stay with me, Boden." Heath kicked his horse gently, mainly controlling the animal using his hands and pressure from his thighs. He surged ahead, but Justin was riding his pa's fast bay, so there was no being left behind. His mount was a near-perfect horse, and one that loved a challenge.

Yet their galloping had more to do with getting home than winning a race.

"Cole, couldn't you please stay in bed for just a couple more days?" Angie didn't try to get bossy. She'd seen how Cole reacted to that with Mel, Sadie, and Justin. He just did exactly the opposite of what he got ordered to do.

Cole came up to Angie, frowning. "Haven't Justin and Heath come home yet?"

Angie had to swallow hard to clear her throat enough to talk. "No, and I didn't expect them to be gone so long."

"Is supper ready?"

"Yes. I was just coming in to ask if you're ready for me to bring in a plate."

"I'll eat at the table. I managed breakfast. I'm about half out of my mind from lying around. Surely sitting in a chair won't harm me."

Angie didn't see herself winning any arguments with Cole, a man who clearly had a will stronger than her own. "Come on out. Mel's gone home."

Cole frowned over that, too, and Angie imagined he was remembering their earlier fight.

"Sadie and Rosita are putting food on the table right now. A chair won't hurt you one bit."

With a nod of satisfaction, Cole rested his hand on her back to urge her out of the room. They walked into the kitchen. Sadie had made a plate up for Cole, and while she arched a brow in displeasure, she didn't nag. She sat the plate down and grabbed a platter of fried chicken and another of Rosita's wonderful biscuits as Cole settled in at the head of the table. Sadie sat down just around the corner from Cole on his right. Angie sat around the corner from him on his left. He wondered if they planned to cut his food for him. Maybe spoon-feed him?

Rosita came and sat beside Angie. He enjoyed female attention to a point, but he was long past that point right now.

The sun was low in the sky, and Sadie looked out the kitchen window compulsively.

Then her tense shoulders relaxed. "Here they come. What could have taken them all day?"

Cole heaved a sigh of relief just as Angie did. All three of them smiled at their matching sounds. Rosita stood and made short work of putting a plate at the other end of the table, another one beside Sadie.

They were just in place when the back door swung open. Justin came in first, inhaled, and said, "Rosita's fried chicken. That's the best welcome—"

"Justin, what happened?" Angie stood so quickly her chair slid backward and tipped over. "You're coated in blood."

His lighthearted greeting faded. He looked down at himself. "I've got to go and change." He left the room, and his footsteps could be heard pounding up the stairs to the second floor.

Heath went straight to the basin to wash up. He wasn't nearly as bloody, though there was a splatter here and there. He moved to the table and sank down beside Sadie as if he had little strength left.

"I hate to say this . . ." Looking grim, his eyes slid from Cole to Rosita, then to his wife. "Miss Maria is dead."

Sadie grabbed his arm. "Not Maria." Her voice broke as she went on. "No, please . . . not that. Not one of the ladies from Safe Haven."

"We think the gunman was shooting at Justin. The first shot was closer to him and barely missed him. Then there was more gunfire, and three bullets hit Maria. She ended up saving Justin's life." He reached for a chicken leg, but his arm dropped back. His expression said the thought of food wasn't welcome now.

Those at the table sat there stunned. Angie too, even though she hadn't known Miss Maria long. And what she knew of her was sad. Maria spent every free moment closed in her bedroom. She wasn't one to talk much or welcome anyone. She was given to melancholy and long prayers, all done on her knees, her face nearly to the floor as if begging for forgiveness.

The children lifted her spirits, and Angie could tell she loved them. But it had worried Angie that the children were under pressure to cheer up their teacher every day. That seemed the opposite of how it should be. Orphans should be surrounded by people who were aware of their hardships and who did their best not to burden them further.

But Angie knew that Sister Margaret and Sister Louise had loved their downcast friend, and they'd done their best, as had the children, to keep her spirits up. They would be heartbroken. She noticed tears sliding silently down Sadie's face. Heath wrapped his arm around her and pulled her close.

Just then, Justin came back into the room. As he settled at the table, Angie had one more thing to say. "What a noble way to die. Maria gave her life for a friend—there's no greater love. God is gathering her into His arms right now. I know she was a woman of faith. She is happier now than she's ever been, secure at the feet of Jesus."

That brought everyone's head up, including Justin's. Angie saw everyone's eyes brighten and their shoulders square. Sadie dabbed her handkerchief at her eyes. Heath reached for the chicken.

Quietly, Justin said, "Thank you, Angie. It was a terrible thing to have her die in my arms, to die in my place. I feel so ashamed—I should have moved faster. I should have protected her." He closed his eyes for a long moment, then opened them and lifted his chin. "But you're right. For someone to give so sacrificially, we need to respect that she died that way. I needed to hear that because I hadn't gotten there in my thoughts yet. I hope I would have on my own, but I'll do it sooner because of you."

Rosita said, "Let's all take a moment to give thanks to God that He sent Miss Maria into our lives. And pray for her happiness as she goes to a better place."

When they went back to eating, Justin told them what had happened. He included that Heath had driven the gunman off before a bullet could find Justin. They spoke of the sheriff and Sister Margaret's grief.

"I have to go back. They were already shorthanded." Angie gave Cole a wry smile. "And you are well—not full strength, but in good shape. You no longer need someone sitting with you at all times."

"I don't know, Angie." Justin stopped eating his chicken, held in two hands. His eyes were shadowed with worry. "The orphanage is where this shooting occurred."

"But weren't there bullets fired out here, too?" Angie reminded him. "Where in the entire West can a person be ensured of complete safety? Where in the whole world?"

Justin got a stubborn look that usually foretold of an argument and orders being issued.

She held up the flat of her hand. "I thank you for thinking of my safety. I plan to tell Sister Margaret that we all should stay inside or maybe play outside the front door rather than the back. It's cold out and we have a lot of plans for Christmas next week, so I don't think the children will mind. I'm sure she's thought of many precautions already. But I have to go back. Two elderly nuns can't run the orphanage themselves. And I won't protect myself while the children go without care and my beloved aunt is overwhelmed by work. If they're in danger, it makes me a coward to stay away when they can't leave."

The silence at the table seemed to have weight.

Finally, Justin nodded. "We've lost the light. It would be best if you could wait until tomorrow to go. You'll be escorted on the trail to town."

"Thank you. I will go back in the morning." Angie smiled through her sadness. She had enjoyed her time here, watching this family love each other, even when they squabbled. All the more reason she needed to get back to town and help her aunt, her only remaining family.

She rose to begin gathering the dirty dishes, then stopped and looked at everyone. "As dangerous as it is here in the West, it's the best place I've ever lived. I love it here."

She turned quickly, afraid of what she might see in their eyes. The best she could hope for was pity.

13

Justin didn't give a lot of thought to what was proper in his life, but it was mighty hard to get rid of Angie the next morning, or he should say, get her home to the orphanage. And it all came down to propriety.

"A woman should never ride out alone with a man." She spoke it as if it were a commandment straight out of the Good Book.

"I thought that was a rule for young women. Aren't the rules for widows a little easier?" Honest, he'd never given it a bit of thought before, not until about one minute ago when he'd been stumped by her commandment.

He boosted her onto her horse, and she grabbed the saddle horn to keep herself from going right over the other side. He caught her and centered her on the saddle.

She glared at him until he felt like he might have burn marks on his face. It took him a minute to try to figure out why. "Uh . . . that is, I'm not saying you're not young."

She sniffed and faced forward as they rode, both hands clinging to the saddle horn with the reins twisted here and there between her fingers.

The woman needed riding lessons.

"And anyway, who's gonna be upset? Sister Margaret? I've known her my whole life. She trusts me."

"It's still not proper."

Sadie and Rosita were up to their elbows scrubbing Cole's bedroom upstairs because Angie had stayed in the room for the days she'd been here, and Cole had declared he was moving back in. Then they had Ma and Pa's room to clean. He should've made Sadie quit cleaning to ride along, but they both knew Rosita would do it all herself.

Justin found himself trapped into riding Angie to town. He needed to stay home and take action with his cowhands and root out the traitor. But for the same reason he didn't feel like he could send Angie to town with one of his cowhands. Besides, that'd probably not be very proper either.

"It's not like there's any chance we would behave improperly—that's a concern for courting couples. And we don't even like each other." He said it to reassure her, even though as he spoke he knew what he'd said wasn't strictly true.

Turning the widest, saddest eyes he'd ever seen on him, Angie said, "You don't like me?"

"Well, I like you some."

Her eyes narrowed. "Let's ride faster. The less time together, the less improper it is."

"What exactly do you mean by improper anyway? Is this some high-society rule? I've ridden all over this country with Mel Blake. No one's ever accused us of being improper. And Sadie rides to town with my cowhands as escort. She's in good, safe hands with them." Of course, he didn't believe that anymore.

"It's fine, Justin." Now she just sounded snooty. "Let's just make the best we can of this improper situation."

It seemed whatever he said set her off one way or another. He wanted to apologize, say something to make it better, but every time he opened his mouth he made it worse. Justin found himself daydreaming about a longhorn bull he'd roped and thrown a while back. The bull had been limping, and he needed to check its leg. The slashing horns and churning hooves, combined with fifteen hundred pounds of gristle and murderous rage, was a whole lot easier to handle than one fussy woman.

It had never once in his life before bothered him to ride long distances in silence, but for some half-witted reason right now he couldn't stand it. So he asked the question that was burning in his gut. "Tell me about your life back in Omaha. It must've been real bad. Was your husband a louse? How long's he been dead?"

She stared at him, her hazel eyes wide and worried. There was such vulnerability there, for a moment he regretted asking. At the same time he was even more determined to know.

"M-my husband had been dead over a year when I left Omaha. When he died, I found we were deeply in debt. I had to turn everything over to our bill collectors, and there were some financial troubles at the bank my husband owned. If he hadn't died, there is little doubt he was headed for ruin and possibly prison." She fell silent.

There was no possible way he could help being curious. "So what did you do after he died?"

More silence, until finally she said, "I moved here to be with Aunt Margaret."

Which he knew wasn't a fraction of the story, but from the stubborn set of her chin, he didn't think he could get more words out of her. Not now.

He noticed the high hill rising up on the west side of the trail and the heavy forest closing in from the east. The trail was still wide, but a skilled rifleman would make his shot count. It wasn't a long stretch. Yesterday with Heath, he'd ridden hard past it, bent low over their horses. Of course, they'd ridden like that the whole way home.

That was beyond Miss City Girl's riding skills.

"We walk on foot for a while now." He pulled his horse to a stop, and she was just seconds behind him pulling up her mare. He was already on the ground. Rounding his horse, he reached up and helped her from the saddle so that they stood sandwiched between the horses. He had to pry her hands loose from the saddle and untangle the reins from between each finger.

"Why are we walking? I've never had to walk on this trail before."

"Haven't you been on it only once before?"

Her only answer was to sniff.

"The reason I want to walk is because someone might be gunning for us from the highlands. Walking between the horses is safer."

They continued on quietly, Justin carefully studying the land, his eyes eagle-sharp as he watched for any unexplained movement, his ears listening for any sounds that didn't belong. He kept his nose busy too, knowing you could often smell a man before you could see him.

"The trail widens soon. Then we can ride again."

Angie glanced sideways at him, her expression one of sadness.

"What's the matter, Angie?" Without thinking whether it was wise, he reached for her hand and held it as they walked, wanting to give her comfort. Hoping she could feel his strength and his willingness to protect her from this harsh world.

A tiny shrug of one shoulder wasn't an answer, and then her lips turned down even further. Justin thought they could ride the horses again, but he hoped if they walked just a bit more, maybe she'd tell him her troubles. He might be able to fix them.

Speaking just above a whisper, she asked, "Do you really not like me?"

He stopped in his tracks. Her horse stuck with Justin's and stopped. Facing her, Justin tried not to be such a complete lunkhead. What does a man say to a woman to cheer her up? At the rate he was going, he'd probably make things worse.

He prided himself on being an honest man. But that usually amounted to yelling orders while he and his men herded cattle. Still, he didn't know any other way to be than straightforward. Surely there was a way to be honest without being a half-wit.

"I like you real well, Angie."

She lifted her chin, and there was a spark of hope now in her eyes, peeking out from behind the sadness.

He tugged his leather gloves off and tucked them behind his belt. Without really thinking what he was doing, he touched her cheek with his index finger. He had a cattleman's hands— rough, scarred, and callused—made that way from long hours working in a rugged land. The moment he touched her, he knew he shouldn't have.

Because he found out how soft she was. Instantly a longing awakened within him to touch her again. "When you came to town and collapsed and I caught you, held you in my arms, I thought I held the most beautiful woman in the world."

"But my face was covered with soot. My dress was filthy, and I'm sure I smelled terrible."

"I admit I looked forward to seeing you all cleaned up."

That got a smile out of her.

"You looked so fragile that day, and then when I heard what you'd done for that mother and her three children, giving them all your money so they could eat, going without yourself—"

"Any decent person would go without to feed hungry children. You certainly would."

He brushed aside her protest. "The sad truth is, many people wouldn't. But you did, and I knew that along with being beautiful, you were generous and kindhearted, too."

A tiny smile trembled on her lips. "That's a lot to figure out about one unconscious woman you've never spoken to."

He wished he could turn that smile into a big one. A smile with no hurt, no fear behind it. He wanted to know what had happened to her, and yet he understood completely that a body wanted to keep dark times to themselves.

But the little smile was an encouraging sign. Justin tilted his head. "That's what I saw. Then I took you to the orphanage and saw how much Sister Margaret loved you. I knew you had to be a good woman through and through."

"Aunt Margaret loves everyone. I think that's part of the job when you're a nun."

That gave Justin a moment of concern. "Are . . . are you considering becoming a nun?" He admired and respected Sister Margaret, but the thought of Angie taking the veil was upsetting for some reason.

"Honestly, the idea appeals to me, but there are a couple of things stopping me."

He waited, not wanting to appear too eager to hear what those things were. Because he was all too ready to encourage her in her doubts, which was most likely a sin. He asked for forgiveness even as he braced himself to argue with her. "What's stopping you?"

"I'm not Catholic."

That set his smile loose. "I think they insist on that."

"Beyond that, they ask for poverty, chastity, obedience. I am obedient to a fault, and while I would always do my best to obey God no matter what I do with my life, I think I need to learn to obey people much less. I need to trust my own ideas of how to go on and stop letting people rule me. I'm all too ready to do as I'm told. Aunt Margaret would never abuse that, but many people would."

Like her husband. Had the man insisted on obedience to the point of being a tyrant?

"What was your husband's name?" As soon as he asked, he realized they hadn't spoken one word about her husband while they discussed her putting on a habit. His question really had nothing to do with this, except Justin suspected it had a lot to do with it. And he wanted to put a name to the man for when he daydreamed about punching him.

He had to clench his jaw to hide his anger and stop his demand to know if he'd ever put his hands on her in anger.

Angie gave Justin a startled look, then replied, "It was Edward. Edward DuPree." Then she kept on talking quickly. "And poverty is certainly no problem. I've managed to be poor with no effort on my part whatsoever."

"So poverty and obedience, but—"

"But I've been married. So chastity isn't possible, and I think it's a very strong requirement."

Was it? What if a woman was widowed? Justin didn't ask because he didn't want to consider the idea, and he didn't want to send her hunting for information. And mighty sudden he knew exactly why.

They stood face-to-face between the shields of the two horses, the critters waiting patiently. Justin was less than a foot away from her. Then it was inches . . .

"I think those are mighty good reasons, Angie. I've got one more mighty good reason you shouldn't become a nun."

Her eyebrows quirked. "You do? What's that?"

Justin lowered his head and kissed her. His right palm settled on her cheek. He'd never kissed a woman before, but he showed a surprising talent for it. He pulled away before the kiss could deepen, scolding himself about being improper.

He stood looking into her eyes on the cold December day. They were, for the moment, out of anyone's gun range, and they didn't have a horde of family and cowhands and nuns close around them. When had that ever happened before?

"Justin." His name was more breath than a word. Her hands rested on his chest as she pushed him away.

It was a rejection, and the thought of it slashed through him like an ax. The pounding of hooves then broke them apart.

They both whirled around. Someone was coming around a bend in the trail. Justin's brain came out of its daze. They had no business lingering out here, in a place so exposed. Although he was having a hard time regretting the talk and especially the kiss.

"Let's mount up," he told her.

As Angie reached for the saddle horn, Justin saw her hands were shaking. He was all too happy to take her by the slender waist and lift her onto the horse. He made sure she was balanced, then quickly mounted his bay and they began walking forward, all without speaking. Justin had his hand on his Colt the entire time.

A few minutes later, Doc Garner rounded the curve and drew up in front of them. The man looked exhausted.

"If you're headed out to our place, Doc," Justin said, "I don't think you need to bother. Cole's up and doing well now. He's gonna make it, Doc. We owe you our thanks. You pulled him through, and we all appreciate your help."

A genuine smile of pure relief lightened the doctor's face. "I'm glad to hear he's on the mend."

"I think we're done dragging you out there so often." Justin wondered if that was too optimistic. Pa had been bad hurt in the avalanche, Heath was shot not that long ago, then Cole. Maybe the doctor oughta drop by every few days from now on, just in case.

Angie said, "He's still moving slow, but other than that, it looks like he'll be back to his old self real soon."

The doctor nodded. "Well, if you're sure he's all right, I think I'll go on back to town and not take the long ride out. My wife is beginning to wonder what I look like."

"Head on back with our thanks, Doc."

The doctor gave Angie a curious look. "Is that why you're riding to town? Because your work is done out at the Boden place?"

"Yes, it's time for me to get back to the orphanage."

"Then I can save you some riding, too, Justin. I can ride in with Angie, and you can head right back home."

Justin still had a lot to say to Angie and he wouldn't mind seeing if she'd kiss him again. In fact, he wanted more time alone with her so bad he knew he needed to get away from her. He glanced at her, and she looked right back, a light pink blush on her cheeks.

"Thank you, Dr. Garner," she said with utter politeness. "I'm happy for your company."

The two rode off for town while Justin turned back to pass through the gauntlet again. He bent low over the saddle and galloped like mad. Trying to pound away his frustration and his wide-awake desire to keep Angie, a woman who looked to be the worst possible choice for a rancher's wife, for himself and not let the doctor or an orphanage, and especially not a pair of kindhearted nuns, steal her away from him.

There was another thought pestering him just as bad as he raced for home.

Those snooty society types who'd made the rule about a man and woman riding alone together being improper knew exactly what they were talking about.

14

Cole got it in his head that he wanted to be upstairs in his own room, and Justin had his hands full getting him up there. The stubborn ox.

He wouldn't admit he oughta stay in Ma and Pa's room. Justin didn't blame him for wanting out of there. It was strange to take over their parents' bed. Justin wouldn't have liked it, and he understood why Cole didn't.

Justin offered to get a few men and carry him up. Cole acted like that'd shame him.

They tried slinging his arm around Justin's neck, but Cole almost collapsed in pain. In the end, Cole had walked all by himself. With Justin right behind him to catch him if he collapsed, which he never did. But Justin couldn't exactly trust the half-wit to stay on his feet, now, could he?

Finally, big brother was in his own bed, studying that notebook with the cramped handwriting. Maybe all of Cole's years wasted in college when he could've been helping on the ranch might be worth something at last.

Rosita and Sadie had changed sheets and tidied the room after Angie went back to Skull Gulch, and now they were working in Pa and Ma's room. By the ruthless scrubbing going into the job, Justin could tell they were eager to leave this bad episode behind them.

It was going to take more than a scrubbing to accomplish that.

Cole held a small wooden desk, placed carefully on his lap. He took notes and read, scratched out what he wrote, then took more notes. He didn't have time to talk, so Justin left him to it. Justin's help probably would've just slowed him down. Instead, he tried to remember that he was running a cattle ranch.

He was a fortunate man to have John for a foreman and Alonzo for a ramrod for this last spell. He'd spent all his time worrying over Cole. If not for their help, his cattle might've wandered all the way to Texas.

Besides, if he tore that notebook out of Cole's hands so he could read it himself, Cole wouldn't have a job that'd keep him still. Justin had high hopes he could keep his brother in bed for a few more days. It was Thursday already, with Miss Maria's funeral set for this afternoon, and Cole had admitted he wasn't up to attending.

They'd all ride to services on Sunday and see how Cole held up for that fairly easy ride. It was a long one, and with any luck it wouldn't include a running gun battle.

Once Sunday was over, Justin was firmly fixed on no more pestering of his big brother. He vowed he'd let Cole decide what he felt able to do, even if he did show the sense of a two-year-old child. But it was time to live in the present, not the future.

He strode up to John. "What do you have planned for the rest of the morning? Tell me where to help."

With a tired smile, John said, "Your help would be greatly appreciated, Justin. We've let things slide around here. I've asked the men if any of them want to go to the funeral, but none knew Maria all that well. So work with us this morning, and then starting tomorrow we'll get things back to normal."

While they saddled fresh horses side by side, Justin looked around the corral and didn't see a single soul.

"We're most likely going to be one more man short," he said to John.

John's brows lowered and wrinkles covered his brow. He had deep frown lines around his mouth. Justin realized with a pang that John was getting older, and because he was Pa's age, that meant Pa and Ma were getting older, too. Justin went ahead and threw himself in the getting-older category, as well. Which for some reason made him think of Angie.

"And why is that?" John asked.

Justin forced his thoughts back to John. "Because it's time to find out which man in our employ is a traitor."

"Alonzo is back. Is he still one you're worried about?"

"I don't trust him, but that may not be deserved. I'm not sure enough where my troubles are coming from to fire one man and think it's all over. So instead I'm going to set a trap."

John nodded, his mouth a grim line. "What do you have in mind, boss?"

"Come in for supper tonight. I want Cole involved. Time for that boy to use his brain for something worthwhile."

John gave a hard jerk of his chin, accepting the invitation. "For now, we've got cattle on pasture that's wearing out. I sent five men ahead to start moving them, but they're short-handed."

"Let's ride," Justin said. It felt good to be working again.

Angie stood near Aunt Margaret and Sister Louisa at Maria's funeral, the children at their sides.

The Bodens had ridden into town. Justin nodded hello but stayed with his family at the graveside. The group paid their respects to Aunt Margaret, Louisa, and Angie and then rode back home.

Ramone hadn't come. Angie wasn't sure if it was disrespect or just a man not up to facing more grief.

The children were given quiet time for reading, and classes weren't held for the rest of the day. Aunt Margaret sent Angie to pack things from Maria's room. She looked for anything to give to Ramone, yet Maria had nothing anyone would describe as valuable.

She folded a threadbare nightgown and three dark-colored dresses that were long past their prime. There were a few books that belonged on the bookshelves in the schoolroom. Then she drew open the top drawers in a small wooden chest. It contained underthings and a comb and hairpins. The room was the size of a prison cell. Aunt Margaret said she'd tried many times to get Maria to take a larger room.

Angie wondered if Maria's whole life hadn't been about martyrdom. Had she felt born into shame? Did she believe she didn't deserve even small comforts?

The bottom drawer had similar humble things and of lighter weight, as if this was all she had for the blazing-hot summer months. When the drawer was nearly empty, a small stack of papers covered the bottom.

With a quick prayer, Angie hoped for letters, some sign of a private friendship beyond the orphanage.

Instead they were just a mix of useless old papers that looked like they'd ended up in Maria's room somehow and been forgotten. Some were letters about the origin of the orphanage written from a priest. Father Wharton appeared to have been the clergyman in charge of this area, because the letters were about raising funds and sending children to stay. Interesting, but so old they were more pieces of history than anything to do with Maria.

Angie heard children moving in the hall. They had a break for cake and milk every day at this time. Sister Margaret's voice joined with the children, talking to Sister Louisa.

"Aunt Margaret?" Angie waited for her sweet aunt to come in. With her head covered in her nun's wimple and dressed in her black habit, Aunt Margaret came in, a sad expression on her face. She mourned Maria deeply. They'd been friends for thirty years.

"How can I help, Angelique?"

Angie winced inwardly. She had been so awful to Aunt Margaret for years. Her mother, then her husband, had demanded the distance, but Angie had gone along and wouldn't excuse herself. It was a shameful thing. One of Angie's rudenesses was to insist on being called Angelique. It was a much finer name than Angie, or so her mother had insisted, with Edward agreeing completely.

Aunt Margaret had complied humbly to all their arrogance. She was trying to change to Angie now, but it was hard after years of being so careful.

"Have you seen these?" Angie showed her the stack of papers from the drawer.

Her aunt's brow furrowed as she took the papers and studied them. "Why, I haven't seen these in years. I knew they'd been misplaced, but in the constant swirl of duties, I'd forget for long stretches of time that I'd once had them."

"They were in Maria's bottom drawer. I suspect she forgot she'd kept them."

Smiling, Aunt Margaret held them close to her chest. "Thank you for doing this."

"It's a sad job, made much harder by the way Maria died. But the work isn't difficult."

Nodding, Aunt Margaret's eyes shifted to the few boxes of Maria's things. "We will go through them. Perhaps some of her things might fit the older girls." She hesitated, then said, "But they are worn and dark. The dreary clothes were a match for her temperament. I think it would be best to give them away elsewhere." Margaret leaned forward to look in the drawer. "There is another paper at the very bottom."

Surprised, Angie studied the bottom. "I didn't even notice it. It's the same size and color as the drawer." Angie tried to pick it up, but it was stiff, maybe from age. She pried at it with her fingernails, yet it would not come. Finally she pulled the whole drawer out. "I still can't get it."

"Try loosening it with one of Maria's hairpins."

There were a few resting on the top of the chest. Working at lifting a corner of the paper, she bent it enough to get ahold of it. She pulled the brittle paper out only to see it was a piece of wallpaper faded to an antique shade of white.

"It's just to line the bottom of the drawer. All that to remove a drawer liner." Shaking her head, Angie grabbed the drawer to return it, and it swung a bit when she held the drawer with one hand.

Aunt Margaret caught her arm. "What's that?"

Angie glanced at her aunt, then followed to where her eyes were fixed. The drawer. Aunt Margaret took the drawer and turned it completely over until they could see the underside. A large envelope was stuck to the bottom. The other papers they'd found might have been forgotten, but not this.

Angie could see the envelope wasn't yellowed with age. It had been put here recently enough, and Maria had to have hidden it herself. Angie looked at Aunt Margaret. "Why would she hide this?"

Her always sensible aunt said, "Let's find out."

Angie reached for it and realized her hand was trembling. For no rational reason, she was sure the envelope contained something important. Definitely something Maria didn't want anyone to see. Angie tugged at it. It had been secured simply by being shoved into a back corner of the drawer. The wood held it on only two sides, so it lifted out easily.

Angie extended the envelope to Aunt Margaret to open. But Margaret hesitated before taking it from her. Angie knew her aunt and Maria were old friends. Was Margaret afraid the letter would say something to show Maria in an unflattering way?

The envelope had a strange address written on the outside. Aunt Margaret flipped it over, carefully folded back the flap, and withdrew a single sheet of paper. She set the envelope back on the chest and then unfolded the paper. Her look of nervous anticipation was replaced by a frown.

"What in heaven's name is this?" Aunt Margaret turned the paper so Angie could see it.

It seemed to be a series of lines drawn on the paper. They were irregular, not a straight line or a square corner anywhere. The misshapen blocks had been placed side by side and filled nearly the whole page. The odd part was that the boxes had a bold, black X drawn through them.

One was left without the X mark, however.

"What do you suppose it is?" Angie asked.

Aunt Margaret pointed first to a small drawing inside one of the blocks, then to a curvy line near the drawing. "I think this is the Cimarron River, and this right here is Skull Mesa. If I'm right, these markings might be property lines. And those lines are around where the Bodens live. This must be their ranch." Looking up, Margaret added, "It's one of the few that hasn't been marked off."

"Marked off?" Angie felt her mouth go dry.

"Yes, as if someone's doing something to these holdings one by one." Aunt Margaret jabbed a finger at the drawing of Skull Mesa and the unmarked area around it. "And it looks to me like the Cimarron Ranch is next."

15

"You expect me to climb in that?" Chance wasn't afraid of much, but this was just asking for trouble.

"I told you I was going to spirit you away and be careful no one followed." Dr. Radcliffe gave Chance a look that said more clearly than words that he was a busy man.

"So you're going to spirit me away and somehow I end up being a real spirit?"

"No, you don't have to die. Don't be ridiculous."

"There's a lot that's ridiculous about this situation." Ronnie folded her arms, but she didn't throw the doctor out of the room.

With a sinking feeling, Chance got the message. She wasn't going to fight the doctor over this.

"But I'd think this would offend your professional pride."

"Not at all." Doc Radcliffe seemed overly cheerful, all things considered. "I haul people out of here in one of these all the time."

"I'm guessing most of 'em are dead, though." Chance looked at the wooden coffin. "There's no way there might be a mix-up and they accidently bury me, is there?"

"No." The doctor waved that away, but Chance thought the man was way too casual about the whole thing.

"Ronnie, make sure I have my gun before I climb in there."

"Mrs. Boden won't forget anything." The doctor removed his wire-rimmed glasses and polished them with a white kerchief he pulled from his back pocket, as if he put people in a casket every day. If he did, that made him a mighty poor doctor in Chance's opinion.

"You'll have to empty the room of all your belongings."

There wasn't much. They'd traveled mighty light when they came racing up here.

"So I get in the coffin and Ronnie walks out pretending like she's mourning?" Chance hated to make Ronnie even pretend such a thing.

"You seem like a very strong, straightforward, and honest man, Mr. Boden."

Instead of saying thank you, Chance braced himself.

"Which is why you seem to have no notion of how to sneak around."

"I do prefer to face my troubles head on, Doc. And instead of sneaking, I'd rather just punch my enemies in the face."

"Hmm . . ." Doc Radcliffe seemed obsessed with a speck on one of his lenses. Maybe he was afraid he might end up being one of Chance's "troubles."

"The thing is, Mr. Boden," he said and cleared his throat as if half the Rocky Mountains had lodged in there, "Mrs. Boden needs to be in the casket with you."

Chance slapped a hand over his eyes and groaned. He peeked through his fingers to see Ronnie staring in horror at the wooden box, one hand clutching her throat.

The doctor glanced nervously over his shoulder. "One of the nurses working here last night thought a man was watching the hospital with a bit too much interest. He kept back in the shadows most of the time, but she has sharp eyes and knew he was there."

That got every ounce of Chance's attention. The men John had warned him about might already be here.

"We have little choice, Mr. Boden. We must get you out of here. We will lose a patient and carry him out in that wooden box." The doctor nodded at the casket. "It's not just a sneaky thing to do, it also provides you with excellent care. The straw-filled wagon will cushion your ride. The solid wooden box is good support for your leg while you're being transported. I'll direct the driver to take you to a house, where your family awaits to hold the funeral. No one will know what became of you. You'll then be taken to a place where you'll be safe and have all the time you need to heal."

Chance thought of the danger. Was John right? Had those attacking his family really sent someone this far to finish what that avalanche had started? He looked at the box, then at Ronnie. Then he glared at the doctor, who refused to flinch from Chance's gaze. That impressed him because Chance had made some mighty tough men flinch.

"We'll do it," he finally said.

"When do you need us to climb in there, Doctor?" Ronnie plucked things up and laid them inside the pine box. "I'd as soon wait to get in myself until the last minute."

"The days are short. The sun has set, and I'd prefer to do this under cover of darkness. The last minute is right now."

Ronnie's jaw clenched, but she just folded and packed faster. His wife was packing a coffin like it was a valise. Not for the first time, Chance wished badly he could just go home.

Ronnie said, "That's everything. Now, how do we get my husband in there?"

"If you'll notice, Mrs. Boden, there's a latch you can release from inside the casket."

Shaking his head, Chance muttered, "That had to terrify the undertaker."

Ronnie undid the latch, and the whole side of the casket swung down.

The doctor laughed. "I rigged it myself. No one knows about this but me. Even the men carrying you out don't know."

"I hope they don't forget what they're about and accidentally bury us."

Ronnie looked at him, and he was pretty sure she growled. "Stop bringing that up, Chance," she said.

Ronnie and the doctor helped him hobble the few feet to the strangest thing he'd ever ridden in. Once they had him tucked in, Ronnie climbed in beside him. It was a mighty tight squeeze.

The doctor swung the side up. "Mrs. Boden, can you reach the latch?"

Ronnie did it with only a minimum of twisting around.

The doctor lowered the lid, and as he did he said, "Now you two behave yourselves in there." He laughed and slammed the lid shut. Chance heard him leave the room.

"You know, Ronnie, I could have just limped out the front door and shot whoever was watching us. Instead we're locked into the world's smallest prison by a man we really don't know all that well." Chance sighed.

"I have both our guns." Ronnie pressed one into his hands. "We can fight our way out if we need to."

"Ronnie, there's no one I'd rather be locked in a coffin with than you."

She punched him in the chest. Chance suspected it was the only place she could reach. As long as they had some spare time and he was this close, he kissed her.

Justin had been out of the saddle too much the last few weeks. As he stood from the table, he was full to the point of pain.

Rosita worked magic with a roast and she'd outdone herself, celebrating Cole being up and about. The aroma of the savory meat and the sweet apple cobbler lingered and made the house comforting. He eased himself into a leather chair in the office and considered his aching muscles.

Cole set himself up behind Pa's desk, which irritated Justin on a normal day. Today he didn't mind—much.

His brother was still pale, still moving slow, but up and around, healing. Justin didn't like being all foolish and sentimental, but he had to admit, Cole looking so much better was a bright light amidst all the dark troubles that swirled around the Boden family.

John sat in a chair straight across from Justin, on either end of the settee where Sadie sat with Cole.

"It seems to me," Justin said, "we've spent every minute since Pa got hurt just defending ourselves and reacting to trouble. Today we turn and take the trouble straight to those who've asked for it."

Heath slapped the arm of the small settee, and his eyes flashed with anticipation.

Cole nodded in satisfaction.

John said, "High time."

With a graceful move, Sadie took Heath's hand. She looked worried but determined.

"I've got a plan to flush out whoever is betraying us," Justin began. "Tomorrow I want to—"

"I've got some thoughts, too." Cole interrupted. "I want us to do this legal so we can arrest—"

"Hold on, Cole." Heath talked over Justin's big brother like a man who'd had plenty of big brothers of his own. "I have an idea or two about this myself. I think—"

Cole was off, yammering, using words as long as he could conjure them out of his overloaded brain.

Personally, Justin had always thought that a person who'd been to college had too much of the common sense educated out of him. Of course, Cole was about the only person he knew who'd been to college.

Heath, well, anyone who knew that Heath had three big brothers would be able to see how a youngster learns to speak up.

Justin inhaled deeply, ready to shut them both up no matter how loud he had to yell, when a commotion drew his attention.

Justin leapt to his feet, took one long step to the desk, and pulled open the center drawer while being mindful of Cole's tender belly. He grabbed the gun he'd been keeping close to hand at all times.

He saw Cole produce a gun from a bottom drawer, and Heath pulled one he'd tucked behind a picture propped up on the mantel. Nope, two guns. He handed the second to Sadie.

All four of them were armed in seconds. They cocked their guns at the same instant. No one wore a holster inside as a rule, but they'd all made sure to have a loaded weapon close to hand.

Justin rushed for the door, Heath a step behind him. Justin reached for the knob. He wasn't leaving Rosita to face an intruder alone. Then he heard her speaking to someone in the kitchen. There was an urgency to the exchange, but no fear coming from Rosita.

The voices were definitely moving closer, and he recognized the other voice. As fast as they'd appeared, all of the guns vanished. They were all seated calmly when the door opened.

Angie had come back to the CR, and Justin had no interest in fighting her off. When she came in, Justin rose to his feet. "How did you get here?"

That seemed to stun her into silence for a moment, as if that wasn't what she wanted to talk about at all. "Uh . . . I rode."

"By yourself? In December? In the dark?" He saw her tremble to control her mouth and remembered what she'd said about being too obedient her whole life. She seemed to be fighting the reflex to be obedient right now.

Into the silence she spoke quickly, quietly. "I may have found out the root cause of the trouble you've been having. And it's possible that the man who shot Maria wasn't gunning for you at all, though I doubt he'd have objected to killing you."

"What does that mean?" Justin strode to her side.

She handed him a single sheet of paper, and he found it surprisingly hard to tear his eyes away from her. But he forced himself to look down.

He knew exactly what he was looking at. He'd seen maps of the land grants before. Pa had more than one book in his office that had a version of this same map. The difference was that this one had a black X marked on nearly all the land grants. One of the few left was the CR.

"Maria . . . what does this have to do with her?"

"We were cleaning out her room today, and we found this. It was deliberately and very well hidden."

"Let's see it, Justin." By the impatient tone in Cole's voice, Justin wondered just how long he'd stared at the map.

He handed it to Cole. Sadie and Heath got up and rounded the desk to see what was going on.

Cole's jaw tightened as he considered it.

Heath said, "This looks like someone is doing something to all the old land grants. And whoever it is, he's close to getting what he aims to get."

Cole nodded. "Justin, you know the area ranchers better than I do. What's going on? What do these Xs mean? I know these haven't all changed hands."

"There's been an effort to strip the land grants away from their owners, but they aren't all gone." Justin caught Angie's arm and towed her along with him to look down at the map. He tapped on it. "This one's the Merino grant, the one

straight to the north. As you can see, it's been marked off.
But I know for a fact the land has been passed down through
the family."

"Well, it's not exactly in their hands," Sadie said. "There
was only one daughter, and since her wedding five years ago,
she's become a hermit. She was always a social woman who
loved parties and pretty dresses, but there hasn't been a party
at the Merino ranch in years. Her parents have both died since
she married. Her husband isn't a friendly man, and he's not a
very good rancher."

That sent a ripple of surprise through the room.

Frowning, Justin tapped another spot on the map. "This one
got taken away and given to one of the governor's cronies. And
this one"—he pointed to another—"has been broken up since
the last owner died with no children."

"No children?" Heath asked in a harsh voice. "Or no living
children?"

"I think he lost two boys in the war, and another one, young
enough not to go to war, broke his neck in a fall from his horse.
But that was years ago."

"A slow, steady takeover of a huge portion of the territory,"
Cole said, staring past them all, his expression forbidding.

"We know whoever is behind this is playing a long game."
Sadie's grim words reflected what they all knew. The shooting
of Grandfather Chastain was one of the opening rounds of
this quiet war.

"If we study this map real hard, I think we're going to find
out that each and every one of these ranches has somehow come
under the rule of the governor, or his people."

Shaking his head, Justin said, "No, I know the governor. He's
a decent man. He's no conspirator trying to steal land grants."

"He's decent, but is he strong?" Cole asked. "I know him,
too, and he's let a lot of the running of this territory be handled

by underlings. The governor likes the ceremonies of his job, but he doesn't hold the reins tightly."

"Maybe that's part of this," Sadie said. "Some governors are easily managed, others are too watchful. That might explain why it's taken thirty years. The men behind this have to pull back with their scheming at times."

"But then comes a new governor who isn't vigilant and the plan revives." Justin spoke past a tightly clenched jaw. "Someone is trying to take over this whole part of the state."

"Not someone." Rosita's voice drew their attention to where she stood in the office doorway. "Rebels. Rebels trying to get the land back for Mexico. *Viva México.*"

The words of a revolution.

16

Angie knew she'd as good as shot a flaming arrow into the middle of the Boden family.

She had to do it. Riding out here alone, on that contrary horse, was terrifying, but she'd waited until the orphanage had settled down for the night, then snuck away, telling no one. She knew Aunt Margaret would have forbidden it. Yet the Bodens needed to know without delay. Speed and secrecy were both vital. And now she had to get back. Hopefully Aunt Margaret would never know about her dangerous decision to ride off alone at night.

The ride home was just as threatening, but Angie hoped to be tucked in bed in the morning with Aunt Margaret none the wiser. She also knew what she might face with the Bodens if she rode off alone. An escort, of course, and most likely it would be Justin.

The memory of the kiss they'd shared was like a living thing inside her. Her desire to be loved and, even more, to be taken care of was strong. She'd spent her whole life handing her care over to others, and she was finished with that. She couldn't be the woman God wanted her to be without standing on her own two feet. She'd promised God she would find her own strength, the strength He gave everyone to be a person of faith instead of a weakling who did as she was told, even when it was sin.

And while Edward was a cruel man with words, he wasn't physically strong. Mostly he ignored her. Still, she'd found a way to survive and be a faithful Christian, quietly, within a marriage she was too weak to refuse.

With Justin, the strongest man she'd ever known, she would never find her own backbone. Learn her own mind. Stand up for herself. And one more ride with Justin might seal her fate and put her into his keeping. Something she wanted more than she feared, but she hadn't impressed herself with her wisdom.

When Rosita came in with her talk of rebels, everyone's attention was riveted. Rosita paced toward the fireplace and all eyes were on her. Angie took this moment to slip silently away.

She was careful to walk as silently as she could down the hallway to the kitchen. She was a woman who had spent most of her life trying to avoid the notice of her mother and then later her husband. She could move quietly.

The kitchen door opened and closed without a creak. She was in the saddle, careful not to gallop, even though the back of her neck itched as if the hairs were standing straight up, urging her to run to the safety of the orphanage. A galloping horse would only draw attention and she'd be caught in minutes. Also, she'd probably fall off.

Once she was out of the ranch yard she tried speeding the horse up, but there was such a terrible bouncing that she immediately went back to walking. It was an old mare, after all, the horse that pulled Aunt Margaret's buggy. It was in no way a speedy creature, so the walk suited them both, except for her desire to get home quickly.

The darkness increased, pressing down on her like falling stones. She remembered why Justin made her dismount and walk when he'd ridden home with her. Gunmen might be lying in wait. The horses would shield them on both sides.

Though she hadn't reached that narrow stretch yet, she felt those rifles now, aimed right at her. The man who'd shot Maria could be aiming at her right now.

Then she heard hoofbeats behind her . . . gaining fast. Her fear of imagined things turned to terror. This was real. Her heart pounded and she fought to breathe. She kicked her mare to that terrible shaking pace and clung for her life.

Those attacking the Bodens might think she was a danger to their plans, just as they must have thought Maria was. Terrified that she would meet her end alone in the dark, she leaned lower and urged her poor mare to a greater speed.

The hooves thundered, drawing closer.

Why had she done this reckless thing? Aunt Margaret would mourn. She'd never know if the promise hinted at in Justin's kiss would grow into something real. She'd never prove to God she could be the woman He had created her to be.

The hooves were upon her now. A dark arm reached over and caught her horse's reins. She whimpered as much as any helpless prey, and her horse was pulled to a halt.

"What are you doing, woman?"

Her terror turned to relief so quickly that it left her feeling dizzy.

Justin!

She glanced sideways at him. He was furious. In the cold, his breath came as a white cloud and for a moment she thought of a fire-breathing dragon swooping down from the sky.

She'd never been so happy to be captured by a dragon in her life. It took every ounce of self-control to keep from throwing herself into his arms. But his ferocious glare helped keep her back.

It was then she realized how many times her husband had looked at her with anger and how she'd cringed and tried to dodge his cutting words. Never once had she considered throwing herself into his arms.

With Justin she felt no need to cringe, no need to placate. Not because he wasn't going to yell at her—he very likely was—but because his words, even if harsh, weren't going to cut away at her soul.

She wasn't quite sure how she did it, but all of a sudden she was in his arms. Sitting in his lap.

"Don't ever scare me like that again."

She braced herself for the scolding of her life. And considering her ma and husband, that was saying something.

Justin's head dropped forward. It felt too heavy to hold upright. In fact, his forehead rested against hers when he asked, "Angie, what am I going to do with you?"

She pulled back and looked at him. Blue eyes caught the starlight and gleamed at him. She seemed scared . . . scared of him? Scared of riding alone in the night? When she flung her arms around his neck, he decided it was the long, dark ride.

He held her close, just let her cling to him and calm down. He had to get her back to the ranch. Turning his horse, with hers in tow, he didn't ask if heading for the CR was all right with her. She'd demand to be taken home just as soon as her head cleared, so he hoped it didn't clear anytime soon.

The feel of her in his arms jostled a few words loose. "I think, Miss Angelique DuPree," he began, sounding very formal, "you are going to have to let me come a-courtin'."

Those blue eyes blinked, then focused strictly on him. Then his words soaked in, her eyes widened, and she shook her head. Saying no.

A sharp change from the lively confidence he'd been feeling, even as he spoke of courting a woman who would be helpless on a ranch.

"Justin, I can't. I promised God I'd learn to stand on my own. I'd stop letting others rule my life and try to become the woman He made me and live as He wished. Live the best Christian life I could."

None of that made much sense to Justin. "You can live a good Christian life while you're courting me, Angie. I'm a believer."

"No, that's not what I mean."

Since he'd guessed wrong the first time, Justin just waited. He had time. They were still a fair stretch away from the ranch.

It occurred to him then what she was fretting about. "Is this about your first husband?"

She looked away, not meeting his gaze for the first time since he'd caught up with her. Which he took to mean that he'd guessed right.

"You can tell me all about that low-down coyote if you want, and I can promise you I'll never act like he did. Then you can—"

Angie covered his mouth with her fingertips to stop him. Both of his brows arched in surprise.

"Yes, my reasons for wanting to discover some strength inside of myself has to do with him, and also my mother."

Justin waited in silence.

"Edward had all the polish and grace of the finest of wealthy citizens."

While Justin wore broadcloth and denim and buckskin.

"I had none of that, so he and my mother worked as a team to try to make me presentable in society." Her hand left his mouth and traced a line from beneath his eye to his chin.

"Your mother, too?"

"Yes, she raised me to say, 'Yes, Mother,' and say it quickly. I never had a thought of my own, at least not one I was allowed to speak."

"You seem to speak your mind to me."

She gave him a shy smile. "I've had the same thought myself. You've scolded me and fussed at me, but you don't pick away at my soul."

"What?"

Angie reached up and rubbed a gentle finger across his forehead. "You get furrows here when you worry. Did what I say worry you?"

"It's an unusual thing to say—I don't pick away at your soul?"

"I've watched Aunt Margaret scold the children at school."

Justin chuckled. "Sadie said she's mighty stern."

"Oh, yes, she is. But when she scolds there's kindness behind it. She tells the children to lower their voices, but she wouldn't tell them their voices are ugly. She will scold them for not finishing a school lesson, but she won't tell them they are stupid. Whatever correction she gives them is always backed by her— her—" Angie's voice broke.

Justin knew exactly the word she was searching for. The word she'd never found from her mother. "It's always backed by her love?"

Angie pressed her face against Justin's chest and managed a tiny nod of agreement. A young woman agreeing that her mother didn't love her. A terrible thing.

Angie turned her face so she rested her cheek against his chest. "I remember Aunt Margaret coming for a visit once, back in Omaha, years ago. She is my father's sister. It was then that Mother told her so rudely to call me Angelique, and only that."

"That name's a mouthful."

"If she ever slipped and said 'Angie,' Mother corrected her. By the end of the week, Aunt Margaret called me Angelique without fail. Her visit came while Father was alive and we lived in lavish style. With servants and fine food and the best clothing. Aunt Margaret made such a long trip, but I think she missed us and just wanted to be reminded she had family. Mother treated her like she was poor relation, as if her nun's habit was an embarrassment. Near the end, Aunt Margaret spoke of her orphanage and asked if we'd be interested in donating to it."

"I'd guess that didn't go well."

With a tiny shake of her head, Angie said, "There we sat in our fine drawing room, with our silk dresses and delicate china, with servants all around. Mother acted as if Aunt Margaret were a beggar on the street. Mother as good as threw her out of our house." She looked up at Justin and pressed her open hand on his chest, right over his heart. "Even after that, she still wrote to us over the years, always kind letters, full of faith and encouragement and love, but she never visited again. Can you understand how I never dreamed I could go to her when my husband died?"

"A lot of folks would've been done with your family after that." Justin noticed that he'd asked about her husband but Angie had talked only of her mother. Was her mother the worst part of the story or was she unable to talk about her husband? Maybe she still grieved. Even if he'd left her in poor circumstances, it didn't mean she hadn't loved him. Maybe that was what stood between her and saying she was interested in having him come calling.

Of course, she was in his arms and didn't seem to mind. So he hoped he could get past any other reasons she had for not welcoming his attentions.

The horses' hooves clopped along, hollow and quiet in the moonlight. The winter breeze had no bite at the moment. As he rode, he considered what Angie had said. Was he foolish to try to get to know her better? A man with all his troubles, who really wanted to protect a woman, would tell her to stay as far away as she could, at least until there was no more threat.

"So when her letter arrived asking if I'd come out and work

for her, it was like I held a miracle in my hands. God had answered my prayers, had noticed my struggles out of all those who suffered in the world."

Justin hugged her tight. "You had a rough life, Angie, but things are good for you now. I'm the one who shouldn't be thinking of courting. You know Pa had his leg badly broken?"

"Yes, I heard about that. He's in Denver under the care of a special doctor."

"Well, when Pa was hurt, it was mighty serious—men can die from a break where the bone cuts through the skin. Ma was at his side caring for him, as was Sadie. Ma left Sadie alone with him, when out of nowhere Pa told her he'd changed his will. He'd planned for the changes after his death, but because his injury was so dangerous, he said he was going to enforce those changes from the minute he left for the doctor. He told her, and we read it in writing later, that we all had to move home to the CR. I was already there, but Cole lived in his own house in Skull Gulch and ran the family's mining operation. And Sadie lived with Cole and worked at the orphanage."

"I've never heard of such a thing. Can a man order his children to move home?"

"No, but he can leave his ranch and mines and all his money to a low-down cousin if they don't."

Angie gasped just a bit, and her arms tightened around him as if to lend him support.

"The only way to keep the CR after Pa's death—and he'd gone off to Denver in very fragile condition, so his death could have happened at any time—was for Sadie and Cole to move home to the CR that very day."

"I'm sorry to say it, Justin, but your father sounds like a complete tyrant."

"I can see that it sounds that way, but my pa only wanted us to appreciate the ranch left to us by Grandfather Chastain, my ma's father. Pa was always saying Grandfather Chastain died on this land, his blood soaked into the very soil. He'd given his life fighting to save it for his daughter, and now that legacy was carried on by Pa and Ma. But Pa didn't think we appreciated it enough. He wanted us to be closer to each other and to our birthright, the Cimarron Ranch. He wanted us to love the land and our heritage."

"That's why Sadie quit at the orphanage. All I ever heard was that she was needed at home. But it opened the door for me to come west."

Justin rested his chin on top of her head and was silent for a moment. Then he said almost reverently, "I hadn't thought of it that way. Pa's threat to disinherit us brought you here."

"He saved me from a terrible life."

A life that had left her bone-thin, wearing a dress that was in tatters, without an ounce of strength left in her.

It came to Justin, a verse he'd heard, something about all things working together for good for believers. It was humbling to remember how defiant he'd been about Pa's edict. He sure hadn't taken a moment to appreciate it, for heaven's sake. And he'd never for one second wondered about what good could be done for someone else, someone far away, cold and hungry in Omaha.

What Pa had set in motion brought this woman into Justin's life, whom he cared for more every day.

And if he pushed and sweet-talked her, he was pretty sure he could talk Angie into joining her life to his. Which was how it should end up if a woman took to sitting for long rides in a man's arms—which would leave him with a ranch wife who didn't know the kicking end of a horse from the biting end, and at the same time plunge her into deadly danger.

He thought of the note marking Sadie as bait and how Heath's name had been added to that list.

Angie's name would go on there as well the minute anyone knew they were involved, because Heath's had been added before he married Sadie. And Angie could be used as bait just as surely as Sadie. What might a man do if the woman he was courting was kidnapped and held on threat of death if that man didn't hand over his land?

He needed to get her away from him, and keep her away. And he'd tell her that just as soon as he wasn't carrying her home on his lap.

17

If she really wanted to prove to God that she wasn't a weakling, that she could live her life as a Christian and stand on her own, she really ought to get off Justin's lap.

Angie hadn't paid much attention to anything but him since he'd caught her horse and dragged her out of the saddle—at least not since she'd gotten over her terror. And because she'd been so shaken when she was afraid someone evil was after her, then so relieved when it was Justin, she'd recklessly shared some of her painful memories of Mother, which seemed much like a woman *not* standing on her own, but rather handing her problems off to a big strong man.

Which left her weak, afraid, cowardly. In short, a failure. She believed fully that God loved her and forgave her and had her name written in the Book of Life.

That wasn't the same as Him being pleased.

About one year into her two-year marriage to Edward, Mother had died. That's when Angie recognized how lost she was and how hopeless was the life she'd been living as the obedient shadow, first to her mother, then later to her husband. Realizing that had led her to make her peace with God.

Angie had begun living as she believed God wanted her to. No one listened to her, of course, and she'd been a long way from the courage of shouting her faith from the rooftops. But she lived on and spoke the truth as God showed her. No one had much to do with her at that point, because Edward had cut her off from nearly everyone and everything, and that included attending church. By then, Edward spent most nights with one woman or another, which frankly was a relief to Angie. He was gone all day, too. She'd foolishly assumed he was working.

Within that narrow existence, her mind and her words were true to her faith. In her own quiet way she strove to honor God.

With Mother gone and Edward mostly gone, Angie's life became one of ease. Servants and fine clothes and a mansion to sleep in.

And then Edward died. She hadn't been given a moment to grieve, nor to feel profound relief. The shocks had come too fast, and soon she was out on the street with only the black widow's dress she'd had on. With everything gone, she'd found the only work available was at a harshly demanding factory that paid pennies a day. She rented a pitiful apartment that was tiny, cold, and none too safe, and still she could barely afford it. But through it all she'd done as she believed God would have her do.

And she wasn't going to stop now. She tore herself out of her deep thoughts and lifted her chin to demand Justin put her down and let her ride her own horse as they headed toward Skull Gulch.

That's when she saw the Bodens' ranch yard. In the dark, she hadn't noticed their direction but assumed he was taking her home. Her only protest was that she shouldn't need an escort and she most certainly shouldn't make the ride on his lap. She'd never thought to insist he take her home.

"I have to go back to the orphanage."

"I'll take you in the morning."

"No, Aunt Margaret will worry."

A deep sigh ruffled the front of her hair. "So you snuck off in the night without telling Sister Margaret where you were going. You didn't even leave a note?"

"Justin, stop criticizing my every word and action and let me ride out of here." It was a wonder to think she spoke to him in such a way. Edward would have torn her apart for it.

"Admit it, Angie, you were never so glad to see anyone in your life when you figured out who'd grabbed you. If you ride out of here now, it's the same long ride in the pitch-dark. That trail is no fit place for a woman to ride alone at night. Which means I have to go with you, and I don't have time right now."

"The men who attacked you wouldn't have known I was out. They like to dry-gulch people—you said that yourself. They have to know ahead of time that someone is going to be vulnerable."

"Maybe that's right, although if they saw you ride in they had time to set a trap. But it's not just whoever's conspiring against us—outlaws ride the trails at night."

"What are the chances—?"

"As do mountain lions and rattlesnakes."

"Rattlesnakes and mountain lions don't *ride*."

He rolled his eyes toward heaven as if looking to God for strength. "And there are wolves and bears."

"There are bears around here?" She gripped the front of his shirt.

As if bears were her biggest problem.

"And scorpions and poisonous spiders."

"What's a scorpion?"

"It's a five-inch-long bug with a vicious bite."

Angie flinched. "This sounds like a very harsh land."

"You won't like Gila monsters neither."

"M-monsters?" Angie was losing her desire to ride on alone.

"Not to mention some wicked plants that'd bite you if you left the trail, which ain't hard to do in the darkness."

"The plants most certainly do not have teeth."

Justin chuckled as he rode toward the barn. "They ain't exactly teeth, but you won't know the difference."

"Well, my goodness, what does this territory have such awful things for?"

"New Mexico Territory is a beautiful land. Our cattle get fat on the lush grass, and the white mountain peaks to the west are as pretty as anything on God's earth. But there's plenty of desert and rock. And in a desert nearly everything bites or stings or stabs. I think growing up hot and dry just makes plants and animals pure mean."

She wondered if that held for men, too.

"Add to that your horse could step in a gopher hole, throw you, and you'd break your neck."

"I'm quite good at staying in the saddle, thank you." She touched her neck nervously.

Justin laughed. She took exception to that, but he didn't give her time to protest. "And if you don't fall to your death, you might fall partway with your boot hung up in the stirrup, and you could be dragged like that all the way back to town. You'd be right down on the ground disturbing all number of spiders and snakes, and that's if the horse doesn't stomp a hoof on your head."

Angie decided maybe riding by herself was a poor idea. "Can we head for town at first light?"

Justin rode his horse into the barn through wide-open doors. He swung down as a cowpoke rushed forward to take the reins of both critters.

"Thanks, Windy."

The cowhand grunted and led the horses away.

Justin kept Angie in his arms as he walked toward the house.

Angie kept her chin down, and she spoke to her hands, twisted together in her lap. "I really did think you needed to know about that map right away."

"And you were right."

"I thought of asking Sheriff Dunn or Dr. Garner or Parson Gregory to ride out with me. Beyond that, I didn't feel I knew anyone in town well enough to trust them. And I certainly couldn't ask Aunt Margaret or Sister Louisa."

"That's wise on your part." His voice was flat, some might even call it sarcastic.

"So I took the chance. I know it was reckless, but I thought if I just risked it this once, I'd never do it again. It's not my wish to cause you worry, Justin. And I have no desire to do hazardous things, nor do I believe I'm a particularly lucky woman—which is how I often end up in bad situations." She knew that beyond all doubt.

They paused as they reached the back door. Justin stopped so suddenly, all her attempts to explain herself dried up. He set her on her feet and reached for the back door, but instead of opening it, he looked down at her. His dark blue eyes were shadowed by his hat and the darkness.

"I admire that you were brave enough that you warned us right away, and I'm glad to hear you'll never do it again. But, Angie, what if you find another clue and decide it can't wait? I don't know if I can trust you. And I don't know if I can bear the thought of you being in such danger."

She thought for a moment that he was going to kiss her. Despite the little scolding she gave herself about not wanting his affection, she realized she wanted it desperately.

Then he straightened as if he remembered himself and then pulled the door open to the bright lantern light of the Bodens' kitchen. "I really don't think you know a lick about this land. No one would go out riding at night over those long miles if they did."

No more than the absolute truth. Was he saying this to remind himself of why he shouldn't get mixed up with a woman who'd lived in a city all her life? Or was he calling her stupid?

"How am I ever going to keep you safe?"

That wasn't his job, but he pushed her gently but firmly into the kitchen, then took her hand and headed back to the office where she'd interrupted the family gathering not that long ago.

She followed him because she didn't have much choice—his grip was firm. But she didn't delude herself. She'd have followed him anywhere.

And that was all wrong. She had to stay away from him.

From this moment on, she must never let herself be alone with Justin again.

Justin didn't want this time alone with Angie to end. His mind wandered to arranging another private ride. One where no one was liable to shoot at them. That way there was a much better chance they'd have themselves a good time.

He held tight to Angie's hand and slowed his pace as he walked to Pa's office just to draw out this short spell of being with her because he liked it so much. But he knew that it was fleeting. This had to be the last time.

The family barely glanced up when Justin came in with Angie in tow. Heath's wild eyes flickered to their joined hands, then flashed with humor, but he kept a straight face. Sadie and Cole acted like it was business as usual, which in a way made Justin more nervous than Heath's silent teasing.

Rosita was sitting by the fire and stood. "I'll get a room ready for you, Angie." She hurried out. Rosita would always rather be moving than sitting.

Justin had left them debating how they'd set up the cowhand who'd been reporting to Dantalion.

Cole leaned back in Pa's chair behind the desk. Justin was used to him claiming that spot even though it chafed something awful. It wasn't as if Justin wanted the chair; it just seemed like it ought to remain empty, waiting for Pa's return.

John was gone, so Justin turned a couple of heavy chairs to face Cole.

Justin escorted Angie to the one farthest in the room, to keep an eye on her in the event of another escape attempt. He asked, "What have you decided?"

Cole's mouth looked pinched, but he said, "We're going to do it your way. I agree that Skull Mesa is probably not necessary."

"What about Skull Mesa?" Justin had missed that part of the conversation.

"I sure would like to climb that old beast." Cole ignored Justin's question.

"We'll do it one of these days," Heath said with a smirk. "I can get you to the top from two different directions in about half an hour. Easy."

Cole and Justin both glared at Heath. They'd been trying to climb that mesa all their lives—and their pa before them. Heath, taking Sadie with him, had gotten to the top on his second try. He'd gone up one way and come down another, using the path seen from the top but invisible at the bottom.

Heath was a climbing fool and knew some fancy tricks. He claimed he'd spent most of his life climbing around in a cavern. Justin had a hard time believing that. What sort of cave was big enough to climb?

Cole sketched out their plan.

Justin was fiercely satisfied that they were using his. He'd barely gotten it told before he noticed Angie's runaway attempt, so he'd left it to them to hash out.

"I've got to ride to Skull Gulch as early as possible tomorrow to get Angie home." Justin narrowed his eyes at her. "She took a big risk riding out here alone, but she thought we needed to see that map. Thank you, Angie."

"That's so brave, Angie," Sadie said. "God bless you."

Some might say brave. Some might say stupid.

"Mighty tough woman," Heath said with a nod.

Justin was mighty sure Heath was wrong about the tough part.

"We appreciate it, Angie," Cole added, "but we hate the thought of you in danger. We have to find a way to make sure you're safe. Justin, talk to Sheriff Joe tomorrow about riding out with Angie if she finds something else we might need to know. Now that it looks like Maria was involved . . ." He stopped talking for a solemn moment.

Justin remembered the quiet, courageous woman who'd saved his life. Her funeral had been a somber affair. With the children all there, tears were shed aplenty.

Cole cleared his throat and went on. "There might be more clues come to light at the orphanage."

Angie looked startled, as though she'd expected the Bodens to scold her.

Justin had kinda expected it, too. Just in case he failed to mention it before, he said to Angie, "I can see why you thought it was real important to bring the map to us. Thank you. I doubt I can get you to town early enough to keep Sister Margaret from being upset, but we'll get you there as fast as possible."

Justin had another thought. "Heath, why don't you ride in with us? I think it's high time we had another talk with Ramone. If Maria knew about this, there's a good chance Ramone does. I'm pretty sure he was hiding something from me when I questioned him before."

"Nope." Cole cut off Justin's planning. "Someone else had

better ride her in. I want this thing settled. There's no reason
we can't spring our trap tomorrow."

Justin had been looking forward to the ride. But then he'd
thought of "proper," opened his mouth and invited Heath along,
so the ride was ruined anyway. Since Justin was a man of action,
it suited him to get on with it. "I agree. In fact, taking Angie
home will explain the absence of a few people we need to get in
place. Heath, you take her and let Sadie ride along, too. Then
instead of heading back to the ranch, you can . . ."

They planned the next morning a bit longer before Justin
said, "All right, let's get some rest. Maybe after tomorrow we'll
be on our way to putting an end to all this nonsense. Maybe we
can enjoy a quiet Christmas without anyone gunning for us."

A chill crawled down his spine then, as if his confidence was
just asking for trouble. There was plenty that could go wrong,
but it did a man no good to worry.

Rosita came in at that minute. "Everything is ready. Angie, I
found some things that will fit you among Sadie's nightclothes."

Sadie nodded in satisfaction.

"Thank you," Angie said as she stood. "Thank you all."

They gratefully ended the long day.

"Just set it on the table there."

"You want us to help get the lid off, Dr. Radcliffe?" A deep
voice sounded a bit too interested, like maybe he enjoyed seeing
the occasional corpse.

"No, thank you. We'll do that tomorrow when the guests
arrive."

Chance sure enough hoped no guests arrived. And he also
wondered how a man with such a fine reputation and an honorable profession could be such a smooth liar.

The door shut, and soon after the lid lifted.

"Hey, Doc." Chance blinked at the lantern light. The casket had been black as pitch.

Ronnie didn't say anything. Instead, she unlatched the side of the coffin and let it swing down. She hopped out like a woman escaping the worst nightmare of her life—and why wouldn't she?

"It was a nice, quiet ride, honey. What's the hurry?"

Ronnie smiled while her narrow eyes seemed to threaten him. "Let's get you out of that pine box, Chance." She turned to the doctor. "And let's find a less horrifying way to travel in the future."

The doctor chuckled. "I don't think this will be necessary again."

Ronnie and the doc eased Chance's legs around so he could sit up, the doctor handling the broken one with great care. Then they helped him stand, balancing his weight on his one good foot.

"I asked the sheriff to make sure a bed was made up on the ground floor. Let's get you in there so we can stop jostling you around."

"The sheriff?" Chance asked. "He's involved in this?"

"He's your landlord and your next-door neighbor." The doctor eased Chance's arm around his shoulder. "He just married the woman who lived in this house. She hasn't moved any of her furniture yet, so the place is livable. And you've got a man close by who's so tough, no one's going to start trouble within a mile."

Ronnie held on to him from the other side, and together they all moved slowly toward the bedroom.

Chance didn't want any trouble finding him with his leg still on the mend, but if he could walk freely, he'd welcome whoever was hunting him. He'd like to end all this once and for all.

The two of them helped get him settled in bed. Chance nearly collapsed from the effort of the short walk. Yep, he was useless.

"I've got to go. Make yourselves comfortable. I informed the sheriff that there might be danger coming for you, so he'll be stopping in to talk come morning."

"Doc, before you go, how much longer will I have this cast on my leg?"

The doctor scratched his head thoughtfully—or maybe his head just itched. "You're a mighty fast healer, Mr. Boden. I think one more week in that cast is enough. Then I'm going to put on another, much smaller and of a lighter plaster, and get you some crutches."

Right now Chance had plaster from his foot all the way to the top of his thigh. "With the bone healed, though not strong yet, you'll be able to get along with a cast from right below your knee to your toes. I still don't want any weight put on it, but you'll be able to move around better and the plaster will weigh half as much. The smaller cast will need to stay on for another month."

"A month?" Chance wanted badly to get home.

"You had a very severe break, Mr. Boden, and I want your leg solidly knit before you're standing and walking on your own. And you must admit that patience isn't your strength. If I trusted you to be careful, I might not make you remain in the plaster for as long. But you're already chafing to fight whoever is pursuing you."

Chance fumed, but blast it, the doctor was right. "Can I go home with the lighter cast and crutches?"

"I want you completely healed before you leave my care. You're one of the most severely injured men I've ever treated. And even I admit I couldn't have done it without the fine care you received right after the break."

Doc Garner in Skull Gulch had helped, but most of the credit went to Heath Kincaid. While Chance had been out cold through it all, he'd heard all the details. Garner had ridden to Denver with them and told them what Heath had done.

"I'm not going to release you to go running off until I'm sure you can't do any new damage to yourself."

Despite his seeming to relish the trick of slipping Chance out of the hospital and then joking about the coffin, the doctor was dead serious when it came to medicine. Chance would have to step right over him to head for Skull Gulch.

He didn't want to leave footprints on such a fine man. He didn't even want to go against his advice. Yet neither of those wants was necessarily enough to stop him.

18

"Cole, you shouldn't be out of bed!" Justin shouted loud enough to shake dirt down off the barn rafters.

The men were saddling up, getting ready for the day. Not a one of them missed Justin and Cole scrapping. And that was just how Justin and Cole had planned it. They wanted to make sure everyone heard them making the day's arrangements.

"I told you, I'm fine." Cole headed for his horse, kept in a stall inside until it learned to get along with the other horses. It had been living in town with Cole, and the feisty stallion hadn't quite found the right herd yet.

Justin grabbed Cole's arm hard enough to stop him in his tracks and made a fist. "If you're well enough to be out here riding, you're well enough to take a punch."

Cole turned to face him, his eyes flashing rage.

Justin almost smiled, but then caught himself. That'd ruin everything.

"I have to ride out to the mines today." Cole yanked his arm free of Justin's grip. "It's been a week."

"We've had reports brought in. Go study them."

"The last I heard from them was Monday. It's been a full

workweek since then, and someone should have checked in. I'm worried that they didn't. Something must've gone wrong. I'm well enough to—"

"Just shut up for a minute," Justin snarled. Fighting with Cole was his favorite pastime.

"I plan to take it slow, so I'll be gone all day—"

"I said quiet down!" Justin said. "I'll go."

"You've got a full day's work."

Justin looked around at his men. "I can head out to the mine after the noon meal. I don't have to take it slow, so I can make a fast run, get the report you're so worried about, and still be home by supper."

Cole didn't respond. Instead he glared at Justin and breathed hard through clenched teeth. He knew good and well he wasn't up to the long ride. But their plan had included Cole losing this fight, so anyone with bad intentions would know exactly where Justin would be riding. And that he'd be alone.

"Fine, but I want your word you'll get out there and back today."

"Even if I have to ride long after dark, I'll get back here. Anyway, it's a shorter ride from here because you've been starting from town. I'll cut nearly two hours off your time."

"I checked Pa's office this morning and Monday's reports weren't there. Where'd you put them?"

Justin dragged his Stetson off his head and whacked himself in the leg, as if Cole's question made him half-crazed with impatience. "I tucked them away. Let's go, I'll have to get them for you."

He looked up at Alonzo. "Get the men started. I want to bring the cattle up from the east pasture, and I want a head count on the closest herd to the south. I'll catch the cowhands heading south and help with that before I ride for the mine."

Alonzo was in charge because John had ridden with Heath, Sadie, and Angie. As if it took all three of them to get Angie safely to town. All the more reason for Justin to keep busy, so he wouldn't think about how much he'd wanted to escort her in.

"Here he comes!" Heath ducked low, not wanting to give his position away.

"That's Windy." Sadie hissed the words. She was a good partner and knew how to keep quiet and stay out of sight.

Heath looked at her and saw the hurt of betrayal. He hesitated to say more. But he needed her to get beyond hurt feelings and be ready if this turned into a fight.

He pulled her close and whispered, "He can't have any business on that trail, Sadie. Justin sent him along with the drovers to bring the cattle closer. Here he is, as if he dropped back to return to the ranch, and then instead of going back he's heading up that old trail."

"The same one where we fought Dantalion."

All the sadness vanished from Sadie's expression, replaced by fury. "He's trying to find Dantalion and report Justin's trip to the mines this afternoon. They're planning to waylay him and kill him."

Windy—that was the only name Heath had ever heard him called—vanished into the woods. Heath inched his head up. When he saw no sign of their prey, he grabbed Sadie's hand and headed through the woods toward the trail Windy had taken. He'd been in some tight spots in his life, but he'd never tried to catch an outlaw and hold a woman's hand at the same time.

Marriage changed a man.

Heath's instincts were to get Sadie far away to somewhere safe, but he knew how his wife felt about that and knew just how tough she was. She'd wanted to go, and he respected her enough to see that she'd be a mighty big help if he needed one.

They followed Windy along, he on horseback, they on foot. But the trail was so winding and treacherous that Heath figured they could keep up well enough, and it was hard to trail a man when you're seated high on horseback. They stayed after him for ten minutes, reached the top of the incline, then started down. He wasn't far ahead.

"What will he do when he can't find his partner?" Sadie kept up so well, Heath had to hustle or she'd leave him behind.

"They must have some signal they send each other. Windy will send the signal—or maybe he already did somehow. He may think he's meeting Dantalion."

Heath came around a curve and saw Windy dismount. With a darting grab, he tugged Sadie back behind the cover of trees. He noticed how she was tugging him back just as hard. She'd seen Windy the same time he did, or maybe a second sooner. They'd all but walked right into him no more than twenty paces ahead now. They crouched behind scrub trees and watched. But of course Dantalion wasn't coming, he being dead and buried, after all. And Windy could have no reason to have come up this trail but a traitorous one.

There was no sense waiting another minute.

With a squeeze of Sadie's hand, Heath let her go and drew his gun silently. He didn't cock it; Windy would hear that. He heard Sadie arm herself, too. Heath didn't protest. For one thing, she'd do as she pleased, so why waste his breath? And for another thing, when a body went to chasing down an outlaw who had a rifle in his saddle scabbard and a gun in his holster, well, being armed seemed like a right fine idea.

Windy hadn't impressed Heath as being all that sharp. The man didn't look around him, didn't seem aware they were close or worry anyone was following. But then he'd fooled them all into thinking he was loyal, so Heath took him seriously.

He caught Sadie's eye and nodded for her to go into the woods to the right. He wanted them coming up from two directions. With a single nod of agreement she melted silently out of sight. He really loved that woman.

Slipping into the woods to his left, he inched forward, choosing every step to avoid snapping twigs or crushing dead leaves. With each pace forward he closed the distance. Meanwhile, Heath kept a sharp lookout for anyone else coming to meet Windy. It'd be reckless to rule out other conspirators.

Two more long paces and Heath had his quarry within grabbing distance. Windy was facing away. A quick look and Heath saw Sadie barely visible in the underbrush across the trail. Their gazes met, and Heath held up a hand, hoping it kept Sadie in hiding. He nodded at their target, holstered his gun, drew in a deep breath, focusing on Windy while never forgetting the man was armed.

He hurled himself forward and slammed into Windy's back. They landed hard on the trail.

Windy gave a startled shout, then attacked as fast and hard as a striking snake, landing an elbow against Heath's cheek. He was a skinny man and none too tall, but he was wiry and quick. He struck again and then raked a spur down Heath's leg.

He'd nearly gotten free when Heath clobbered him in the side of his face, then flipped the wriggling fool onto his back and plowed another fist into his chin.

Windy lay flat on his back, and Heath let out a sigh of relief to have the man subdued. He was sitting on top of him and he moved to disarm the man, letting go with one hand to reach for his pistol. The second Windy was free, he brought a roundhouse punch straight into Heath's gut. Heath tumbled backward. Dazed, Heath scrambled to grab the thrashing, kicking man again before he could get to his gun.

But Windy didn't reach for his gun. Instead he sprinted forward and leapt onto his horse. Heath's hand flew to his six-shooter and drew it even as he swung around. A shot rang out and blasted into a tree just inches behind Windy's head. Sadie had joined the fray.

Windy spurred his horse, jumping into a gallop. He bent low over his horse's neck as another bullet missed him by a hair. Vanishing downhill, away from the ranch, he rode around the closest of a hundred curves in the trail.

Heath ran forward, Windy's gun peppering his back trail. Heath threw himself flat on his belly just as he rounded the curve. He had his gun out and aimed just as Windy reached the next curve and was out of sight again.

Footsteps pounded behind him, so Heath rolled onto his back, expecting another attack. Instead he saw Sadie standing there in her blue skirt. She had her smoking gun gripped tight, aimed straight at . . . nothing. No one was there.

She said in disgust, "I missed him. I had two clear shots."

Heath jumped up and dashed down the trial. "We might be able to get him from above. You can see the lower parts of the trail from up there," he said, pointing. He rushed forward and then realized, this high up, no part of the lower trail showed. He'd be running for a long way, and by then Windy would be gone.

Gasping for air and still reeling from Windy's blow, Heath turned to see his wife only a few paces behind him. "You are the best kind of woman there is, Sadie Kincaid."

She grinned, then gave him a sassy nod. "Don't you ever forget it, Heath Kincaid."

As he stood, breathing hard, Sadie's eyes focused on his cheek, and she reached up. He caught her hand before she could touch the bruise. It was bound to pain him if she did.

"You're hurt." Sadie closed her fingers around his hand. "I won't touch it. I don't want to make it feel worse."

Heath said, "I reckon I'll have myself a beauty of a black eye come morning."

She smiled, her eyes brimming with kindness. "I'll still love you, Heath, even if you spend a few days not being so pretty."

"I appreciate that, Mrs. Kincaid." He looked in the direction Windy had ridden. The frustration was like a maddening itch, but on foot there was no chance of catching him.

"Let's go home." He turned toward the uphill stretch of the narrow path. "We may not have him, but we identified the coyote and he's gone from the ranch for good."

It wasn't a very satisfying end to their trap, but there was nothing to be done about it now. They headed down the heavily wooded, twisting trail to the ranch yard.

Heath and Sadie entered the house through the kitchen door. Once there, Heath turned toward his tough little wife. "Now, I need to thank you properly for saving my life." He then dragged her into his arms.

19

Justin, who'd left his crew to support the story they'd told about his going alone to the mines, rode into the ranch yard in time to see Heath enter the house with Sadie a step behind him.

Justin made short work of stripping the leather off his horse, then turned the animal out in the corral to roll in the dry winter grass.

Running to the house, he found Heath and Sadie, arms wrapped around each other, kissing.

"Will you two knock that off?" Justin's voice jerked them apart.

Sadie rubbed her lips, which did a poor job of hiding her smile. Heath just grinned like a cat full of cream.

"Did you find out anything?" Justin thought they seemed mighty cheerful if the plan had failed.

"Windy." Sadie's eyes lost their spark of humor and went narrow, angry.

"Windy?" Cole came into the kitchen from the direction of Pa's office. "How long's he been working here?"

"Better part of a year." Justin knew he'd been here for spring roundup. "For certain before Pa got that avalanche sent down on his head."

"We saw him come back from the south." Heath had a bruise forming on his face.

"Don't look like Windy came along peacefully." Justin fought down the grim disappointment.

Heath lifted a hand to his cheek, then pulled back, not touching it.

"That looks mighty tender." Cole went to the sink and got a cloth wet and wrung it out. He handed it to Heath, who tossed it on the table.

"I reckon Windy is even more tender than me right now." His eyes went bright as he looked at Sadie. "My little woman fired twice at him and drove him off when he would have killed me. That's the second time you've saved my life."

She moved into his arms and hugged him tight. "Please stop getting into the kind of mess that leads to you needing your life saved."

"I'll do my very best, Mrs. Kincaid."

"You shot at a man twice and he's still alive? That's plumb shameful, little sister."

She just smiled at him and didn't say a word. The kind of thing a very confident woman would do.

Justin shook his head. He had to face the fact that his sister was one tough western woman. "You're sure he's the traitor?"

"He'd ridden out with the other men, but either he made some excuse or just dropped back until they didn't notice him leaving the group." Heath explained quickly what had happened.

"That must've been where he and Dantalion always met to exchange information."

"I thought this was about someone trying to stir up trouble with Mexico. There ain't nothing Mexican about Windy."

Justin nodded. "Maybe we're wrong about the whole revolution nonsense. That never made no sense anyway."

He wondered again what it all meant. They'd figured out Viva México, but what in the world did *cuidado* have to do with it? Something about Juarez maybe. He thought he'd heard it called cuidado. Though it was a long ride away, it was one of the closest towns over the Mexican border.

Heath said, "I'm sorry I couldn't hang on to the slippery varmint."

"Yep, I'd have liked to get some answers from the man," Justin said grimly. "Our troubles aren't over, but at least we don't have a spy on our payroll anymore."

Angie caught Melanie's attention with a nearly silent hiss.

Mel grinned and came over. The last child went into the dining room to eat. "What is it?"

"Shhh."

Mel whispered with an irreverent grin, "I feel like we're the naughty children trying to get away with mischief."

Angie frowned. "Aunt Margaret is furious with me for riding out to the Boden place last night." She'd gotten home early, only not early enough. Aunt Margaret was awake and worried nearly to the point of collapse. When Angie walked in, her worry was replaced by anger. Angie had never seen her aunt that angry before. It was impressive.

"As she oughta be. That was a reckless thing to do."

"But don't you ride home alone to your pa's ranch every day when you're done with school?"

"Yep, but not at night. And besides, my family doesn't have trouble like the Bodens. I don't think of my ride home as dangerous and neither do my folks. The truth is that, except for out at the CR, things have gotten mighty peaceable in this part of the country. It's a shame someone's out there stirring up trouble, but I trust Cole and Justin to get to the bottom of it soon."

"I need to help them, and I want you to help me. I think Justin would be less furious, along with Aunt Margaret, if I were with you."

Mel arched a brow. "What are you up to now?"

Angie wished Mel had just said yes instead of asking questions. "Justin is running himself ragged with his pa gone from the ranch and this trouble boiling all around him. He mentioned talking to Ramone again, and I thought maybe I could do that for him."

"Now, Angie, I think it's best if you just leave it to the Bodens. This is men's work."

Angie plunked her fists on her hips. "And when, may I ask, Melanie Blake, have you *ever* admitted there was such a thing as 'men's work'?" She knew her friend hated being called Melanie and so she needled her with her real name.

"Do *not* call me Melanie." She said it in a threatening way, but then she ruined it by letting a sheepish grin slip out. "Now, it's all different when you're talking about me, Angelique."

Angie didn't like hearing her own full name any better than Mel did hers.

"I'm tougher than most men and a sight tougher than you'll ever be. If it were my problem, you're right, I'd wait for no man. But I'm a whole lot better at taking care of myself than you are. I wear a gun and can draw it quick and put my bullets right where I want 'em. I can swing a fist that'll take all but the toughest men to their knees. I can outride, out-rope, and out-bulldog every man on our place, except Pa. And he's slowed down some over the years—I'll beat him one of these days."

Angie believed every word. "So does that mean it would be all right for you to ride alone to the Bodens'?"

Mel frowned as she gave that some real thought. "I've never hesitated to do it before. I rode out there after their pa got hurt."

"You mean in the avalanche that broke his leg?" Angie asked. Justin had talked about that just last night.

"Yes, and it was a terrible break. Heath's quick thinking and medical skill may have saved his life, but it absolutely saved his leg."

"How'd Heath get his doctor skills?"

"He spent time riding with the cavalry or something like that. He worked with an army doctor."

"I never heard that."

"Yep, then Doc Garner rushed out to the Bodens and found that Heath's treatment made it possible to save the leg. He knew a man in Denver who'd done some special work with breaks that cut through the skin, and the doctor convinced Chance and Veronica it was worth a try to get to Denver. And from what Sadie has told me, it looks like they saved the leg. Chance is gonna be a long time gone, but he'll be back—walking and able to run his ranch again."

"And all this trouble started when Justin's pa broke his leg?" Angie had heard the story but only in bits and pieces.

"They've had two or three more attempts on their lives. Heath got shot when someone opened fire on the Bodens from the top of that big mesa by the Boden place. Then Cole got shot. Maria, too, the day Justin came here." Mel shook her head when she mentioned that.

Angie remembered how Mel and Cole had fought when Mel came to visit. "You're not safe, Mel. The risk can come to anyone who gets close to a Boden."

Angie looked at Mel. They were both good friends of the Bodens.

"Maybe I oughta ask Pa what he thinks before I ride over there again. The trouble does seem to be all around them."

Angie knew the Blake Ranch wasn't one of the old land-grant holdings. But it was a large spread all the same. Just how safe were they? If someone wanted the land grants, why wouldn't they want *all* the land in these parts? If there really was a revolution, they certainly wouldn't leave any land behind. She was tempted to tell Mel everything and warn her that she might be in danger. But did the Bodens want anyone else to know? It seemed to her that they'd been pretty secretive about it all.

The indecision was enough to drive her mad. She had to talk to Justin right away. It could be a matter of life and death to the tough and fearless Mel Blake.

"Angie, where are you, dear?" Aunt Margaret's voice was raised but it sounded friendly. Something Margaret feigned for the sake of the children. Angie now understood Margaret's temper was formidable.

"I need to talk to the Bodens again," she whispered to Mel. "How am I supposed to do that if I can't go out to the ranch?"

"Angie, Mel, I would appreciate your help." The words and tone were nice, but Angie knew a threat when she heard one.

Mel had heard Margaret's voice just as well as Angie did. She immediately started toward the dining room. "I'll think of something."

They both hurried along, not wanting to face the wrath of Sister Margaret. Before they entered the dining room, Angie got an idea and asked Mel, "Could you teach me to be as tough as you?"

Angie had never heard laughter that loud come out of Mel Blake.

Aunt Margaret gave them a look of confusion when they stepped into the room. "What on earth are you laughing about, Mel?"

Mel laughed all the harder.

Angie got straight to work. Not because she was so consci-entious—though she was—but because she'd never hit anyone before in her life, and starting on someone as tough as Melanie Blake was a really poor idea.

And then she remembered what tough really was. What would it take to be tough enough not to be intimidated by a cranky nun?

20

Justin led a group from the ranch into church on Sunday.

Well, he didn't exactly lead, because Cole rode along, strong and straight. And when Cole was in on something, he liked to think he was the leader. Because Justin felt a little sorry for his healing big brother, he didn't squabble over who was in charge.

They didn't make good time, as Justin didn't want to push Cole in any way, yet his brother held up just fine. Justin was so pleased to see him looking so good, it was all he could do to keep from smiling right at him. Which would be so strange that Cole would think Justin had gone pure mad.

Sadie and Heath rode along, as well as most of their cow-hands.

Justin planned to talk some more to Ramone after the service. Alonzo would be there because he visited his father as often as possible. That was just as well, because Justin didn't want to be accused of being hard on a weak old man.

He wanted to be mighty hard on Ramone—he just didn't want to be accused of it. So Alonzo's presence would make Justin behave.

Angie was in church, sitting with Mel and her pa and ma,

and a crowd of hands from the Blake Ranch. They were sitting toward the front, and Angie was fidgeting and turning around like she was plagued with an itch.

She saw him come in and whispered to Mel, then got up and came over to him right in front of everyone. "I need to talk to you after church." Her voice was so serious and earnest that he was sure this had something to do with the troubles at the ranch. "I have to say some things you might need to know."

Then she turned around and rushed back to her seat so quick Justin couldn't grab her. He'd have dragged her straight outside and demanded to hear what she had to say right then, even if they missed a few minutes of the service.

That woman had a knack for tormenting him, and there was no denying it. Now he had to pay attention to the sermon while his brain was hopping around wondering what in the world that woman had found out.

If today hadn't been Sunday, which brought the family to town, he was sure as certain she'd've come riding out to the CR again, and alone just like before. The woman didn't have a lick of common sense.

Of course, she was worried about them and wanted to help. And heaven knew, with Maria's death and Ramone staying here in town, there might be things to find out.

Right then the pastor called for everyone to bow their heads in prayer, or Justin might've gotten up and made a scene by hauling Miss Angie outside.

Justin waited outside the church, feeling as impatient as a longhorn bull kicking at the gate to a green pasture. From the way Angie was hurrying, he knew she'd come as fast as decency allowed.

She rushed up to him. He'd stayed behind while the rest of the family walked on toward the street.

"What is it?"

"I was asking Mel about how dangerous it is to ride out alone."

"Angie, I told you—"

"Stop!" Angie shoved the flat of her hand right at his face. She stopped a bare inch from his nose. "Let me ask you this."

Justin clamped his mouth shut. That was what he wanted, for her to talk, so he needed to give her the chance.

"Mel said she rides alone all the time, just not at night." Her hand came up again before Justin could start on the many differences between a tough western woman like Mel and a city girl like Angie. "What I want to know is, if someone's interested in a revolution, why would they ignore other big ranches? You saw the same map I did. They put the Xs only on the land grants. I want to know if you think the Blakes could be in danger, too. Yes, the land grants are maybe the easiest to steal because they have ownership problems that can be twisted and questioned, but I wanted to warn Mel about the dangers of her riding out alone, and I wasn't sure if you wanted me to tell anyone about the exact sort of trouble you're having. And I also want to know why they'd ignore holdings like the Blake Ranch."

That stopped Justin from saying whatever nonsense he was no doubt going to say. He had noticed that he usually said whatever was the worst possible thing when he talked to Angie. Every time he did it, he swore to use more sense next time, and then he'd just go right ahead and mess up again.

He caught her arm and said, "I think we need to ask your questions to my family. But I think you're right. We should warn the Blakes."

He didn't have to drag Angie anywhere, because she headed for where the Bodens stood faster than he did. It warmed his heart. She really did care about his family.

John was standing nearby, so Justin waved him over to listen, too. Justin had Angie repeat her worries to Cole, Sadie, and Heath.

When Angie finished, Justin said, "I've never thought a thing of Mel riding around alone. She's as tough as any man."

"There's nothing manly about Mel." Cole sounded gruff, like for some reason what Justin said annoyed him. But it was nothing every man, woman, and child—Mel included—hadn't said about her all her life. Maybe Cole wasn't as healthy as he let on.

"I think we need to warn the Blakes. It's not just women who might be in danger. No one should be riding alone. Are there other ranchers around who should hear this tale?" Justin's eyes narrowed as he thought of a few. "It's been my inclination to handle this ourselves. And I especially thought so when we've been trying to find out who's been spying on us."

With her arms crossed, looking worried, Sadie said, "But now that we know it was Windy, and he's lost his position to pass on news about us, we owe it to our neighbors to warn them."

"It looks like most of the other land grants are already beyond helping." Justin saw Mel and her folks, Jack and Myra, heading for their horses. "The folks in charge of them are working with our enemies. But plenty of regular ranchers are still in charge of their own places. Pa and Ma would be mighty disappointed in us if we didn't warn their old friends of possible danger."

He jerked his head at the Blake family. "Let's go talk to them now." Justin led the way.

The rest of his family followed along. Angie stuck with them too, which seemed right to Justin, and he questioned himself as to why.

The Blakes knew a lot of it, because Mel had talked plenty to Sadie and Angie. But Angie admitted she had hesitated to share Boden private business with even someone as trustworthy as Mel. Justin admired a woman . . . well, come to that, any person who thought before they spoke.

When they were finished, Jack said, "I didn't even realize that your pa's injury was an attack. And there have been two more shootings?"

"Out at the ranch, both Heath and I were shot on separate occasions," Cole said. "But there were three shootings. You're not counting Miss Maria from the orphanage. We consider the attack that killed her to have been aimed at Justin. And she definitely had evidence in her possession that makes us think she was part of this."

"Are you sure they were after Justin or had they become worried that Maria might tell all she knew and ruin their plans?" Jack asked.

Cole and Justin looked at each other and both shrugged.

Justin said, "I can tell you for sure that whoever started shooting at us might've been after me, but they didn't give a hang if Maria got hurt. It was full daylight and she was standing right beside me. The first shot seemed to be aimed at me. She jumped in front of me. I took that to mean she knew men were after me, and she was willing to die to save me. It was a mighty brave way to die."

Jack looked at his daughter with one arched brow. "You knew all this, Mel?"

Myra chimed in, "And you didn't tell us there was such danger in the area?"

Mel had a swagger that she couldn't control. She didn't look one speck repentant. "The way I understood it, the trouble was all aimed at the Bodens, and they wanted to handle it quietly. So I didn't pass on details. Now that they're talking about it, I'll be glad to add anything I've learned, although some of this was new to me. So Angie and Sadie were holding some of the details back." Mel's blue eyes narrowed as she looked from Angie to Sadie.

Sadie grinned. Angie wrung her hands. Justin wondered if that was because Angie had to work with Mel every day.

"One thing's for certain," Myra said as she rested her hand on Mel's back. "You mustn't ride out alone anymore. We can't be certain that these outlaws, whether they are after a revolution or just land thieves, won't come for our family, too."

"But Ma, I've been riding the trail to town alone for years."

The Blakes left for home on their guard, and Justin heard Jack adding his own voice, very sternly, to Myra's new rule.

As they saddled up, the glare Mel gave Angie, who she clearly blamed for limiting her freedom, was a little scary. Justin hoped it didn't scare Angie right back to Omaha.

Once the Blakes rode away, Justin turned to the group. "We're going to have a talk with Ramone now. Angie, you searched Maria's room. I want you to come along with us. I'm not letting Ramone lie to me again, and if he denies Maria had that map, you can tell him exactly where you found it."

21

"You don't need all of us there." Cole spoke before Justin walked the short distance to where Ramone was staying.

"I'm going to stay here and talk to some more of our neighbors," Cole continued. "I want the word to get out about this danger. I regret that we haven't warned them. It felt personal before, but now that I've seen that map, I think ranchers in the area need to have what information we've got."

Heath said, "That's a big job. Sadie and I will stay here and help."

Angie found herself walking off with Justin alone. She was quite sure that at some point, not that long ago, she'd promised herself she'd never be alone with him again.

"Angie, I could see that you wanted to ask me about the danger to the Blakes and others mighty bad. Thank you for waiting for us this morning. It's a good sign that you're learning the ways of the West."

But Angie could tell that what he really meant was *never ride alone again, ever*. She decided to goad him just a bit. "I asked Mel if she'd help me learn to ride and shoot and be better at all the western things she knows about."

Justin stopped in his tracks and pulled Angie to a halt. "Uh, I don't think you should probably be shooting a gun."

"Why not?"

"Because you could do a lot of damage. What if you shoot something you weren't aimin' for?" He pulled her close, his eyes wide with alarm.

"Well, of course I won't shoot what I aim at, not at first. But I'll get better."

"What if you shoot someone or yourself?" His hand slid from her hand to her upper arm.

"I'm sure Mel will have me practice somewhere I can do no harm."

Justin stared down at her as if he were either struck dumb or had so much to say that he couldn't get out a single word.

Feeling tired, Angie was sure it was the latter. When had Justin ever stopped lecturing her? "Wouldn't you like me to be safer? A woman alone, like I am, can't count on someone else to protect her."

"You were riding some better the other night. You don't need to learn all these things."

"I was hanging on by my fingernails every time I got that old mare to go faster than a walk. Mel said she could handle herself as well as any man riding alone, and she'd teach me to be just as tough." Angie was making this all up, since Mel hadn't been able to talk for laughing—although she intended to ask Mel again and nag her until she did show Angie a few things. But she made it sound like Mel had agreed just to annoy Justin, who seemed to want to handle everything for her. But he was always so far away he was useless.

"She might teach me to rope a steer, too." She'd heard of roping cattle, and a steer was some kind of cow, but it was beyond her what you'd do with it once you had it roped.

She didn't tell Justin that, of course.

"Can't you keep busy letting Sister Margaret teach you how to cook and sew? And being a teacher is a fine womanly task. Concern yourself with that."

True, she needed to learn those things along with shooting.

"I don't suppose you know how to collect eggs."

"You mean collect them from the store?"

"I'll take that to mean no. How about milk a cow?"

"Is that why Mel said she could rope steers? You tie them up before you milk them?"

Justin sighed. "Did you ever plant a garden back in Omaha?"

"Oh, yes. Before Father died, Mother and I had the most beautiful roses. It was one of the few things we did together that came close to being pleasant." Angie hadn't noticed any roses around town. Maybe she could plant some.

"Are there things a woman can learn to make a fistfight fairer between her and a man?"

Justin turned her and marched her on toward Ramone's house. "You're not getting into any fistfights. Just stay inside the orphanage and you won't have to fight for your life."

He made it sound like an order, and Angie bristled. "You have no right to tell me what to do, Justin Boden. You're not in charge of my life. In fact, I want you to—"

Justin hammered hard on a door, and only then did Angie realize they'd reached Ramone's house. She also realized Justin didn't want to talk to her anymore.

It was a big old shame because she had a lot more things to say to him, and she was considering shouting them at the top of her lungs.

Ramone swung the door open. Angie would have stepped back if Justin hadn't been right behind her. She'd never met Ramone, though she'd heard of him. No one had mentioned the dreadful scar that disfigured the entire left side of his face and had left him with a white, empty socket where his eye should be.

He was ugly beyond Angie's ability to find her voice.

Alonzo came up behind his father on the left. "Padre, let them in."

Ramone turned to give his son a hard look. When he revealed the right side of his face only, Angie saw that he'd once been a handsome man. Now, though, he was left scarred, quite old, white-haired, and generally worn down by life. Even so, he looked so much like his son that she was suddenly confused about just what his story was. To go from fine-looking to being disfigured must have been a shocking and dreadful change.

Struggle could make a person stronger, or it could break them and turn them into someone who was ugly on the inside. Which way had Ramone been changed? Was he a friend or a very dangerous foe? She knew Justin was suspicious and had come here determined to find out what was what.

Going by his expression, she guessed he wasn't going to leave until he got some answers.

⁓✢⁓

Justin had a list of questions for Ramone, and the man wasn't going to be allowed to dance around them this time.

Whatever Maria had known about those land-grant holdings and a revolution she'd learned from Ramone or people he had a connection to. To Justin's way of thinking, that meant Ramone was an accomplice to murder.

Shouldering the door open, Justin pushed past Ramone and Alonzo. Ramone wasn't strong enough to stop him, and Alonzo must've remembered Justin was his boss.

Justin kept Angie by his side as the two of them sat down on chairs near the kitchen table in the one-room dwelling. A narrow bed had been pushed against one wall, with two chairs facing the fireplace, a couple of wooden crates tacked on the wall for cupboards, and a small wooden table under them that served as a counter and held a dishpan. The house didn't amount to much more than that.

"Last time I saw you, you were bone-thin and mighty weary, Ramone. You're getting stronger." Justin hoped the man didn't intend to use that strength to cause trouble. He kept his eye on Ramone, watching for any sign of what he was thinking or feeling.

It wasn't hard to figure out.

Ramone hesitated for far too long. Finally he stepped closer to Justin and said, his voice low and urgent, "You must leave, Señor Boden. They will kill me for talking to you, just as they killed Maria."

"Tell me what you know, Ramone. We'll keep you safe."

"That is not possible. They are too strong, too determined. We will help them and keep their secrets or we will die."

Studying the man in silence for a moment, Justin said, "I've already been seen entering your house. If someone's watching you, the damage is done."

Ramone's hands began shaking. His face blanched even with his dark complexion. His breath was too shallow. Every movement spoke of terror. He then nodded, taking a seat at the table. "You are right. My death is assured. It is time to stop running and face them as a man. Instead, I act the coward and keep their secrets when all should be exposed to the light of day." He folded his hands together until they formed a single fist and bowed his head low.

He looked like a man resigned to death, as if he wanted to die in prayer. Alonzo rested a hand on his father's back as if to comfort him.

"Please, Ramone, do it." Angie reached out and touched Ramone's folded hands. "You speak of yourself as if you are a coward, but it's they who are the cowards. Hiding behind bushes, shooting from cover at unsuspecting men and women. If someone like you would face them, as a few of the Boden men have done, these dangerous men will slink back into the shadows like the frightened vermin they are."

Ramone lifted his chin and looked at Angie. "You speak with more valor than I." He nodded slowly but steadily. "You are right—to make everyone who hears of their plans cower is the only way they can win."

"But win what?" Justin leaned forward. "Is there truly a revolution coming?"

Ramone turned to meet Justin's eyes, and for the first time Justin saw some backbone in the man. Justin had no tolerance for weaklings, and he'd judged Ramone to be one. But now, looking straight into this man's ravaged face, Justin could imagine his pain and fear and desperation. He'd learned it when Dantalion had killed Grandfather Chastain, then scarred Ramone brutally and promised he'd hang if he didn't run. Afterward, he'd lived his life serving a tyrant of a father and had been cast out by his father's angry, betrayed widow.

The life he'd led could beat the strength out of anyone.

"The truth is your only hope to survive this. Tell me what's going on and I'll go with you to the sheriff and make sure he understands the danger you're in. He'll protect you."

Ramone, his jaw a tight line, replied, "I can't tell you much, Señor Boden, but I can tell you that it is true. The murmurs are everywhere. Some people speak of it with longing to be back with Mexico, but few are so foolish as to think they can win a war with the United States."

"Tell me what you know."

"There are few in Skull Gulch involved." Ramone gave him some names, none of them men Justin knew. Still, he promised to pass the names on to the sheriff right away.

"I have met with the ones I know and they are a ragged bunch.

We have been told there are others, many others throughout New Mexico Territory. These men know nothing but their discontent. Dantalion must have been planning this clear back to when he killed your grandfather."

"You heard of this revolution talk way back then?"

Shaking his head, Ramone said, "No, but why else would he still be involved?"

"You're assuming he's behind a rebellion, but maybe it's something else. We knew Grandfather was paying off someone in the territorial governor's office. That doesn't sound like a coming war. That sounds like powerful men pressing their thumb on a citizen. Yes, there is definitely talk of an uprising, but could this talk be a way to stir up trouble? Or is it a distraction to keep us from finding the real problem?" Justin just didn't see how they could turn reclaimed land grants in America into Mexican land—at least not without a war.

Which reminded Justin of Maria's last words. "And what does Juarez have to do with it?"

Ramone's brow furrowed. "Juarez? I came through Juarez on my way back here from Mexico City. But I knew no one there and I've never heard it spoken of when they talked of a revolt."

"Maria mentioned it. She whispered it as one of her few dying words. Why would she speak of Juarez if it weren't important?"

"She said Juarez was involved?"

"Not exactly, but I figure it's what she meant. She said '*Viva México* and *tener cuidado*.' Cuidado means city, doesn't it? And the full name for Juarez is Cuidado Juarez."

"No, it's *Cuidad* Juarez."

When Ramone said it, Justin realized that wasn't the word Maria had spoken. "Then what does *tener cuidado* mean?" Justin was upset with himself. He'd thought he knew and so hadn't bothered to ask.

"It means 'beware,' and 'Viva México' could just be a remark about loving Mexico and wanting that country to be well."

Justin swallowed. "But Maria wouldn't talk of loving a country she's never been to with her dying breath. No, she said it because she'd heard talk of a revolution and was warning me: Beware the revolution."

He'd almost talked himself out of it, decided there was something more going on. But for Maria to say it with her dying breath . . .

He turned to Angie. "We're going to the orphanage so you can pack up. You're coming with us. Now."

22

"I want you to move in with me."

Those weren't Justin's exact words, but that was what Angie heard.

"What? No!" Angie pressed her hand to her throat and fought down the strange combination of thrill and fear.

Justin was a pure temptation to sin. By that she meant sin by not standing on her own. She veered her mind from a host of other possible sins that popped into her head.

"You have to come. Here I stand, ready to throw this door open, wondering if I'll face gunfire because Ramone is connected to this, but then I'm supposed to take you back to the orphanage and just leave you?"

"Why would anyone think I'm involved?"

"For the same reason Heath's name showed up on the list. It's not just the Bodens; it's all those close to them. And you just walked across town holding my hand."

"You were dragging me. That's not the same thing."

"You went into Ramone's house, when he is afraid he's being watched, and now we leave—all of us together. How could someone who's after the Bodens *not* think you're involved?"

"But I'm not involved! And Aunt Margaret needs me."

"I'm going to talk to your aunt. It's been a struggle to keep help since Sadie quit. She needs to hire someone else."

"But I like my job!" She thought for a moment and added, "I don't get paid, you know."

"Neither did Sadie." Justin frowned. "We'll figure something out so she can get along without you. Why not send the orphans to the Skull Gulch school?"

"I think there was some trouble. Some folks thought orphans weren't fit company for the other children."

"Well, that's just plain stupid."

Angie raised both hands. She agreed, but didn't know what to do about it.

"Whatever troubles there are, you're not going to stay at the orphanage."

"I want to. I love my aunt and I'm not abandoning her." Although an idea came to Angie that might solve the whole thing and at little expense. But was it fair? Would it work? Should she—

"Not only might you be in danger, but you might endanger everyone else there if someone decides to do you harm. What if one of the children had come outside when they were shooting at Maria?"

With that one sentence, Angie knew he had her beat. She didn't dare stay if it meant putting her aunt and the children in peril. "When in the world am I ever going to be in charge of my own life?"

Justin looked back at Alonzo and Ramone. His eyes met Alonzo's. "You ready for this?"

Alonzo drew his gun, and it wasn't the first time Justin wondered if he could trust the man—a man who now had a gun at Justin's back.

Being in charge of a ranch was proving to be nothing but a trial. Pa oughta just toughen up, stop coddling his broke leg, and come home. Running the ranch was Pa's job after all, and Justin wasn't sure he was handling it all that well in his absence. He wished he'd written to his folks and encouraged them to return home by Christmas. Pa could heal up here and yell orders at everyone from a chair in the barn.

And speaking of orders, as they strode across town toward church, where Justin would tell his family Angie needed time to pack, he'd just ordered this beautiful, troublesome woman to come home with him.

He was probably right about her being in deadly danger, so he didn't see how he could do anything else. But he'd decided—although he tended to change his mind at odd moments—that he oughta stay away from her to keep her safe, not drag her into the middle of it all.

Justin glanced between his big brother, who thought he knew everything, and his new brother-in-law, who was besotted with Sadie, and wondered who a man should go to for advice about women.

He wished he had time to write a letter and ask his folks to come home. Tending Pa would give the woman something to do. He'd've done so too if he wasn't worried about getting out of town before he got shot. And before he left town . . .

"We have to stop at the sheriff's office, and we need to stick together."

Angie just followed along. Her life was so out of control she was just doing whatever she was told. The sad part was this was how she'd lived most of her life.

When they reached the door, Justin knocked hard, then went

in. The sheriff stood slowly from his desk, as if he were the most relaxed man who ever lived. Angie was sorry the man had to work on Sunday.

Arizona Watts rose from his cot in the cell. Angie hadn't seen him except briefly at the Bodens' house, where Justin had brought him after Cole's shooting. Then the sheriff had come and taken him away. He'd been in jail ever since.

"You Bodens about to admit you've made a fool's mistake and let me out of this cell?"

Justin smiled in a very mean way, then turned to the sheriff. "I've got a list of names I want you to check out. I think we might find the men who will testify against Watts here. But I think we should talk about it outside."

He'd just thought of that and said it to goad the prisoner.

"We don't need anyone to testify against Watts. I heard him confess with my own ears." The sheriff fell in line with them and went outside, stepping well away from the door. "I meant to catch you before you left town, Justin, but I couldn't get away. My deputy was supposed to come and take over, only he never showed up."

Justin handed the sheriff the list of names Ramone had given him, men he'd met who talked of revolution. Justin told the sheriff to stand guard over Ramone or have his deputy do it, at least until all these men were rounded up.

Cole had some questions for Ramone. Sadie and Health listened and talked quietly between themselves. Alonzo had his gun drawn and his back to the group, most likely keeping the memory of how his aunt Maria had died right in the front of his mind.

"Give me until the day after Christmas on this, Justin. There are ten names here and I can probably shove them all into one cell, but I'm not gonna be able to hold them long and I won't without more than their unhappy talk. Grumbling ain't against the law in these parts. Besides, if I go and arrest them, I'll have to feed 'em. And with Christmas coming, they'll probably expect turkey with all the trimmings."

"Why do you need extra time?"

"The day after Christmas I'll be moving Watts. That's what I wanted to tell you. I wrote to the state capital to see if he's a wanted man. I just got word that a territorial judge has asked for him to be transported to Santa Fe. I have a man riding up to take Watts into custody. I've written up our evidence, and I'll swear to it before the judge's man. We won't need to go. As soon as I get him sent on his way, I'll round these men up." Sheriff Dunn waved the slip of paper. "I'll send word to you when they're locked up. I hope this'll help us get to the bottom of what's been going on. Getting Watts out of the cell will help, especially if we have any chance of scaring him about what these men might know."

Justin nodded. "I'll wait to hear from you. Tell that man transporting Watts to be real careful. He seems fearless, and anyone handling him should be wary."

"We should have brought Mel home with us, too." Sadie hugged Angie after they got her settled in the Boden ranch house. "She's always fun to have around."

Angie hated to stop Sadie's cheerful excitement, but . . . "It's not a party, Sadie. Justin's trying to keep everyone from getting killed. He probably trusts Mel's father to protect her, but he's not quite so sure about Aunt Margaret."

Aunt Margaret was tough, but considering poor Maria's fate, Angie could understand that.

Sadie sat down on the freshly made bed in her parents' room and folded her hands in her lap as if settling in for a chat.

Rosita came in at that moment. Her black eyes went between Sadie and Angie in a solemn way. Her expression spoke of affection and deep concern. "I had the notion of giving you each a gift for Christmas, but I decided it was time now for the gifts. There's been so much strife here, and I thought it right to remind you of the special season."

She extended her hands, each with a string of beads dangling from it. "The colors caught my eye in the general-store window a few days ago. These are made by the Pueblo people. I thought something bright and beautiful might lift all our spirits. I have one for each of you. Some of the beads are from colored stones, others from the clay dug out of the ground and painted."

Angie lifted the string of beads from Rosita's hand. Each bead was a different color, from bright red and glittering white to darkest black. There were at least twenty beads on the necklace, including earth tones, one the natural color of clay. "It's beautiful."

"I thought they were pretty things, much as you two girls are pretty things. And I like the idea of you wearing stone strung on leather. That way you can carry a bit of the land around with you and be reminded of your own strength."

"I'm not sure I have much strength," Angie said.

Rosita pressed a strong hand gently against Angie's cheek. "You are strong, *niña bonita*. You are here, aren't you? Though your life has been hard, you have survived. Your spirit is not crushed, your heart is unbroken."

The words lifted Angie's spirits. She looked from Rosita to the necklace, and it was as if Rosita's encouragement shone out in the bright beads. "I will always cherish this, Rosita." She slipped the necklace over her head and let the beads dangle. "I shouldn't wear it now. I should save it for special times."

Rosita drew five strings of the beads from inside her dress. She must always wear them inside her clothes, because Angie had never seen them before. "No, wear them all the time. If you aren't dressed up fit for a necklace, drop it inside your collar. There are those among the Pueblo people who think of certain beads as good luck or a special protection. These are superstitions, and I put my trust in God, but for me the necklaces are a reminder of God being near and of the beauty of His earth. I would be proud if you would keep it with you."

"I will, I promise. It'll be a reminder that I do have strength, even if I must look deep inside to find it." Angie smiled and kissed Rosita's weathered brown cheek. "It's the first Christmas gift I've received in years. My mother and husband thought such things were for children, but I'm surprised how much this touches my heart. Thank you, Rosita."

Sadie gave Rosita a hug and whispered words that must have made Rosita happy, because she smiled as she patted Sadie on the back.

"Now," Rosita said, "what more do we need to do to settle you in?"

"Are you sure I should stay here?" Honestly, Angie was feeling a bit uncomfortable. "It's your parents' room, Sadie, and besides that, Cole was in here not that long ago." It felt intrusive and overly personal to sleep in a bed a man had recently vacated. "You said there's a fourth bedroom upstairs?"

"A room, yes, but there's no bed in it. There are boxes stored in there and very little floor space."

"I could sleep on blankets on the floor."

"It's proper for you to sleep down here," Rosita said. "That room upstairs is near to Justin and Cole."

Angie didn't feel comfortable about that either.

If they wanted proper, they probably should have brought Mel along—on the condition that Mel brought her mother. But Sadie was a married woman and therefore a good enough chaperone, and Rosita was better than good enough. She was as watchful as Aunt Margaret.

Angie nodded, accepting the room.

Rosita smiled and bustled out.

"Now," Sadie said in a falsely cheerful voice, "because the big, strong men are trying so hard to keep us safe, which means they'd like to lock us in the cellar with an armed guard posted in the kitchen . . ."

Angie had to admit that Sadie knew her brothers and her husband well.

". . . I think we should stop worrying about the terrible crimes that have been committed against my family and plan Christmas." Sadie's tone suddenly wasn't a young woman enjoying a visit. She was a tough frontierswoman with a gift for sarcasm.

"You don't seem like a woman who ignores danger, Sadie. Which makes me wonder if you're not cooking up some plan to fight these awful men."

"It's high time someone had a plan, Angie."

By the time Sadie was done explaining, Angie wondered if she hadn't oughta move out of the Bodens' bedroom and go hide under their porch. Maybe Rosita would bring her food.

23

The day after Christmas the sheriff rode up while Justin stood in the barn pitching straw into a clean stall.

All had been peaceful at the CR and they'd had a fine, if simple, Christmas. No one had given much thought to presents, but they'd gotten a nice box from Ma and Pa. Ma must've had time to shop some in Denver.

Justin tossed aside his pitchfork as the sheriff emerged from the stall with the light of victory in his eyes.

"We need to talk privately." The sheriff looked around the barn. There were three other cowhands close by doing their morning chores. Justin knew he still didn't trust them and that only made it more impossible to believe the peace would last.

The two men stepped out into the chilly, clear December morning, away from the cowhands.

When they'd put a good amount of space between themselves and the barn, the sheriff said, "We've identified Dantalion."

Justin stopped so fast that he almost skidded on the frozen ground. "What did you learn?"

"It wasn't easy. I wrote to several of the lawmen around here with a description and I got no answers. They all promised to ask around. Finally this morning the man from Santa Fe, the one who came to pick up Arizona Watts, brought me a letter from the U.S. Marshal down there."

"He knew Dantalion?"

"He sure enough did. He's been around the territorial capital a while, and Sam, the Marshal, was suspicious of him a time or two."

"For what?"

"Sam's suspicions were vague. There's been a few incidents where bad things happened. A rancher's only son and heir died under strange circumstances. A herd of cattle was rustled so skillfully, no one knew they were gone until they'd been driven across the border. Another rancher had money trouble that came from one piece of bad luck after another, and he finally sold out to a man Sam didn't trust."

"And he thought Dantalion was behind all this?"

The sheriff's eyes narrowed. "There was no proof. That's why there are no wanted posters. He'd never been caught or even accused of anything. But Dantalion would show up in Santa Fe, and sure enough there'd be trouble. It happened a few times too many, and Sam had begun some investigating. He had to be real careful, though. Dantalion knew some people high up in the government, and without solid proof, Sam might've found himself with powerful enemies."

"Like the governor?"

"He didn't say that in his letter, but I wondered. What he did say was that he ran across the letter I sent around in an odd way. He was in the sheriff's office, waiting for the lawman to come back. They were supposed to have a meeting. A breeze came down the chimney and blew some burning ash out onto the floor and along with it the letter I'd sent. It'd been thrown on the fire but had fallen to the side and hadn't caught. Sam picked it up to toss it back onto the fire. He read a few words and realized it was the kind of thing the sheriff would've usually shown him. So why had it been tossed away?"

"He recognized the description?"

"Yep, especially because he was already suspicious of the man. And now he suspects the sheriff was covering up for Dantalion. My letter also told him Dantalion was dead. Sam got to thinking the sheriff might've run off to pass that news along."

"Does Sam know who might've been behind Dantalion's crimes?"

"He's got some ideas, but he needed to ask a few more questions. He said there'd be another letter in a day or two. He's a good lawman and nothing makes him madder'n a crooked sheriff. Sam also said he has an idea that might get to the bottom of everything. I think you oughta consider it."

Justin was all for someone having an idea.

Sadie had a terrible idea.

Angie knew better than to go along with it. But what else could they do? This trouble dragging on and on was wearing them all down.

She sat up, rocking in a chair in Chance Boden's office, near the glowing embers of the fire. Sleep was beyond her.

All she could think was how many years she'd lived like a coward, keeping silent, always afraid. She'd lived like that most of her life. And she'd promised God she wasn't going to do that anymore.

Here was her chance to show a little courage.

They had to find out what all the strange happenings and talk of revolution meant. And dangerous as it was, Sadie's plan would work . . . if they lived through it.

Angie thought of Maria's sacrificial death to save Justin and knew it was what love truly should be. She prayed for peace, for some certain knowledge that what Sadie had planned was God's will. Or if not, that God would shut the door firmly in their faces.

The door swung open. A man's silhouette showed in the dim light.

"Can't sleep?"

Just as she'd hoped and feared in equal parts. Justin came in and they were together. Alone together.

He crossed the room and slid over one of the chairs from beside the couch and took a seat beside her. With a sigh he lowered himself into the chair. He was fully dressed. She sat there in her nightgown and robe.

The room was quiet and peaceful, and she couldn't bring herself to care about her appearance.

"Aunt Margaret sent a note out to the ranch today saying Stephanie is working out well as a teacher." Angie had suggested they let some of the older girls take over the teaching.

Margaret had given the job to Stephanie, who was only sixteen. She wrote of how impressively the girl handled her classes. There were two other older children, both girls, who might be able to help, too. When the boys reached sixteen, they always left to find work. The girls, if they didn't marry, stayed a bit longer.

Now Aunt Margaret spoke with enthusiasm of how this would train the girls for a teaching job elsewhere.

"Chances are Sister Margaret isn't even gonna need a teacher again. She can raise her own." Justin stretched his legs toward the fire and folded his hands in his lap. He rested his head against the chair back, the very image of a relaxed and easygoing man. Which of course Angie knew wasn't even close to the truth.

"What're we gonna do about this, Angie?"

"I thought the sheriff came with new information. We can—"

"I'm not talking about the fight we're in. I know what I'm gonna do about that."

"You do?"

"Yep."

"What?"

"I'm gonna keep after the varmints pesterin' us. I'm gonna fight and keep fighting. And I'm never gonna let any man steal one single square foot of the Cimarron Ranch."

"Then what did you mean?"

"I mean what are we gonna do about the fact that I can't find myself alone with you without wanting to kiss you? And all I've got to offer you is to buy into our fight and risk your life." Justin hesitated before he went on. "To ask you to consider being part of my life is to invite you into danger. But more than that, it's a life you've never expected. It's harsh, with hours of hard work, horses you can't ride, clothes you can't sew. Burning heat in the summer, with every wild plant and animal trying to bite you or poison you. It's no life fit for you."

His words struck hard. "What you really mean is that I'm not fit for this life."

Justin sat up and leaned toward her. "I just think you'll be unhappy out here. There is nothing of the city, very few comforts."

"That's something Mother would say, something Edward would say."

Justin jumped out of his chair. "Don't you compare me to your mother. I haven't said a word to tear at you like she did."

Angie stood just as fast. "You just did."

Justin breathed hard but didn't speak. His hands flexed as if he was making fists. Then he forced them open, then made fists again. She was quite sure he wouldn't punch her, so she thought it was his way of fighting for control.

"However you heard it, what I meant was you wouldn't be happy here. This is no life for a woman who has worn silk and bonnets, who grew up on paved streets without a single rattlesnake in sight—even if she did it in a home with no love."

"You don't know what you're talking about." She slashed her hand through the air so close to him that Justin flinched. "A home with no love is a terrible place, no matter the comfort. I'd rather sleep on dirt floors and wear one calico dress the rest of my life than have a home without love."

Another stretch of silence. "Tell me about your husband."

"My mother—"

"No, last time I asked you about your husband, you talked of your mother. Tell me about Edward."

She turned from him and stared into the fire. "What I began to say was Mother picked Edward for me. He was much older and humorless, but he seemed like a decent man and he was rich. To Mother there was no decision to be made. Of course I must marry him. I tired of him as we courted, and when I told Mother I wasn't interested in marrying him, she informed me our money was gone. She borrowed money against the value of the house for years to survive. But it was all gone. The bank was going to foreclose. She said if I didn't marry Edward, we'd be out on the streets. The thought scared me witless. I was used to being under her thumb, doing as I was told. I didn't have the courage to stand up to her. I convinced myself that although Edward wasn't good, he was good enough.

"Our marriage happened fast, and for a time poverty was a thing of the past. He lived in a fine house. We had servants and the best clothing. We wanted for nothing. Mother lost the house and came to live with us. When Edward was severe with me, she approved. They formed quite a partnership to run my life."

"So neither of them would let you make your own decisions?"

"Never. Mother died about a year after I married. That's when I began to think of eternity. I read my Bible and made peace with God. Edward paid little attention to me by then and was gone day and night, yet he wouldn't let me leave the house—"

"Wait," Justin interrupted. "What do you mean he wouldn't let you leave the house?"

That caught her attention. "Edward insisted I stay home. He thought the world was too dangerous and I had poor judgment. He accused me of spending too much money. He found fault with my few acquaintances—I wouldn't really call them friends, but I met them to walk in the park occasionally. Edward made it difficult to do these things, and at the beginning of our marriage I was determined to please him. By the time I got tired of that, there were no acquaintances left to gather with. He had control of all the money, so I didn't have a dime to spend. His stories about the dangerous world outside our house had made me afraid."

"If he was gone day and night, how could he make you do anything?"

"The servants spied on me and reported to him. While she was alive, my mother reported to him. I left a few times, and he made me very sorry I'd done it." She paused, shrugged her shoulders. "I don't want to talk about my tyrant of a husband anymore. He could force me to stay home, but he couldn't control my heart and mind and soul. I found a way, in my secluded little world, to be a woman of faith. I promised my heavenly Father I would learn courage, grow a sturdy backbone, and stand up to Edward one day. At the time, I imagined insisting I be allowed to attend church. Even that was too much for me to ask.

"A year after Mother died, Edward was shot and killed in a card game. I only knew about it when the police came to my door. They told me he was a gambler and he'd been living on an inheritance, but it was all gone now. Creditors were there only hours after the police left. Edward had run up bills for all our furniture and clothing. The house itself was rented, and I didn't even know it. They took everything and forced me out with the black dress I'd donned on news of Edward's death." Angie glanced at Justin. "It was the same black dress I was wearing when I stepped off the train in Skull Gulch. I was cast into the street, the horror Mother had threatened me with before, with no idea how to survive on my own. I knew then the pressure I'd felt to be strong and brave was because God saw that I was going to need every ounce of strength and courage I could find."

Justin caught her arm gently and turned her to face him. "What did you do?"

"I knew no one. After a lifetime living in Omaha, I couldn't claim a single friend. All the servants had been dismissed, and the wages due them went unpaid, so of course they were hostile. One of the maids said she was going to hunt for work in a factory. I knew she was one of Edward's most faithful spies, so I expected and got no help from her beyond that factory's name. I found the factory and got a job—a terrible, dangerous job—then found a place to stay in a rat-infested rooming house.

"I'd been living there and working fourteen-hour days in that factory for nearly a year when Aunt Margaret's letter arrived." She lifted her chin. "I know how to live through hard times. I know how to get my hands dirty and work. I've been hot and cold before, Justin." She poked him hard in the chest. "Don't you tell me what life I'm fit for. I've gone through worse times than *you* ever have in your big, rich house. And now I find myself spending time with a man who believes I only want finery and ease. A man who is too much like Edward."

"Don't say that." Anger flashed in his eyes as he pulled her against him. "I'm nothing like him."

Angie closed her eyes. From her complete lack of fear of him, she had to admit he was right. "No, you're not. You wouldn't hurt me, but you'd take over my whole life because you thought you knew better how to run it than me."

"But I do."

Angie found herself able to laugh at his manly confusion. She shook her head and didn't respond.

"If taking over your whole life is what you call me keeping you safe, well, that's just a husband's God-given duty. I want . . ." Justin fell silent and slowly leaned down until his forehead rested against hers. His grip on her arm was more of a caress. "I'm sorry if I sound like Edward. Can you forgive me?"

And those were words Edward had never once said.

"Now it's my turn," she whispered, "to say I'm sorry. You sound nothing like him." Without making a decision to do such a thing, Angie kissed him.

She'd never kissed him before. He'd kissed her and she'd gone along, but she hadn't started it.

Justin finally broke off the kiss because he knew he should, then raised his head a few inches. "Let's talk about you letting me court you, Angie."

A log snapped in the fireplace and sent up a shower of sparks that caused her to jump. She stepped away and turned her back to him. "No, Justin. Nothing has changed. I admit I'm drawn to you . . . but I need time. Even if you're kind and decent, I know myself. I will lean on you. I'll allow you to be my strength rather than find my own."

"Angie, we'll figure it out. Together."

"No, we won't. I want to go back to the orphanage. Aunt Margaret won't think it's right for me to live under the same roof as you, no matter that we have chaperones around."

"I'm not letting you go back. So you have to—"

"Not let me?" She turned to face him. "There you are, dictating to me."

"No, that's not what I meant at all."

"What else could you possibly have meant?"

"What I would have said if you'd let me finished was, I'm not letting you go back to town, so you have to marry me. There'll be no long courtship, because your aunt would be right. We shouldn't be staying under the same roof when we have feelings for each other. I think you're safer out here. I want to kiss you when the spirit moves and not feel like I'm treating you with disrespect. All those things you worry about—riding alone, being improper—are absolutely right until we're married."

He studied her face. Her blue eyes catching the flicker of the firelight. Her blond hair pulled free of whatever had been restraining it before.

"You honor me with your proposal, Justin, and I think in time we might suit. But I have to say no right now."

"So it's no for now, but you are considering it? And in the meantime, you will stay here and let me protect you?"

Nodding, Angie replied, "I would love to have your protection, Justin. I understand it's a new country and right now there's a special threat that makes it even more dangerous than usual. I will agree to a courtship, but like I said, I need time."

Wanting to sway her from her stubborn refusal, he leaned down to kiss her. But she quickly pressed her fingertips against his lips and said, "I'm leaving—before I forget why I should."

It hurt that she didn't care enough about him to see he would let her find her own strength within the marriage. A flash of anger goaded him. She should be eager to marry into the Boden family. It was a long step up for a woman who'd been near starvation not that many weeks ago. He felt the arrogance in his reaction.

She was right that he had it in him to be a dictator. A kind-hearted one, yet that didn't give her room to test her own strength. And a woman needed strength in the West.

"I think it's wise that you go. Good night, Angie." He couldn't keep the disappointment out of his voice.

She rushed out of the room as though she were running away from him, leaving him before the crackling fire—alone.

24

The sheriff rode in before breakfast, and Justin's jaw clenched until he thought he'd crack his teeth. Sheriff Joe wasn't part of what he saw for the day. He had work to do and a reluctant woman to corral. His day was full.

"I've got men in jail, Justin. I found six of them *hombres* Ramone mentioned, all of 'em Mexicans. They're telling some strange stories about a revolution, but they're a ragtag bunch and not a one has the fire in his eyes that fit with a fighting man. I'm not sure what's going on, but I think they may know enough to help us find who's behind all this. I want you and Cole to come in and talk to them. I'd like Rosita there too, because most of 'em don't speak much American. Rosita can translate your questions and their answers. Let's see what we can get out of them."

Heath was in the next stall, saddling his horse. "I want in, too. I'd like to look them in the eye when we ask if they were part of a plan to use Sadie as bait."

"Do we have to do this right now?" Justin heard a little bit of a whining tone in his voice and it shocked him into silence.

The sheriff, Cole, and Heath all looked at him in alarm, no doubt wondering if he'd lost his wits.

"I can't hold these men for long, Justin. I arrested 'em on one man's word, and even if they are grumblers who wish they could go back to being Mexican, they haven't broken any laws. A man's got a right to complain, after all."

"Is something wrong?" Cole asked, looking worried.

Well, Justin wasn't going to let the men out of jail just because he wanted to convince Angie to marry him. The answers he could get from them could be a matter of life and death. "No. Nuthin' is wrong—I'll go get Rosita and we'll head out."

It was still mighty early. Sadie and Rosita were in the kitchen fixing breakfast. There was no sign of Angie. He knew for a fact she'd had a late night. Nor could he see himself explaining things to Sadie.

"Can you come with us, Rosita? We need to ride to town to question some men the sheriff arrested. Ramone gave us a few names of the ones he overheard talking revolution, but they don't speak English. We need a translator."

Rosita nodded, grabbed a towel, and wiped her hands. She plucked a heavy coat off a peg by the back door and pulled it on with Justin's help.

"We don't know when we'll be back, Sadie." Justin wanted to say a whole lot more. "Uh . . . is Angie up?"

"I haven't seen her, and I wonder why. She's usually an early riser."

Justin let out a sigh. "This might take a while. We'll probably miss dinner." With a sinking feeling in his stomach, he admitted the truth. "And if there's any evidence to follow, it might take all day. So who knows about supper?"

"Are you all right, Justin?" Sadie asked.

He ushered Rosita out, then shut the door behind them with unnecessary force.

Angie woke up happier than she'd ever been in her life.

She'd said yes to letting Justin court her. He hadn't liked her hesitation, but he'd agreed, and she felt like maybe, sometime in the future, she'd find the courage to bind her life with a man again.

She threw off her covers and leapt out of bed. She looked over her three dresses, not a one of them black. She was done with widow's weeds.

Aunt Margaret had helped her sew them. Though her aunt always wore the most severe nun's habit, she had sewn children's clothes for years, including clothes for mostly grown girls, so she knew her way around a ruffle.

The dresses were yellow, blue, and pink, each scattered with tiny flowers. Angie had watched Margaret sew. She'd tried to teach Angie the way of it and all with a smile, clearly enjoying working with the pretty material.

That thought stopped her in her tracks. Into the silent room she whispered to herself, "I should talk with Aunt Margaret about Justin. I could use her wisdom." Grabbing the blue dress sprinkled with white daisies, she donned her clothes quickly and hurried to the kitchen to see Sadie busy working.

"How late did I sleep? I'm so sorry. How can I help?" Should she mention that she and Justin were courting, or would he rather announce it? Maybe he had already. Or had he decided to wait until they were together? Or not talk about it at all?

Sadie was kneading bread. She looked over her shoulder and smiled. "I'm glad you rested well."

"Is Justin here?"

Sadie's smile turned to a mischievous grin, as if she knew the question was more than idle curiosity. "No, he rode off this morning with Heath, Cole, and Rosita. Heath didn't know how long they'd be gone, but he said not to worry if they were late for the noon meal and even supper."

Angie was so disappointed, she felt like she'd taken a blow. "This is our chance, Angie." Sadie dropped what she was doing, went over and took her hand and began pulling her toward the stairs.

"Our . . . our chance?"

They hurried up the stairs, where Sadie took her into the room she and Heath shared. She closed the door firmly and leaned her back against it as if afraid Angie would try to escape.

Sadie had a furtive look in her eyes, and since there was not much sneakiness in her, Angie knew exactly what was going on.

"You know we have to do something, Angie. This can't go on."

"But to try to catch whoever is after you ourselves, what if—?"

"You know they had the word *bait* by my name, don't you?" Sadie strode to a wooden chest with four drawers. She pulled the top drawer open and produced a gun. Angie knew it was a revolver, but her store of gun knowledge was extremely limited.

"Yes, I saw that list. It made my blood run cold."

"Well, this is our chance to do something. I sent word to Mel a little bit ago. She'll have to slip away from her pa, but she said it'd be easy." Sadie did something and the pistol flipped open sideways on some kind of hinge. She spun the revolver, watching close, then snapped the gun back together.

"Mel's coming?" Angie swallowed hard. Now they were putting someone else in danger. Although Angie had to admit that Mel and Sadie were pretty tough women.

Of course, the men were tougher, but they weren't making any progress. Every time they felt like they were getting somewhere, the door slammed shut.

"I thought it was best." Sadie grabbed a holster off a nail on the wall and fastened it around her waist. "I mean no offense when I say I need someone tougher than you to help me. Heath and my brothers would absolutely forbid us to go. Rosita too. There are a few cowpokes left on the place, but they will soon be heading out, probably for hours. This is the perfect day to carry out our plan." She shoved her gun into the holster, then went for her coat.

Our plan?

Angie felt a twisting in her stomach. She was almost certain this was strictly *Sadie's* plan. Trying to look on the brighter side of things, she said, "If Windy was the only traitor, no one will even know we left the ranch and no harm will come to us."

"Finding out there's no one left to betray us wouldn't be as good as catching the outlaws. But it's better off than we are now. If someone lies in wait for us, we'll catch him. Mel and you and me together can handle it."

Angie wondered if she'd be made to shoot somebody. She really hoped she didn't have to. Mel had shown her a few things—after she'd stopped laughing—but it didn't begin to qualify as real training.

"I even know what we're going to say to let the word out with the hired men, so if one of them is a traitor, they know where to send their outlaw friends."

"What are you going to do?"

"I'm going to tell the men who are still around the ranch that we're headed out to climb Skull Mesa. Then, after our climb, I'll say I'm going to show you around the ranch, maybe even ride all the way to the mines."

"You're going to lie?" As if a lie was the worst of their sins.

"Nope, we really are going to climb Skull Mesa and then go for a ride."

With a little gasp, Angie looked out the bedroom window. Skull Mesa.

The long, narrow mesa that for generations had been de-scribed as unclimbable. That is, until Heath had found a way up. Angie had heard Heath teasing Justin and Cole about how easy it was. He made it sound like he and Sadie had just strolled up its side to the top. By the Boden brothers' reaction, Angie knew they were among the men who'd been thwarted by the big old hill. And now they'd been so busy, they hadn't had time to let Heath show them how he'd done it.

"Besides, it'll be fun to tell Cole and Justin you got to the top before they did. That'll chafe for years." Sadie's laugh was just this side of evil.

Angie wasn't sure if she wanted to do something that would upset Justin for years. "Once we're done climbing, where exactly are we going, and how is anyone going to find us, even if they do notice you leave? Will they come after us themselves or will they need to find their cohorts and pass on the word that their chance to catch you and use you as bait has come?"

"We're just going to ride out, give them a chance to make a move." Sadie frowned. "I'm the one who should do it because by using the word *bait*, I think they're saying I'm not to be killed—which is exactly what they tried with Pa and Cole. Heath got shot protecting us all, so there was some gunfire there."

The deep lines on Sadie's forehead told Angie more than words just how much Sadie cared about her husband and family. "I'm not letting them be hurt again. I just can't."

Despite believing this was a dreadful idea, Angie understood Sadie's need to care for those she loved.

"Since they want to catch me, they won't just shoot from cover like they did before. They'll have to show themselves. I'd guess there's gonna be two of them, maybe only one. They've never come in a pack before. With you and Mel there to back me up, we'll be ready for them."

Sadie went to another drawer and pulled out a second gun. "If we get a chance, I'll let you practice your shooting some more."

"Sadie, this seems like a poor idea. It's extremely risky, and Heath is going to be furious with you." And Justin with both of them, but Angie hoped Heath's feelings might sway Sadie.

"There are some risks, I'll admit that. All I can say is there's a good chance my plan won't flush anyone out. But if it doesn't work today, we can try it again until it does."

Somehow, Angie didn't find that very comforting.

Sadie handed the gun to Angie. "Wear your winter coat. The pockets are big enough for the gun. Besides, it's a chilly day."

Angie looked down at the weapon. It was a dead weight in her hand, cold and threatening. She said nothing because no words came to her. And also because she was too busy trying to keep all the blood in her head from rushing to her feet. And if she swooned, she wasn't going to be much help.

The doctor spent what seemed like hours hacking at Chance's leg with an old saw.

Well, not exactly his leg. He cut the plaster wrapped tight around it. Doc Radcliffe wasn't being all that careful, in Chance's opinion, and he braced himself for the bite of that saw.

It never happened, but Chance felt like the whole experience was created to make a man feel too exhausted to walk.

The doctor had probably planned the whole thing for just that reason.

When the bulky cast finally came off, Dr. Radcliffe spent a long time examining Chance's leg. There was an ugly scar across it, and his whole leg was skinnier than it had been. The doc bent the leg at the knee while Chance gritted his teeth to keep from shouting out in pain.

"It's normal that the knee hurts. It hasn't bent for over a month." Next, the doctor twisted Chance's foot, exercising the joint.

It was all Chance could do not to punch Radcliffe in the mouth.

"I'm going to put a cast back on so that the bone is held tight, but this time I won't go above your knee. You'll soon work the stiffness out of it and be able to sit up comfortably and handle the crutches enough to walk. I'm covering your ankle and foot with plaster to stabilize your tibia."

"My what?"

The doc smiled. "Sorry, I try not to use doctor language my patients don't understand. The tibia is the bone you broke, the main bone that connects your ankle to your knee. The new cast will take pressure off your lower leg. Best of all, you'll have a lot more freedom, be able to get around now."

"High time." Chance fought to control his impatience that had worn his temper clean out. "Not blaming you, Doctor. I appreciate your help. And I will be careful with this cast."

"I said before that this newer, lighter cast needs to stay on a month, but I've decided that if you can hold on for two more weeks, most likely you can ride the train home while wearing it."

The doctor held up a hand to stop Chance from getting excited. "That's no promise. I'll make my final decision two weeks from now. But if you're careful and you keep healing as fast as you've done so far, I think two weeks will be enough. I see no reason a train ride will harm your leg. Dr. Garner back in Skull Gulch is a skilled man. I'll want him to wait two more weeks before he cuts the cast off. My guess is you'll heal even faster once you're home. And maybe whatever trouble is following you will ease up by then."

Chance knew he'd still be unable to ride with his children and fight at their sides. But he could guard the house. One of John's recent letters told about Justin posting sentries and their suspicion that one of the hired men was a traitor. Chance couldn't imagine leaving Sadie home alone, which meant they had to leave someone behind to protect her, which cut down on the number of men Justin could ride out with.

When the doctor was finished wrapping his lower leg in the

much smaller cast, he washed his plaster-coated hands in a basin of warm water and said, "You stay right there in bed for the rest of the day. Let that dry thoroughly. By this evening you can get up and move around on the crutches, but don't put any weight on that leg. And be careful—a fall could set you back a long way. The crutches are awkward to use, so start out slow until you learn to handle them."

Chance was feeling encouraged just looking at the new plaster. "I'll do as you say, Doc."

The doctor gave him a suspicious look, then donned the black suit coat he'd shed. "Mrs. Boden, try and keep him off that leg. Two more weeks is all I ask."

"He will behave, Doctor. I will see to it." She gave Chance a sassy smile over her shoulder, then walked Dr. Radcliffe to the front door.

"I think we can try standing now." Ronnie pressed on the cast as she'd done many times.

The sun had set, and Chance had been careful not to even flex the muscles of his broken leg. He wanted his time in this cast to be short.

He sat up and used his hands to lift his broken leg off the side of the bed, following with his good leg. Ronnie leaned the crutches next to him, then reached out.

"Wait." Chance waved off her hands. "Let me just sit here a minute. I've been lying down for so long, my vision just went black. Give it time to clear. I don't worry about it when a couple of people are on hand to hold me up, but I don't want to collapse on you and knock you into a heap."

She smiled and sat beside him until he said, "Now, let's get me to my feet. I'll stand there until I make sure I won't black out."

She stood in front of him, and he grabbed her wrist while using the bedside table to brace himself. He lurched to his feet, or foot, and stood facing her. His vision seemed to turn into some kind of tunnel, with black all around and only a narrow bit of sight straight ahead.

He waited it out. Before long, the world turned to its normal brightness. "It's all right," he said. "Now the crutches. I'll just take a few steps to make sure I can find my balance."

Ronnie leaned forward and kissed him, then she propped the crutches under his arms. "I have a feeling you're going to get out of here real soon, husband."

25

Justin, Cole, Heath, and Rosita, along with the sheriff, swung down off their horses and tied them in a line outside the jailhouse. The sheriff led the way in and sat behind his desk.

There were six men lolling about in the only cell the town of Skull Gulch had. Two of them sat on the narrow bunk. One leaned against the bars, his back to them. The other three were sitting on the floor, arms wrapped around their knees.

They were dressed in rags. The clothes were filthy, and they all looked downtrodden. Not a one of them looked one bit dangerous.

The sheriff said, "I've got some men here who have a few questions."

"When is the noon meal, Sheriff? If you keep us locked up, you have to feed us." The man spoke with a heavy Mexican accent, though his English was easy to understand.

The sheriff groaned and glared at Justin. "I'm not keeping them if you don't find some wrongdoing. I have to feed them out of my own pocket. The town pays me back, but they're mighty slow about it."

Justin looked at Cole, who nodded back at him. It seemed

to Justin that in the normal run of things, Cole thought all talking was Justin's job.

Turning to the jail cell, Justin said, "Tell us what you know about this revolution we've heard you're talking about."

Expecting defiance and resistance, he was surprised by their reaction. Weren't revolutionaries angry about something? Instead, all but one of the men stared back at him with blank expressions.

The man leaning against the bars spun around, his eyes wide with fear. "We know nothing, señor," he said. "Please let us go. We mean no harm."

Scared, just like Ramone. Through gritted teeth, Justin said, "You're not going anywhere until you talk."

Sadie shocked Angie into a near fit when she put britches on. Sadie offered her a pair, and Angie felt her cheeks heat up until she thought her hair might catch fire.

"It's a lot easier to climb with trousers on. At least wear them under your skirt. It's cold out and we may be gone a long time."

"I've got woolen underwear on, surely that's enough warmth."

Sadie shrugged. "Suit yourself, but you're failing the first test of being tough."

"This is a test?"

Sadie nodded.

"And how is insisting on ladylike clothing a failure?"

"Just is." She badgered a bit more, called on Angie's common sense, and finally Angie agreed to wear pants under her skirt. It was the most outrageous thing she'd ever done in her life.

They saddled up and were riding for the mesa just minutes later. They didn't have to make any excuses about what they were doing because the men were all out working.

They climbed a rope ladder for the first little while. With trousers on, Angie handled it with ease. The rope was new and sturdy, no signs of wear. Sadie was so familiar with it, Angie figured Sadie had helped put the rope there.

When she reached the top of the rope, she stepped out onto a good-sized ledge that had plenty of room for both of them. "I can't imagine why anyone thinks this is hard to climb."

Sadie laughed.

"I can't believe you've found a way up," Mel shouted from below them.

"Come on. Cole and Justin haven't had time to climb it yet."

"Yeehaw!" It was a shout of joy.

Angie backed carefully away from the edge in case Mel's enthusiasm somehow knocked her over.

Mel scrambled up the ladder like a limber squirrel. She had on britches just like Sadie.

This was a new kind of world out in the West. Just yesterday she'd gone with Sadie to collect eggs. The hens were nasty things that pecked until Angie's hands were sprinkled with tender little sores. Sadie laughed at Angie's suffering, told her the chickens had her buffaloed, which made no sense at all. While talking, advising, and laughing, Sadie quickly moved down a row of nest boxes, pulling eggs out from under one hen after another. The hens didn't bother her at all.

And now she was climbing a mountain and wearing trousers.

Which reminded Angie of the heavy gun in her pocket. The frontier took some getting used to.

She thought of the strangely absent Justin Boden. Did he really have something to do? Or had he just come to his senses after she'd agreed to become involved with him, and now he was avoiding her?

Another thing she'd probably have to get used to—a broken heart.

Sadie led the way up what was nearly a staircase, walking carefully in sections, while Mel brought up the rear. Mel caught Angie a couple of times when she stumbled backward, so the order of this line was no coincidence.

At last they reached the top. "You said there was rubble up here that had to be from old houses?" Mel headed toward the mounds of rock.

Angie didn't think she'd have realized they used to be buildings if Mel hadn't mentioned it. But what else could they be? The top of the mesa was close to level. Grass and some scrub brush covered the rocky ground, with nothing to suggest the piles of stone had occurred naturally.

"Not old houses," Sadie said, "*ancient* houses. Looks like they've been abandoned for thousands of years."

Mel approached the nearest mound while Sadie picked the one farther on. Angie wandered around looking at the stones, searching with curiosity. She heard Mel and Sadie talking, exclaiming about the wonder of it all. Mel was excited to be up here. Sadie was thrilled to be back.

Angie saw something fluttering and white pinned beneath a stone. As she walked toward it, she realized it was a weathered piece of paper. She got a firm hold of it before lifting the fist-sized rock.

It was a wanted poster.

"Look at this."

There must have been something in her tone, because Sadie and Mel hurried to her side.

Sadie studied the picture. "That's Dantalion, the man who set off the avalanche that nearly killed Pa. He's also the one who shot Heath and Cole, or hired the men who did."

"The same man you say died on the trail you and Heath were on?" Angie asked.

"Yes, but the poster has a different name with the picture. Web

Dunham. And it's dated years ago, in Missouri. He's wanted for murder." She raised her eyes from the paper. "Far as I know, he's not been seen around these parts since he killed Grandfather Chastain. This might be why. He left the area, committed his crimes somewhere else. If we take this to the sheriff, maybe we can find out where he was all this time, and even better, who his friends are. There's a good chance whoever paid Dantalion that gold we found in his pocket is the same person who wrote those notes with the terrible handwriting."

"We need to get this to the sheriff." Angie saw a way to live through the day. "You wanted to lure out your enemies, but using this new information about Dantalion might be a better way to end the trouble."

"But this is our chance," Sadie argued. "I'm so exhausted by the worry and danger. I want this over, the attackers punished, and *today* is the perfect day."

"No, Sadie. We're not going."

Sadie blinked at Angie's stern tone. "What did you say?"

"You heard me."

"This is my plan. You agreed to it. If you're too afraid to fight—"

"Don't speak to me like that. You know the length of time it's taking to solve this is grinding on all of us. You just said you're exhausted by worry. But that's a long way from it being a desperate situation. Your plan is fraught with danger. There might come a time when we have no other choice, but today is not that day. Especially now that we've found a clue that could help us unravel a mighty big knot."

Sadie rubbed a hand over her mouth. It was as if she were trying to hold her next words inside. Angie well knew that Sadie didn't like taking orders, especially from someone not nearly as strong as she was. But common sense had to prevail.

She glanced over at Mel and saw her fighting a smile. Plunking her hands on her hips, Sadie said in a disgusted voice, "You're right. As much as I want this fight over with, it's unwise to take unnecessary risks. Let's go home."

Angie had braced herself to stand against Sadie's arguments, and when she agreed, Angie could hardly believe her ears.

Mel gave a sigh of relief. "I'll head for home, too."

"Will you be all right, Mel? You have a long ride home and we won't know if you made it back safely."

"I was willing to face my ma and pa's anger in order to make this trap we were setting safer. This morning I managed to convince two groups of cowhands, riding in opposite directions, that I was going with the other group. They'll be home for dinner and find out I'm missing. I left Ma and Pa a note sayin' what we are up to. If I go home right now, no one will even know I snuck off. But if I run into trouble on the trail, they'll find out and begin searching. After that, the alarm will be sounded soon enough."

It wasn't enough, but Angie had little choice but to accept it. They descended the trail to the ground and then split up. Sadie and Angie had their horses put up and were back in the house in short order.

As they entered the kitchen, they looked at each other, and Sadie said dryly, "You're growin' quite a backbone there, Angie."

"I'm just so relieved to be safe again, I could cry."

They stared at each other for a moment, then burst into laughter.

"Now, I need to get out of my coat and riding boots. Then we can get back to work."

"I'm going to my room to change out of these dreadful trousers." The two walked side by side down the hallway. "Let's make the best supper for the men and Rosita they've ever had, and while they're eating we can brag about climbing Skull Mesa."

Sadie nodded. "Maybe I can teach you how to take biscuits out of the oven before they turn black."

Angie definitely needed to learn that.

Sadie's voice dropped to a whisper. "And let's never tell them about my plan!"

Angie nodded as they parted ways. Sadie headed upstairs while Angie turned into her bedroom.

She closed the door and walked to the nearest chest of drawers. She didn't sit down because she was afraid she might not be able to get up again. Her knees were shaking, and it wasn't because she was so glad to be safe. It was because of the way she'd spoken to Sadie on top of the mesa.

It was the boldest she'd ever been in her life. And she'd convinced Sadie to abandon her plan, and now they could relax in the shelter of this house. Wherever else they'd run into trouble, no one had ever attacked them here.

A rough hand covered her mouth and ruthlessly dragged her back against a hard body.

Justin held the door for Rosita and then he, Cole, and Heath followed her out of the jail.

"What a waste of time that was." Justin slapped his hat against his pant leg to keep from shouting in frustration.

"Someone is stirring up trouble with these folks." Heath stared into the distance, thinking. "It sounds like it was Dantalion from their description. But they mentioned others. One of them could have been Windy, but I'd never be able to swear to it. He looks like a lot of other cowpokes. There has to be a way to find the men they're talking about. Those folks look so scared, though, I doubt they'd point to the right man even if we did catch him."

Cole crossed his arms and frowned. "There had to be something in what they said that'll give us a direction to hunt. Let's get some coffee and go through all of it again."

"We can do that on the ride home." Justin thought of his bride-to-be. It was past the middle of the afternoon now. He wondered if she'd gone hunting a noose yet.

"No. The sheriff said he's going to hold those men a few more hours," Cole said, "but then he's letting them go before supper so he doesn't have to feed them. He had to pay for breakfast and dinner himself, and he can't afford a third meal. If we think of more questions we need to ask, I want to do it before he unlocks that cell door."

That's when Justin remembered that he hadn't punched Cole in a long time. He also remembered why he liked doing it.

"You men have this talk," Rosita said. "I will run to the general store and buy a few things we need. Then I'll go to the orphanage to see if I can be of any help. Pick up the supplies and come for me at the orphanage if you need me to listen in on more questions. Or if you are done, get me when you're ready to ride home."

"You need to eat, Rosita. Come with us to the diner."

With a smile she said, "I will not starve, but thank you for asking." She crossed the street without saying more.

"Having Rosita there made all the difference," Justin said. "You could tell that those varmints were ready to talk amongst themselves, then agree on an answer. With Rosita there to translate, I think we got the truth out of them."

"A mighty useless truth." Heath kicked at the board sidewalk as they headed for the diner and went inside.

It was long after the noon meal and none of them had eaten. They were lucky there was any food left. Soon they were digging into beefsteaks, mashed potatoes, and gravy. They had the place to themselves, which gave them freedom to talk openly.

"Six men, all of 'em layabouts. They are discontented. That

makes them willing to complain to folks and stir up trouble." Cole looked to be preparing to go through the whole talk they'd had with the men in jail.

Justin slowly and quietly lowered his right hand to his lap so he could clench his fist without being noticed. He did his best to keep any sign of irritation off his face.

Cole really didn't deserve Justin's impatience. It made perfect sense to talk through what they'd learned before leaving town. And neither Cole nor Heath had any idea of how things had changed between him and Angie.

Before they had debated what other questions they might've asked, they heard the hoofbeats of a galloping horse moving at a reckless speed. Horse and rider thundered past the window of the diner.

A harsh voice whispered, "Don't make a sound, Sadie."

Angie's heart nearly pounded out of her chest. Her throat went bone dry. Her mind raced like a rabbit. Through her terror she heard the strange man's words. He was here for Sadie. Bait.

And he planned to use her to trap and kill the others.

There was no doubt in Angie's mind that he intended to kill Sadie, too. The bait died after the fisherman landed his catch.

If Angie denied she was Sadie, he'd do something awful to her and then go find Sadie. Maybe if Angie didn't fight him, once they'd left the house, she could convince him he had the wrong woman and he'd let her go. If she disappeared, Sadie would be on alert. Justin would get home to protect the ranch, Cole and Heath with him. Maybe they'd send a search party for her. Of course they would.

Despite being upset at him for his absence today, she couldn't hold on to any doubts. Justin would come. She trusted him completely. She realized as she thought it that she hadn't expected to trust another man ever again. Now the knowledge that she did washed over her like a purifying rain, and her heart changed. Healing had begun.

Justin would come, all of them would. They'd find her, save her, and catch this man.

If Angie struggled, made any noise at all, it would bring Sadie running, and there was no one else in the house. So she remained silent, for now.

"You're coming with me." He raised a gun so it was visible right by her face. He whispered so close to her ear that she could feel the damp heat of his foul breath. "If you fight me, your friend upstairs will hear you and come to see what's wrong, and then she'll die."

As near as she could think in her panicked state, either she sacrificed herself to save Sadie or she didn't . . . and got them both killed. Though she was terrified of what she might face, she let the man drag her toward the window. He thrust it open with one hand and clumsily dragged her through. His grip slipped a bit, and she had a moment where she was tempted to fight back. If she could get even a few paces away and duck behi d some furniture, maybe she'd have a chance.

But he had a gun. And given his boldness in hiding in the Boden house, she had no doubt he would do whatever was needed to accomplish his ends, murder included.

Still she was tempted. She bunched her muscles to jump for cover.

Then his grip on her tightened, the gun was again in her sight, and seconds later she was outside.

It was cold, the wind biting at her. The man dragged her fast across the grassy stretch between the house and the nearest tree line. Once they were in the woods, he gagged her mouth with a kerchief and tied her hands in front of her. They moved deeper into the thick woods. This was the side of the house away from the barn. She'd never paid much attention to it.

They stumbled along and quickly came upon two horses. The man swung her up onto one of the horses and lashed her hands to the saddle horn. He released her and hurried to his horse. Finally she could see him and was stunned.

Arizona Watts.

The last she'd heard, Watts was locked up in jail.

Well, here he was running free. She'd only really gotten a good look at him once, the day she first came to the CR with the doctor after Cole had been shot. Very likely shot by this same man. Certainly if not him, then confederates of his.

He was most definitely part of the gang who wanted to use Sadie as bait.

⚜

Heath rose and stepped to the door to watch for where the rider went. "He's gone straight to the jailhouse. Let's go see what's happened." Seconds later, Heath was outside and hurrying toward the sheriff's office.

Justin threw some coins on the table and caught the door before it slammed shut. Heath was striding down the boardwalk, and Justin went after him, Cole right behind.

The sheriff swung the door open and charged out only to see them and nearly skidded to a stop. "That rider just told me Arizona Watts reached the jail in Santa Fe, and a man from the governor's office arrived within minutes and demanded he be set free."

"What?" Justin shook his head.

"Remember he said he'd walk right out and we'd let him go? Well, it wasn't us, but the rest of his boast came true."

The sheriff kept talking, raising his voice and shouting at the backs of the Boden men. "If Watts wanted to, he'd've had plenty of time to get back here."

Justin ran for his horse with only one thought in his head. *Bait.*

26

Angie did as she was told and realized that, for the first time in her life, it was truly necessary.

If she did the wrong thing, it might mean the end for both Sadie and her. And for Justin and all the Bodens. She hoped and prayed not. But to yell, to fight, it all seemed to lead to death.

They rode along in the woods, twisting around tree trunks and underbrush. Watts had a lead rope tied to the horse Angie was on, so she had no choice but to go along.

They followed no trail. She ducked branches that would have knocked her to the ground. Or with her hands tied to the saddle, knocked her off the horse to be dragged.

The man looked back to check on her every few minutes, and each time his face twisted with malicious satisfaction. Soon they were a long way from the house. She had no way to estimate just how far, but hopefully by now Sadie had found out that Angie had vanished and needed help.

Angie thought of all the times she'd done as she was told when the only risk was cruel words and criticism. Compared to this, why hadn't she just laughed at her mother and her husband

and said, "Do your worst. I'm not going to obey your senseless rules or believe your unjust criticisms"?

With that defiant thought in her head, suddenly Angie realized she was most likely going to her death. So why obey this time either?

Angie leaned down to the saddle horn, used the bit of movement her hands were capable of and pulled her gag off. Then she threw herself off the horse and screamed for all she was worth. The horse reared as she dangled and slammed Angie into a clump of aspens. The lead rope tied to Watts's saddle ripped loose.

Relentlessly screaming, stirring up the horse, trying to draw attention, Angie was swung hard by the ropes on her wrists. Her skin tore. She screamed again and again.

Watts leapt from his saddle and rushed at her. He tripped over a downed branch and fell on his face.

Her horse jumped sideways, stumbled, and went down. She was dragged backward, then flung into the air. The rope on Angie's wrists was jerked free of the pommel and she was tossed aside.

She hit the ground so hard that for a moment she couldn't draw breath. With her hands still bound, she struggled to her feet. The impact had left her dizzy and disoriented, but she saw her horse behind her and Watts behind the horse, which told her the direction of home.

She ducked and dodged trees. Every step took her closer to home and closer to help. Fighting for each breath, she wasn't capable of a scream. Without the use of her hands, each step was more difficult than the last. Branches slapped at her face. Fallen trees tripped her and threatened to twist her ankles.

Finally she managed to free her hands of the rope. That's when she heard thudding footsteps coming from behind. She didn't look back. She knew who it was. And he was gaining.

Frantic, she ran faster now, looking ahead and seeing she'd been taken into the woods just north of the house. These trees bordered the field that led to Skull Mesa. If she was out in the open, she could be seen all the way to the house. She'd have a lot better chance of finding help.

She turned and headed for the open area. As she ran, the trees began to thin. She rushed forward, praying, trying to think as she ran.

At last she burst into the open . . . and plowed into something hard.

She looked up, hoping for Justin. Instead it was Alonzo. Still, she was saved. "There's a man after me!" she cried. "Arizona Watts. He's got a gun. Please, help me!"

Alonzo shoved her backward into the woods. *What is he doing?* She opened her mouth to scream, but Alonzo gripped the back of her head and slapped his hand over her mouth.

"You stopped her in time." Watts ran up, gasping for breath.

So shocked she couldn't quite figure out what was going on, Angie shook her head violently to dislodge Alonzo's hand.

He leaned closer, and she saw his eyes. Angry, dangerous. The eyes of an enemy.

"This isn't Sadie. You've got the wrong girl." A smirk then replaced the rage in his expression. "But Justin will be baited just as surely. He's sweet on her." Alonzo reached for his gun. "But we're not going to have another escape attempt."

Her heart slammed against her chest. Her breathing snagged and nearly stopped.

He flipped the gun over. "This will keep you quiet."

She saw the butt of the gun swinging hard.

And then felt the pain.

Then nothing.

"Watts broke out of jail!" Justin banged the back door open. "Sadie! Angie!"

He'd been in a flat-out panic ever since he'd gotten word of it. Only Cole's ice-cold control kept him from leaving Rosita behind in town.

Sadie came running, dressed to ride, a holster and gun on her hip. "Angie's gone."

"Gone?" Justin's heart wrenched.

"I'm pretty sure she's been kidnapped. Her bedroom window is open. No sign of her around the yard. No horse missing. She didn't take a coat. She left no note. No reason at all for her to be gone like that. Someone must've taken her."

"We've got to save her!" He whirled toward the back door. He took Cole's fist full in the face. No anger, no shock, it just stopped him in his tracks. "What was that for?"

"You're acting like a lunatic." Cole grabbed the front of his shirt and jerked him forward until they were facing each other. "You can't do anything by jumping on your horse. What direction would you ride? Let's first look for tracks out the bedroom window. See which way they went."

Cole nodded at Heath. "You're the best tracker. Lead the way."

Heath darted out of the room toward the bedroom. Sadie was on his heels with Rosita behind her. Justin was about to charge after Rosita when Cole shoved him hard into the doorframe.

Justin, furious, looked at Cole and shouted, "What are you pounding on me for? We don't have time for this."

"No, we don't. So stop and think before you act. You're useless to us right now." Cole leaned closer till they were nose to nose, and oh, Justin was so tempted . . .

Except Cole was right, blast it. Justin was useless if he didn't get himself under control. Fighting to slow his breath and use the brain in his head, he bore down on the terror of Angie being in their enemy's hands. With teeth gritted, Justin regained control, cleared his thoughts.

He took a deep breath and forced himself to speak calmly. "You're right. We have to trail her. Heath can find a direction, then we'll go after her."

"I know you're in love with her, Justin," Cole said. "I swear we'll get her back. We'll . . ."

Cole kept talking, but Justin was stunned into deafness. He loved her? He loved Angie? No. A man didn't go and fall in love with a woman he barely knew. A woman who didn't know a lick about horses, who wanted her hand bandaged when a chicken pecked her. Sure, a man might find a respectable woman and marry her and even eventually, reasonably, love her. But right now, being in love was the worst thing he could do. It would make him weak and irrational.

Justin thought of his panic then, his weak and irrational panic. "You can't know I love her, Cole. Where'd you get a fool notion like that anyway?"

Cole shook his head in disgust. "I've got eyes, haven't I? Everyone knows you love her."

"And by everyone, do you mean the cowhands and the folks in town?" Justin swallowed, but his throat was dry and all he did was scratch it raw. "Do you mean the people who want to use Sadie as bait?"

"Possibly." The anger on Cole's face faded, replaced by a fine thread of concern, then panic. "Probably . . ."

A shout from the bedroom brought their heads around.

"Get in here!" Heath sounded furious.

27

Angie regained consciousness slowly. Her whole head ached. She wished she could keep on sleeping until she felt better.

And then she remembered. Watts thought she was Sadie.

Her near escape. The gun butt crashing down, swung by . . . ? She struggled with her muddled thoughts until they came into focus. Along with the traitor in their midst.

Alonzo.

Her vision blurred, the dizziness mixed with pain. She thought she might pass out again. Clinging hard to consciousness, she wondered how long she'd been out. Where were they taking her?

An overwhelming need for caution had her moving her eyes side to side without turning her head. She didn't want them to know she was awake. Also, her headache made her want to cast up everything in her stomach, and it was worse if she moved.

They'd thought Windy was spying, and Angie very much suspected he was in on this. But Alonzo, Watts, and Windy in league with Dantalion before he died . . . they must all be part of the conspiracy to steal the Boden ranch.

Alonzo rode in the lead.

Watts was next, leading her horse. It was just the two of them who had caught her. Angie was last in line. Because she was unconscious, as far as they knew, and tied up tight, no one was paying her much attention at the moment.

For all the trouble they'd caused, Angie had expected more men than this. Maybe they were headed to meet their cohorts right now and figure out how to bait a trap with Angie instead of Sadie.

The horses moved quietly. She realized they were in a dense woods, following a narrow trail carpeted with leaves soggy from the winter snow. Nothing crackled underfoot to give away their location.

She wiggled her hands, bound and hanging down past the stirrup. Her fingers were free and she flexed them, afraid they might be numb, but they all worked fine.

Her first escape attempt had failed but only by the merest thread. Alonzo had heard her, or been waiting for her, because he knew what Watts had planned. He'd stopped her from getting away.

Next time he wouldn't be in the right place at the right time.

Yes, there would be a next time. She prayed for it, and she prayed to God for strength sufficient for the task.

As she prayed, the beaded necklace Rosita had given her slipped out of where she'd tucked it inside her collar for their long climb. And why would it suddenly hang right over her eyes, after who knew how long she'd been riding?

And right in the midst of her prayers.

Angie thought of the grass carpet that showed no signs that they had passed this direction. But now Angie had an idea of a way to leave a trail. She looked carefully at the men ahead of her, then reached for her necklace and yanked hard. The tough leather thong snapped and several beads fell to the ground.

Closing her hands over the necklace so no one could see she held it, she rode along for a good distance, then dropped another bead. She was afraid to leave more. She had no idea how long they'd be riding.

They emerged from the trees, and the riders turned off the trail sharply and stepped onto a stretch of solid rock. Angie had very little tracking skill, but she could see their riding on granite left no trail at all.

She glanced at the men again, who didn't look back at her. They considered her to be helpless, so why should they keep an eye on her? She dropped another bead. They were all different colors, and she was glad this bead was bright red. It would help anyone who was trailing her to see that they'd left the trail for an unlikely course.

While they rode on, Angie left her clues behind. Anytime they'd turn off, as the trail divided and narrowed, she'd mark their direction and hope the beads didn't roll into a hole or get kicked off the path by her horse.

They followed a twisting path and slipped between boulders that appeared to be blocking the trail. Angie didn't want to underestimate the Bodens, but she was growing more afraid that no one would be able to pick up this trail without help.

She sparingly doled out her dwindling supply of beads. Before she dropped one, she would watch Alonzo and Watts for a time. She didn't want them to catch her leaving a trail, but it was also necessary she remain alert so that if something happened that gave her a chance to get away, she'd be ready.

Right now there was little chance of an escape. She was draped over the saddle, her head hung down by a stirrup, her hands bound. But for now she was doing what she could. Hopefully her time would come with an opportunity to fight back or run away.

Testing each restraint she found her legs tied up, as well. A kerchief was tight around her mouth, and every step took her farther away from help and the Cimarron Ranch.

With no idea how long she'd been in her captors' clutches

or how many miles they'd ridden before she awoke and began marking their passage, finally Alonzo veered off the stone trail. She had only two beads left. Should she mark this turn or save the few beads for later? Without much confidence of what was best, Angie decided to drop one of the beads just as they rode into a small clearing.

Leading to a small campsite that Angie could see had been set up a while, Alonzo reached it and then stopped.

Now that they'd reached their destination, Angie didn't want to be found with the one bead and leather strap in her hands so she tossed them and watched where they landed. If she escaped, maybe the beads would mark her way home.

Angie fought back tears. She had to keep her head clear, but one overwhelming thought pounded louder than any sense of reason. *I've reached the end of the trail.*

Heath stood outside the bedroom window, glaring down at the ground, killing mad. "I've picked up tracks."

Only rigid control kept Justin from jumping through the window and racing down the trail Heath had found.

"And I've got a trail made by two Cimarron horses. One of them's the gelding Alonzo favors."

"Alonzo," Justin said, and froze. He'd been suspicious of him, but then he'd suspected everyone. "It was him who saved us."

"From Ramone," Cole said with his jaw so tight he was talking through his teeth. "Alonzo's shaky, elderly pa. He knew he'd never have to shoot."

"He led us up that trail that saved our lives."

"Nope," Heath said, shaking his head. "Ramone did that. He went up that hidden trail. Alonzo had little choice but to follow."

"I asked him—"

"Justin," Heath cut him off. "Let's get on the trail." Heath looked at Sadie. "I want you with me. We should never have left you here alone."

"I left a large bunch of men around the place." Justin realized he was talking when he should be moving. He'd always been a man who acted fast. Being in love had ruined him.

"Did you leave men here, Justin?" Cole asked. "Or did you pass it on to Alonzo and tell him to keep them around?"

Justin recalled how quiet it'd been when they rode in from Skull Gulch. They'd tied their horses to the hitching post because no one had come out of the barn to lend a hand. He hadn't seen anyone around the place since returning home.

"I told Alonzo. John left with the first work crew so only Alonzo was left to pass my orders on." He strode toward the back door and his horse. The mounts were still winded from the mad race home, but they hadn't the time to change saddles.

"And I expect he told them to get to work, probably as far from the ranch as he could. So the women had no one to protect them." Cole spoke as he came through the door.

Sadie was the only one without a saddled horse. "It's a fact that no one was here. We rode out to Skull Mesa this morning and there wasn't a soul around."

Heath snapped, "Someone quick saddle a horse for Sadie. We have to get started on this trail." Heath leapt onto his horse and headed around the house.

"Ride my horse, Sadie. Heath, get going." Cole sprinted for the barn.

"Cole," Rosita shouted, "take mine. I stay and defend the house."

"It's not safe," Cole said, turning back.

"That's right," Justin agreed. "You're coming with us, Rosita. I'm never leaving someone alone at this place again. I've finally learned my lesson."

"No, I will stay," Rosita insisted. "Now ride. You're wasting time. We cannot leave the CR undefended. I will get John to stay here with me when he comes back."

Justin and Cole exchanged a look. Then Justin studied the stubborn look on Rosita's face and decided he didn't have time to argue with her. Especially since he'd lose. "Thank you, Rosita. Remember your life is more important than any house. Please be careful."

She gave them a firm nod. "I will remember."

The Bodens rode around the house after Heath. Once the three of them were alone, Sadie said in a sickened voice. "They wanted me. Why take Angie?"

Justin mulled that over for a second. "Arizona Watts."

"What about him?" Sadie's brow furrowed.

"I was shouting, remember? When Cole, Heath, and I came in the house."

"I remember, but I was busy strapping on a gun to go find Angie. I didn't understand what you were yelling about."

"You were going after Angie alone?" Justin shook his head. His sister was going after the men who'd come to kidnap her? The thought chilled his gut and made him even madder.

"Watts broke out of jail," Cole said. "He must've taken Angie. Alonzo would have come for you. If Windy is in on this, he knows you. That means someone else did it."

"Someone riding Alonzo's horse." Justin knew that horse. Alonzo had ridden in on the horse, and no one rode it but him. "Yep, Watts is guilty as sin. He never got a good look at you, Sadie, and he might've seen Angie for a minute that night after the attack. From a distance you resemble each other. He thought he knew who he was going after. Or if someone described you, he came looking for a blond woman, probably not knowing there are two women here who fit that description."

Cole nodded. "Watts got the wrong girl."

Sadie's face twisted in pain at Cole's words. "So they took Angie thinking they had me, and now they might decide they have no use for her."

"Keep in mind," Cole added, "the whole point of the kidnapping is to use Angie as bait, and now we're riding out after them. And most likely that's exactly what they're hoping we do."

"So that is their plan," Justin said, "and here we are, the whole family, riding right into their trap." All of a sudden his indignation expressed earlier sounded like worry now. Like the danger had just increased for everyone.

Quietly, Sadie said, "It's not the whole family, Justin. At least Ma and Pa are safe in Denver."

28

Chance's eyes popped open when he heard the floorboards creak. He shook Ronnie's shoulder. She moved in absolute silence, though he heard the whisper of a scratch when she picked up her gun off the bedside table.

He grabbed his own gun, loaded and cocked, and swung his legs out of bed, snatched up his crutch, and hobbled quietly around the bed. Ronnie was already behind the door. She stepped away from it enough that if someone came in, pushing the door open, it wouldn't hit her.

He touched her arm. The night was dark, but his eyes had adjusted and were sharp enough to see her nod. He loved this woman more with every breath, and that was saying something because he'd been breathing with her for over twenty-five years.

Chance had his crutch under his left arm and his gun in his right hand, aimed straight at the door. A squeak out in the hall was the pantry door—Chance recognized the sound of its hinges as it was opened.

Obviously the intruder didn't know where he was going. He'd have to open two more doors, one to the fancy front room and the next to the mostly empty office.

After that he'd make his way to their bedroom.

Chance steadied himself and listened, all his senses on alert. He smelled something he couldn't place at first. Sharp, with a burnt aroma to it. Then it came to him. It was one of those black Mexican cigarettes some of his cowpokes smoked. The intruder in the hall had finished one just recently.

A second door opened. There was no squeak this time, just a whisper of a swinging hinge. Chance drew a deep breath. Two more to go. He shifted his weight to keep from putting too much strain on his broken leg.

He wasn't all that conscious of it aching anymore, but he'd been careful, with an overly attentive wife to kindly remind him of what not to do. The doctor wasn't here now, but Ronnie was a good partner in a fight and she always wanted his best.

Chance took another breath, leaned back against the wall. Another door opened. The office. There was no furniture in there so the man soon swung the door shut.

Silence followed. Chance couldn't tell if the man was walking down the hall toward their room or standing still. After another minute, he sensed the intruder standing outside their bedroom door. Then the knob turned slowly, and the door cracked open just an inch. The man was looking in, studying the room, no doubt seeing it was in use. He'd found his prey.

With a loud bang, the door slammed open. Gunfire exploded into the room. The bullets centered first on the bed, then began sweeping the room, coming ever closer to where Chance and Ronnie were hiding.

"Windy must've gone to check his traps." Watts commented on the empty campsite. "Good, hope he gets something. I can use a meal."

After he haltered his horse and staked it to graze, Alonzo approached Angie and swiftly unhooked whatever held her on the saddle. She kept up her ruse of unconsciousness as he dragged her feetfirst off the horse to stand. The blood rushed from her head and down to her feet. It took no faking at all to let her knees buckle and for her body to pitch sideways from the hot pain.

Alonzo grabbed her before she fell and carried her to an oak sapling. He sat her down so she could lean back against the tree, then untied her feet and hands.

"You should have stayed out of this, Señorita Angie," Alonzo said under his breath. Angie couldn't decide if he was talking to her or to himself. "Bodens bring trouble to everyone they touch."

Angie kept her eyes closed and sagged to the side. She was so dizzy from hanging with her head down for so long, she wondered if she might black out.

Alonzo tugged the gag from her mouth. Whether he was just talking to hear himself or she'd done something to give away that she was awake, he went on, "We're far enough away that no one will hear you scream. But don't do it anyway. I will gag you again if you do."

Angie remained limp. The gag had been too tight. Her face and neck were in such pain that she didn't know if she could have screamed even if she wanted to. But a defiant place in her heart told her that as soon as her face didn't hurt so much from the brutal gag, she might scream just on principle.

Then a wicked throb from the spot she'd been thumped by Alonzo's gun made her decide not to defy him again without a very good reason.

"I know you're awake, señorita." Alonzo sunk his hand deep into her hair and jerked her forward, tilting her head back.

His hand closed over the spot where he'd hit her, and she couldn't control a moan of pain. She flickered her eyes open, hoping he'd believe she was just coming around. He was inches from her, his face filling up every bit of her vision.

Speaking softly, because she really wanted to know, she asked, "Why, Alonzo? I can't figure it out. You don't look like a man who's had a bad life. Why turn to murder? What about the Bodens makes you do such a foolish thing?"

"Bad life, señorita?" he sneered and dragged her to her feet by her hair. "I watched my papa suffer for years because my grandfather was too arrogant to do what was necessary to keep his land. It was Grandfather's by right, then my padre's, then mine. The old Don should have fought for it. He should have begun his own revolution. Instead, he turned his back on that heritage, but he never gave up the anger. He never gave up his hatred of America. I was raised on that hate."

Angie knew part of the story but not every detail. "Then aim your anger at the men who signed the treaty that moved this land into America. It was a treaty signed by both governments to end a war. And if not them, aim your anger at the governor who took away your grandfather's land grant. Chance Boden didn't—"

"Chance had nada to do with it? Is that what you were going to say? Well, you're wrong. My papa had a chance to marry François Chastain's daughter, Veronica. She had shown some interest in him, and Papa would have treated her well. But when Chance Boden came along, Chastain pushed them together. He wanted his daughter married to a man who had full claim to American citizenship. Boden was a lowly pioneer from Boston. But his ancestry was right, while Papa's was wrong. Chastain was on his deathbed, urging Chance and Veronica to marry. That stopped *mi padre* from becoming a partner in what was left of the old land grant. My family would have been restored to wealth."

"But I thought Chastain was afraid of losing his half of the land grant, too. He was trying to save it by picking Chance Boden. If Veronica had married Ramone, they might have lost the land. How was it Chastain's fault that the grant was stripped from the old Don? It sounds like they were friends."

"They were not friends! They were partners—something much more important. Chastain stood like a coward, jumping to the tune of the governor to keep his land, and he said nothing to stop my grandfather losing his."

"But he couldn't have stopped the governor, could he?"

"He could have thrown his half of the land grant in the governor's face. He could have been loyal. Chastain was a mere cowhand who rode with the Don at the time. My grandpapa knew many influential people and would have been given a land grant eventually. But then Chance rescued someone and drew the governor's attention. With that act and my grandfather's connections, they were given this land. And later, when the grant was revoked, the governor who'd arranged it was gone."

"Wait a minute," Angie said. "Are you telling me Chastain, Justin's grandfather, performed a heroic deed, and because the Don happened to be riding along with him, he was given land, too?"

"My grandfather had influence. Chastain would never have been considered—"

"So Bautista took a land grant that wasn't due him . . ."

"He would have been royalty in Spain. It was more than his due. It was his right."

". . . and resented that a common man like Chastain had the courage and strength to risk his own life to save another." Angie couldn't believe her nerve. She braced herself for Alonzo to strike her. "While your grandfather no doubt stayed safely away from whatever danger Chastain faced. And then managed to manipulate the governor into including him in Chastain's reward through pressure from cronies."

"You know nothing of what you speak."

"I know a coward when I hear of one. Bautista was nothing but an arrogant coward. And Ramone, your own father, let Chastain die while his killer, Dantalion, ran free. Another coward."

"My father's face was cut open. He was half blind and unarmed. He knew he'd die if he stayed."

"A brave man could have found a way. Who knows how many others Dantalion has killed through the years while your father lived safely in Mexico City." Angie thought of the wanted poster. Dantalion, under another name, wanted for murder. "Now you're fighting for the rights of your family, rights earned by the Don grabbing the coattails of an honorable man like Chastain. You claim those rights by shooting at people from cover like the worst kind of coward. You're trying to kill men who have supported you and respected you, all while they nurtured a viper in their bosom. And the lowest yet, harming women to gain your own ends, like the greatest of yellowbelly weaklings."

Alonzo slapped her hard. "No one disrespects the family of de Val."

Pain exploded behind her eyes, but she had to go on. The truth was too disgusting to keep inside. "You disrespect your own family with every breath you take." Her voice rose with each word. "You're the third generation of contemptible cowards. It flows in your blood like a sickness."

He struck her again, this time with the back of his hand.

Because she knew he would only hit harder, and maybe do worse than strike her, she said more quietly, "No matter how many times you hit me, it won't change the truth. In fact, slapping a defenseless woman only proves I am right."

His gun appeared between them. He had it pointed at the sky, but his eyes burned with rage. His breathing came fast and loud, the only sound she could hear. She braced herself for a bullet.

Maria's death came to mind, and Angie realized there had been one de Val with true courage. "*Greater love hath no man than this, that he lay down his life for his friends.*" Angie prayed for that kind of courage.

She sensed God whispering into her heart. Yes, Maria's act was true love and true courage. But she had done it to protect a decent man, not because she was taunting a dangerous criminal. In her soul Angie knew—now was not the time to die. Not when it would save no one.

She must wait. She must survive. There might come a time when her sacrificial love would be called for, but not now. So Angie bit back the words she wanted to speak, words that might unleash Alonzo's killing fury. Yet from his rising rage, she knew it was already too late.

"Put the gun away." Watts came up beside Alonzo and ripped the pistol out of his hands.

Alonzo turned on Watts like a hungry wolf, but Watts reacted to that anger without one flicker of fear.

Angie saw then she was right. Alonzo was indeed a coward. And while he might hurt a woman, even kill her, he'd never go up against a dangerous man like Arizona Watts.

"Don't waste your lead until it'll do some good." Watts gave Alonzo his gun back by shoving it into his belly so hard that Alonzo gasped and bent in half.

Then Watts turned to Angie and grabbed her face with one of his rough, callused hands. He squeezed until she had to fight not to whimper in pain. "Goad the Mexican all you want, girl. He's a coward just like you said. I shot his aunt and he never spoke a word of complaint. She was betraying us, and I stopped her. Meant to get Boden too, but there wasn't time. Alonzo's a coward, but a useful one, so I'll take his side over yours."

Watts terrified her, and he did so without shouting, without hitting, and without drawing his gun.

"But you oughta be real careful what you say to me, pretty lady. I can see a way we could kill you right now, and so long as the Bodens don't know you're dead, we can still beat 'em. Keep that in mind when you're workin' your mouth. Arizona Watts ain't a man you can prod."

He released her with a forcible twist of her head that pained her neck something awful. Without looking at Alonzo, who still had his gun in hand, who'd heard the insulting things Watts had to say about him, Watts went back to building up the fire.

When she'd escaped Watts and was recaptured by Alonzo, Angie had thought Alonzo was the leader and the brains behind all the trouble. Now she knew different. Alonzo was no doubt more intelligent than Watts, but out here in the West, toughness won out over a sharp brain and a weak spine every time.

Windy emerged from the woods with three dead jackrabbits, skinned and gutted, hanging from his hand by their back legs. He looked at Angie, skidded to a stop, and scowled. "That ain't Sadie. 'Lonzo, what are you doin' with her?"

"We know who she is." Alonzo pushed Angie back against the little oak, and she cracked her head against its trunk. "No matter. She'll do just fine to bait our trap. Now roast those rabbits so we can eat."

Using force with her and a harsh voice with Windy were Alonzo's way of soothing his pride. Angie wondered if a coward's wounded feelings made him even more dangerous.

Alonzo pulled her hands behind her back so they were around the slender tree. She slouched, hoping her position, when she straightened, would leave her hands some slack. He didn't seem to notice and made quick work of binding her. Once his foul hands were no longer touching her, she gingerly rested her hurting head against the tree.

Carefully she wiggled her hands behind the tree, testing the ropes, while keeping her head bowed so she looked defeated.

Afterward she had hope that she could get free. Only not now. Not with three dangerous men within a few steps of her.

With few other choices, she decided to rest for a while. And while it twisted her stomach to think of food right now, if they offered her part of that roasted rabbit, she'd gladly eat it.

Because she was going to need every ounce of her strength.

29

It took every ounce of Justin's strength not to start raving like a lunatic.

The pace Heath had set was brutally slow. For a time they were in heavy woods, where no horse could move faster than a walk.

"Angie escaped right here." Heath made a sharp turn back and walked alongside the line of horses behind him. He went to the edge of the dense forest. In the distance he saw Skull Mesa, which lay directly across the open grazing land. He crouched and studied the ground. "Yep, these are Alonzo's tracks. He stopped Angie." Heath looked up at Justin, his eyes blazing with rage. "She ran to him. I can tell. He's on foot here so I know it's him. He's wearing those big Mexican rowel spurs he favors. I've seen his prints plenty of times. It's him all right. The man who took Angie was on Alonzo's horse . . . well, it could've been stolen. But there's no way to explain this except for what looks to be the clear truth—Alonzo recaptured her and handed her over to Watts."

Sickened by the thought, Justin imagined her relief, her hope when she saw Alonzo. Then her horror as she discovered who among the men could not be trusted. A man Justin had allowed to stay on his ranch.

Justin swore then and there that Alonzo would regret his betrayal for the rest of his life.

Heath studied the tracks further. "And one of them, Alonzo or Watts, knocked her cold here." Justin, a decent tracker in his own right, saw exactly what Heath did.

"Looks like she went down and lay still for a bit, then was dragged away." Heath paused. "Here all sign of Angie vanishes. Alonzo must've carried her because his fancy boots with the big rowels start diggin' deeper with the added weight."

"Anything else?" Justin asked.

Heath nodded. "There's no sense in all of us wading through those trees. Ride in the open, parallel to me. Watch for more prints. I think as soon as they're out of sight of the ranch, they'll head out here on the grass. There's no trail in these woods so they're blazing their own. Once they come out, we can make much faster time."

Justin led the way. If they could find where Alonzo and Watts brought Angie out into the open, Heath could leave off his slow pace in the forest and they could all carry on their search together.

Minutes later, Justin called out, "Heath, I found it! They came out right here." He then paused, waiting while Heath was hurrying over to meet up with him, Cole, and Sadie. Hope that they would find Angie, that she would be safe, that she would marry him, began to fill every part of his body.

Turning to Sadie, Justin said quietly, "We have to find her, Sadie. I asked Angie to marry me yesterday. She said no, but agreed to us courting."

Sadie's eyes went wide.

Cole couldn't quite manage a smile, considering the situation, but his face brightened and he nodded. "I reckoned you'd think of it at some point. But you're a slow one, so I was settled in to wait."

"I'd hoped to talk more about it with her today, but instead I spent most of the day in town, and then Alonzo stole her away before I got back."

Sadie wasn't saying much. Justin wondered about that. How could Cole have seen how he felt and not Sadie? He thought women were the sensitive ones.

"I never saw you spend much time with her," Sadie said finally.

"Just last night I did."

"When?" Sadie glanced back to see Heath emerging from the woods about a hundred feet behind them, leading his horse. He mounted up and came fast.

"Late last night."

"You mean after we all went to bed, you got back up and—"

"I heard 'em in Pa's office. They were . . ." Cole coughed. "Uh, they talked some and . . . they were quiet some."

Heath approached the group. "You talking about Justin and Angie sittin' by the fire half the night?"

Sadie's head snapped around and she glared at him. "Why didn't you tell me?"

"It's been a busy day, honey. I was gonna, truly."

Justin shook his head. "C'mon. Let's get after Angie." He turned his horse to follow the tracks. He wondered just exactly what Cole and Heath had heard, but he wasn't going to ask and didn't want to be told.

Heath trotted around him and took the lead. They set a fast pace, yet it wasn't fast enough to prevent Justin from doing the hardest praying of his life.

He thought of Maria and how she'd died and prayed no one else would have to offer their life to save the Bodens. Heath pushed faster as if he got jabbed in the backside by God himself and was told to hurry.

Which only made Justin pray harder.

Angie prayed harder than she ever had in her life.

They gave her a few bites of rabbit and untied her hands to let her slip into the trees for some privacy. But Alonzo stayed just a few paces away so she wouldn't try to run. She did rub her hands together, trying to push back the cold. Though the ropes hadn't been dangerously tight, and it wasn't a bitter-cold day, it was growing chillier by the moment as night fell. She was afraid that even if she got lucky and Alonzo tied knots she could loosen, her hands would be useless from the cold.

She hurried back, hoping this time her hands would be bound with less care. Whether it was the best Alonzo could do, or he was just sloppy, she again had a bit of movement available.

As she sat, waiting for her chance to escape, she heard Watts say, "Did Dantalion run off, then?"

Windy leaned back against a rock and lowered his hat until it nearly covered his face. "If'n he did, then we ain't gettin' paid. That makes it time to move on. We ain't gonna be able to kill all those Bodens anyway. You really think we can kill off a whole family—a well-known, well-liked family like the Bodens—and nobody'll ask questions?"

Alonzo poked at the fire, burned down to embers, with a sharp stick. "It wasn't ever gonna be that we kill all of them. Dantalion figured we'd kill the old man and maybe the one son who's ranchin' and, with a little pressure in the right places, the Bodens would just give up and move on. Cole and Sadie were already halfway gone off the land."

"Not off the mines, though. Cole is the one in charge of those mines, and I doubt he'll give them up easily."

"No one said we're after the mines." Alonzo stopped his poking and looked hard at Watts. "Cole has to go too, then."

"I reckon," Watts answered. "But that's all. And Chance's death was supposed to look like an accident. Then we hoped to kill the sons and blame it on your pa, Alonzo. That would have been the end of it. To get those sons, we planned to use the daughter, and possibly the wife, to lure out the Bodens and kill them. Whether Sadie or Veronica died during that didn't matter, but Dantalion didn't think their deaths were necessary. But we didn't plan on the daughter getting married to a tough man, or on Justin finding himself a sweetheart. We never planned on so much killing."

Angie shuddered to hear of her and Justin being discussed by such vile outlaws. The casual way they talked of killing. She took a deep breath. She'd thought all this time she needed to find her own strength, to stand on her own before involving herself with a man again. But she knew now, after listening to these men and seeing the evil in some taking advantage of the weakness in Alonzo, that true strength wasn't such a mystery after all. In fact, she decided to claim that strength for herself. And to stay strong, well, that was something she could do, married or not.

More determined than ever to escape their clutches, she worked at loosening the rope binding her hands. The knots were tight, but she had movement enough that she could pick at them. As she battled her bonds, she waited for her captors to fall asleep.

"We're losing the light. I can't see enough to track anymore." Heath looked up. He'd reached the end of the grassy trail leading through the woods.

Justin hadn't recognized any sign of the riders heading this way. He considered himself well able to read signs, but only Heath's rare skill had kept them moving on this nearly invisible trail left in the thick grass.

Heath had found signs, though. And there was no way off

the trail short of plunging deeper into the woodlands. So they'd gone on.

It was dusk now. As darkness battled the light for supremacy, Justin saw that soon it would be impossible to keep going. They might ride off in the wrong direction, a mistake that could mean Angie's death.

But to stop, to leave her overnight in their clutches . . . Justin wanted to tear down the whole mountain range with his bare hands and rescue her.

"What's that?" Sadie pointed to a slick stretch of rock that looked too steep to climb.

Swinging down off her horse, she rushed to the small bit of color she'd pointed at. Her head came up and she spun around, her eyes wide with excitement. "This is a bead off the necklace Rosita gave Angie for Christmas."

Heath dismounted. "Are you sure?"

Sadie pulled something into view that was hidden inside her shirt collar. "I'm sure. It's exactly like mine. Rosita gave me one, too."

She handed the bead she'd found to Heath, then looked around and picked up a few more lying on the ground. "She must've broken the necklace so she could drop these beads and leave a trail."

"Let's go this way until full dark at least." Justin snatched the beads from Sadie and the single one from Heath. "It'll get us closer, and if she dropped more beads, maybe she did it only at a turnoff. That way we can stop and pay special attention when we reach one."

Heath jerked his chin in agreement.

They headed on up, and when the moon came out full and bright, Justin's spirits soared and he felt the righteous hand of God himself lifting them, showing them the way forward.

30

They posted a sentry.

Angie worked on the knots in silence, doing her best not to show any movement. She tipped her head back against the tree and closed her eyes. To let her head droop forward might feign sleep better, but she couldn't look around with her head down.

Through barely opened lashes she watched Windy take a turn. He sat on a rock and didn't budge, and he'd picked a spot where, if she stirred at all, he'd be sure to see her. He did step into the woods for a time, and she picked at the knots frantically while he was out of sight. By the time he returned, she had her hands free. Now all she needed was a chance to run.

She worked it over and over in her mind. What would she do if she did escape? She had no weapon. She'd be running from three dangerous men, all of them skilled trackers. And how would she find her way back?

Follow the beads . . .

Arizona Watts was the next to stand guard. He was more vigilant than Windy and kept his gun drawn. He walked a circuit in the woods every half hour. She wrapped the rope around her wrists, because she was afraid he might check to make sure she was still bound.

As the night wore on, the full moon rose higher. They'd camped in a small clearing in the woods and so remained in deep shadows. Knowing the night wasn't pitch-black helped her to stay alert and ready for her chance.

And then it was Alonzo's turn. Now Angie was so tired, after such a hard day, she had to fight to keep her eyes open.

But she didn't give in.

She couldn't say the same for Alonzo.

Finally it was time.

"This is taking way too much time." Justin fought to keep the words inside, but it was like trying to clamp a lid on a cauldron boiling over.

Everyone with him—Cole, Sadie, and Heath—turned and hissed, "Shhh!"

Considering he was a long way toward losing his mind, they should at least give him credit for whispering.

What was happening to Angie while they searched? Was she being mistreated? Was she fighting for her life? Was she already dead? He kicked his horse into a gallop. He expected Heath to yell at him. Instead, Heath picked up his pace to catch up and stay even. Sadie and Cole were right with him.

But that didn't make Justin feel any better. It only meant his worries were shared by the whole family.

Alonzo sat on the ground and leaned back against the big rock Windy had sat on. Angie heard his snoring within minutes.

She stood and ducked behind the tree. The sapling was too

narrow to hide her really, but it might confuse someone glancing her way.

No one stirred.

She crept along the side of the clearing, feeling with her feet, hoping to avoid stepping on a fallen branch or twig and snapping it.

Knowing right where she'd thrown the beads, she went directly to the trail that led back home. She found three beads, grabbed them and kept going, being careful to move quietly while putting some distance between her and those awful villains.

Before long she reached a fork in the trail and found her bead, but didn't know for sure which way to turn. Downhill again? That seemed to make the most sense.

If the Bodens were on their way, how long would it take her to run into them? She knew Justin. She knew all of them. Their nature was heroic—they would come as fast as they could to save her.

Another bead at another fork in the trail. She picked it up and proceeded downhill, faster now but not running, not on an uneven trail in the dark. She no longer worried about silence.

And then a shout echoed from above.

"She's gone! Alonzo, wake up!" Arizona Watts sounded killing mad.

Angie's eyes burned with tears. Terror swept through her. She fought both the tears and the terror and kept moving. They'd come after her now. She needed to be silent, to get off this trail and hide, but first she wanted to gain every inch of distance from them that she could.

Horse's hooves sounded from the direction of the clearing.

Every instinct told her to run. Yet she ignored those instincts because her only chance right now was to hide . . . in utter silence.

31

"I can't find a bead, but there were definitely horses up this trail today." Heath crouched by something Justin couldn't see, but it had to be evidence Heath was sure of. He pivoted on his boot and looked back. His face was shadowed by his Stetson, though his tone told Justin all he needed to know. Heath was beyond concerned.

"Is it possible they laid a false trail?" Justin was convinced those beads came from Angie. It was a message saying they were on the right trail. Anything else, he wasn't so sure about.

"They've followed a trail none of us have heard of." Heath peered up the strange stretch of rock. "A good trail, and on mostly solid stone. I think they're confident enough, probably arrogant enough, to believe they're safe from being followed. I doubt they took the time to lay a false trail."

Cole said, "The moon is still low in the sky. We'll be riding in near dark before long. Let's head up this trail and hope we can see where they left it. We've got about one more turn, if we're lucky, before we have to stop and wait for the sunrise."

They'd been walking, leading their horses all night. Justin, sick with worry, clapped Heath on the shoulder. "We wouldn't be this far without your help. Thank you."

Heath looked back at Justin and nodded. "That Angie is a smart little thing, and that's the reason we even have a chance."

Angie slipped into the woods, going by feel more than sight. Touching trees and boulders, searching for something big enough to hide behind.

In the darkness she had no idea where she was exactly. Maybe she'd hide somewhere that, in the light of day, was obvious. Maybe she'd left footprints a five-week-old Hereford could follow.

Fighting panic, she groped her way around a rock that was waist-high and big enough around for concealment. She dropped behind it and stayed quiet for a bit. It was a thin defense against armed men, but it was all she could think to do for now.

She wrapped her arms around her pulled-up knees and steadied her breathing. Resting her chin on her knees, she began to pray.

But her prayer was soon interrupted by hooves moving fast down the trail nearby. It made her wonder how foolish she'd been to take the trail they'd used to bring her here—the very trail the men were riding on now as they looked for her, each of them spitting mad. What if instead she'd snuck deep into the woods up near the clearing? Wouldn't she be safe now?

The self-doubt was driving her mad, and she shoved it aside. Her life was in God's hands. She was ready to follow His leading. Meanwhile, she needed to pay attention to the situation for whatever opportunity showed itself.

Breathing in and out silently, she listened as the hoofbeats came closer, closer, closer.

Then they were upon her. One by one, three riders passed close by. She realized then she hadn't ventured far off the trail at all. She wanted to take a peek at them, but decided against it, knowing it was an unwise move. Instead she waited as they moved on, and remained where she was until she couldn't hear a sound.

A decision had to be made. Though she'd like to stay where she was, hiding like a frightened rabbit, this was her chance to run for help. Staying felt safe, but moving was the right thing to do. These men were still a danger to the Boden clan.

With a sudden resolve, she groped around until she found a good-sized rock, roughly round with jagged edges. Taking the same rope that had bound her hands, she used it to tie around the rock as tightly as she could make it. There, she'd just made a weapon she could swing like a war club, one she could use again and again. Since she'd never heard of such a thing before, she gave the credit to God.

Now she wouldn't be completely helpless. Standing, she slipped out of her hiding spot and started again down the trail.

Those men with their evil plans were now the ones being followed. The predators had become the prey.

"We have to stop." Heath rose from where he was hunkered down. "I don't trust myself to go another step."

Justin clamped his mouth shut before he said something foolish. He hated to admit it, but Heath was right—it was time they quit. If they missed the next turnoff, they might be making a mistake that would take them in the wrong direction.

"Let's leave the trail and hide the horses in the woods." Justin looked around. They were all exhausted. "If you can sleep, try to catch a few minutes. The day will begin to dawn in another hour. As soon as we can see again, we'll head out."

No one protested. No one suggested he needed sleep, too. While they rested, Justin went back to the edge of the trail. His mind was bombarded with all that could have happened to Angie. Though it sickened him, all he could think was he could handle anything, so long as she was alive.

Lord, whatever happens, please, save her life, he prayed.

After remaining hidden for what felt like an eternity, Angie peeked out onto the trail, and in the dim light of dawn she saw the men had left her line of sight. It was a grassy stretch here, a wider trail lined with majestic pines. She hadn't seen trees like this before, so they must've passed this way while she was still unconscious.

She stepped onto the trail but stayed on the edge so she could get out of sight in a moment's notice.

With the rope tied to the rock in hand, she took a moment to tie the loose end of the rope around her wrist. Now she could swing it and not lose it. She felt ready to face her enemies. Which wasn't like her at all, and yet if forced to fight back, she was ready. One good whack on the head would show them. As much as she knew Watts was the man to fear, she also wouldn't mind hitting Alonzo good and hard. Windy was every bit as much a traitor, but it was Alonzo whose betrayal seemed the greatest.

Besides, she owed him. Yep, one good whack on the head deserved another.

She hurried along, slowing, and looking carefully when coming to a turn in the trail. She took notice of any beads she found and picked them up, though she didn't waste time searching for them.

After about an hour of pursuit, she came around a bend and caught sight of the three men. They had dismounted and were talking. She was surprised to see she could make them out at this distance. The day had indeed dawned, the light increasing with every minute that passed.

She stopped cold, prepared to dodge behind a nearby pine. She gripped her rope-and-rock weapon, ready to swing away.

Then, as quickly as she'd stopped, the three men vanished into the woods. Two across the trail from her, the other, Alonzo, on her side.

As if they'd heard something and were hiding just as she'd done.

And the only thing she could think of that they heard was someone coming. The Bodens . . .

They'd have the Bodens in a crossfire and cut them down without mercy. This probably wasn't what they'd planned, but in the end it was what they'd meant by bait.

Determined not to let herself be used that way, she clutched her rock and moved to get herself in place to distract Alonzo, if not with a rock to the head, then with a scream to warn the Bodens.

32

"We're on the right track." Sadie pointed to a bright blue bead.

A whoosh of relief sent Justin forward. Dawn had come at last. He clenched his hands tight over the reins. Despite his fear for Angie, knowing they were headed in the right direction shoved back the worst of his panic. He moved on, leading his horse, his jaw tight, his heart pounding, with nothing but resolve to find her and never let her out of his sight again.

The woman was smart enough to leave a trail in the middle of what would be terrifying to anyone—man, woman, or child. Pride in her swelled his chest at the same time it humbled him. He was never going to question her courage again. And if she had a few things to learn about ranch life, she was more than capable of learning them.

And while she was learning, he just might manage to learn a few things about running other people's lives and about judging someone's toughness. He had plenty to work on for himself before he'd ever again find fault with someone else.

Except maybe Cole.

Even that might be wrong since Cole recognized Justin was in love before Justin did. But if Justin all of a sudden started treating Cole with respect and kindness, it might confuse his big brother beyond repair.

As brave as Angie was, when Justin found the men who'd taken her, he intended to put a stop to the trouble surrounding the Cimarron Ranch.

This treachery was going to end.

Angie didn't abandon silence altogether, but she hurried and if that meant an occasional snapped twig, so be it.

When she knew she had to be close to Alonzo, she slowed and watched where she stepped more carefully. She found Alonzo, the worthless coward, crouched behind a tree, watching the trail, preparing to shoot brave, decent, innocent men like the lowest kind of dry-gulcher.

A step at a time, hefting her rock in her hand, she approached. She fought to keep her breath from speeding up to match her heartbeat. She kept her fear under control. A glance now and then at the trail showed no sign of the other outlaws.

She wasn't good at attacking anyone, having had absolutely no practice. A tree was between her and Alonzo. She closed in on him. Near enough now to swing the rock if she used the full length of the rope, but the tree blocked him. By the time she reached the tree, she had to judge how long she could let out the rope.

Letting it out about two feet, she swallowed hard. To think she was so close to such a dangerous man . . . She heard a hoof on the trail, still a distance away. The Bodens. They'd be rounding the corner soon, and her captors would open fire. She had to keep Alonzo out of the fight.

Raising the rock, she fought for calm, taking several deep breaths. Then, with her jaw clenched, she made her move and swung with all her might. Alonzo must have heard or seen something, because he turned toward her just as the rock smashed him right in the face. With a sharp cry he fell over backward. Scared that he'd still be able to fire his weapon, Angie swung the rope a second time. The rock struck him in the head with a sickening thud.

As Alonzo lay there writhing in pain, Angie fumbled for his gun. She got ahold of it, pointed it into the air, and fired to warn the Bodens. She then rushed off in the direction Justin would come.

Would they stay and fight or run? She'd actually prefer they run, but she didn't want them to leave her behind.

To make sure they didn't, she sucked in another deep breath and yelled.

"It's an ambush! Get down!"

Angie, alive and well. And judging from the direction of the gunfire, she was armed. Firing warning shots—he hoped they were warning shots. Justin was swamped with the most horrible urge to cry. It shocked him so much, he came to his senses. Men didn't cry.

The Bodens vanished, Justin a second behind the others to make sure everyone got away. Sadie, Cole, and Heath disappeared into the woods on the south side of the trail. Justin judged where Angie was shouting from and ran for the north side.

"Angie, I'm here!"

Her feet pounded closer. She made no attempt to be silent, though she didn't shout but ran.

Justin ran for her as fast as she ran for him. He finally saw her, bruised, her cheek swollen, more beautiful than anyone he'd ever seen. They ran into each other's arms just as a gun fired. Justin threw himself sideways and twisted to land under Angie, then rolled to tuck her beneath him.

Judging by its location, it had to be from one of her kidnappers.

Another gun went off, then another, the rain of lead shredding the trees over their heads.

"Alonzo's down."

Justin looked at her and saw the satisfaction on her face, heard it in her voice. "You shot him?"

She gasped, and her eyes went wide. "Of course not."

Since there'd been a shot fired, and he noticed Angie held a gun in her left hand, that was the only conclusion his mind went to.

Then she raised her right hand, which clutched a large rock with a rope tied around it. "I hit him in the head with this stone, then took his gun and fired it to warn you. Arizona Watts and your cowhand, Windy, took the south side of the trail. That's them firing now. Alonzo took the north side, this side, and I snuck up on him and knocked him cold." A nervous giggle escaped her lips.

The gunfire stopped. "Let's go." Justin rose and pulled her to her feet. "Cole, Sadie, and Heath went into the forest to the south. They'll be after those varmints. I want to help grab 'em."

While it was urgent they get moving, Justin lifted her right off her feet and kissed her passionately, almost desperately. "I've been out of my mind all night worrying about you." He tenderly touched a spot on her face that she could feel was bruised. "Are you all right?"

"Nothing that won't heal in a couple days' time." She caught his hand and held it tight. "Let's go catch the rest of these crooks."

"Yep, right now. Then we can go home." Justin's eyes gleamed with pleasure.

They rushed back in the direction Angie had come from to get uphill of the danger. They found Alonzo unconscious. Justin made quick work of tying him up.

"I want him here when the fight's over, not waking up and slipping away from us."

Angie nodded. "I'd have done it, but I didn't want to give up my rope."

They hurried on. A minute later, more gunfire erupted, though it wasn't aimed at them this time.

Justin drew his gun and cocked it. "That's my family, in a gunfight with Watts and Windy."

They'd been running alongside the trail, but now they rushed straight for it. There was no broken path so it was nearly impossible to move side by side, but Angie could tell Justin was leading in such a way as to tuck her body behind his.

Hadn't she just knocked an armed outlaw cold with nothing but a rock and a rope? On the other hand, she felt her heart flutter to think such a strong man was protecting her with his own life.

They reached the edge of the woods. Rather than step out into the open, Justin turned and raced along just inside the forest edge.

"Stay low." They crouched together behind a big pine with branches that went all the way to the ground, providing decent cover. "The way it sounds, one of the outlaws isn't too far into the woods. I'll watch for movement and take a shot if I get one."

"How can you be sure that's not where Cole, Sadie, and Heath are?" Angie asked.

"I'll recognize their guns," Justin replied. "I'd try to get behind these low-down coyotes, slip across the trail, and come at them that way, but I don't want to be where I could get shot by one of my own family. They'd feel mighty bad if they accidentally shot me."

"So would I."

He leaned over and kissed her. "So would I. I plan to spend a lot of years married to you."

"Don't forget I've got my rock. I can help."

"If I can know for sure who I'm aiming at, I'll take a shot, but then they'll divide their attention and bullets will come flying this way." His brow furrowed with worry. "You stay here. Keep this tree between you and those varmints."

Nodding, Angie said, "I'll hide right here behind this tree trunk, Justin. I'll be all right. I've got my rock. You go—do what you need to do."

Before leaving, he turned to her with a grin and added, "You know, you're gonna make about the finest ranch wife a frontier rancher has ever known."

"And don't you forget it," she said, smiling back at him. "Now go!"

33

Yep, Justin figured she would make the finest wife a man could ever hope to have. She knew how to leave a trail, how to escape, how to attack, and how to hide.

He sighed as he left Angie behind, just like he seemed to have to do all the time. And every time he did, danger found her. But the blasting gunfire coming from across the trail told him his family was in danger. They needed his help.

An ugly choice to make.

He forced himself forward. When he was north of Watts, he slipped to the edge of the woods and studied the opposite side. He couldn't make out any sign of the villains. He inched his eyes on down to where his family had to be hiding. Because of his angle on the trail, he was able to see Cole, just a part of his shoulder. Justin watched him every second, wishing he'd lean back just a bit, look this way, and see Justin through the trees.

It was a lot to wish for.

He'd have shouted or fired his gun in the air, but if he did, he'd lose the chance to sneak up on the outlaws. A rustling sound back from where he'd left Angie caught his attention. He looked, tense with worry. What was she doing out from behind the tree? What if she was seen by the wrong people? He then saw her step away from the tree. Thankfully, he hadn't yet gone that far from her.

She looked at him, nodded, and held up her rock. No, she'd kept her rock and found another, this one with no rope. She tossed the rock up in the air as if testing its weight, then flung it with all her strength. It crashed through the branches Cole was crouched behind. He turned his head and looked right at Angie. The relief on his face warmed Justin's heart.

Then Angie pointed at Justin, and Cole turned and saw him.

Cole pointed with his pistol at a gnarled pinyon tree that grew out of a pile of boulders. Steady gunfire roared from there and also from a second spot on past the pinyon. Justin nodded, then pointed at himself and the trail.

Cole frowned, then nodded back. Justin hurried down his side of the woods. The gunfire from his family slowed some with their aim high, firing into the air. Before the villains could notice, Justin darted across the trail and closed on both men, his gun drawn.

Kidnapping a woman was a serious crime. Any abuse of women in the West was considered a terrible act. A woman was a rare and fine thing, and usually even the lowest of villains wouldn't harm one. But they'd run into a group with no such decency. With the right judge, a man could hang for kidnapping and marking a woman. All three men—Watts, Windy, and Alonzo—no doubt knew they faced long jail terms, if not a noose. Watts had held tough when they'd questioned them and managed to walk out of jail. Then he'd come right back to the CR to finish his job.

Justin didn't think Watts would ever talk. And Windy and Alonzo both worked for him while they'd done their spying. They kept their true purpose to themselves the whole time, so Justin didn't underestimate them. But they weren't hardened men like Watts. They were men who might do a lot of talking to save their mangy hides, especially if they knew another man might talk first to save himself and leave his partners to go to prison.

The shooting from both sides had slowed now. Justin's family was being cautious. They knew exactly where he was. A shiver climbed up his spine as he peeked around a tree. Were Watts and Windy on to him?

He approached them swiftly, listening for their guns. Thankfully, they had spread out. If they were side by side, he'd've had trouble subduing both of them at once.

He heard the nearest gun fire and poked his head again around the tree. It was Windy. Within a couple of steps, facing away from Justin. No sign of Watts.

He rounded the tree with a few quick steps and slammed the butt of his gun into Windy's head. Windy went down and flopped a couple of times on the ground like a landed trout. Then he went limp. Justin took his gun, hog-tied him, then looked to see if any of his family was visible. He caught sight of Heath, who waved behind him. He must be within sight of Sadie and Cole.

Heath crawled on his belly straight for Justin. After reaching him, he whispered, "Justin, give me the gun. I'll fire it every so often in hopes Watts doesn't figure out his partner's been taken out of the fight."

Justin jerked his chin in agreement. Then, stooped low, he headed for the still-firing gun. Watts was somewhere deeper into the woods.

Just like he said, Heath shot Windy's gun a few times, aiming it up in the air. Justin glanced around the bushes that hid him and saw Watts firing his gun. He ducked back out of sight and gathered himself to plunge out of the woods at Watts.

He leapt out from cover.

Watts wasn't there.

"Freeze, Boden." Watts's harsh voice came from off to the side.

Justin spun to find Watts with his gun leveled on him, aimed at his head. Too bad for Watts, because Justin's gun was just as well-aimed, right at his belly. It was a standoff, and Justin didn't see any way out of it but both of them dying.

"You're surrounded, Watts. I've got four men riding with me." Well, two men, and Sadie and Angie. "We've taken both your partners prisoner. If you want to live through this day, lay down your gun and come along peacefully."

Watts's response was a guttural laugh. "I'm sick of this fight and only want out. I'm not letting you take me to jail. The man who got me out last time said never again. But I'll let you live if you help me get out of here—if you call off your family and give me a head start. Otherwise your life means nothing to me."

"Have you gotten the word yet that Dantalion is dead?"

The shock on Watts's face made it clear he hadn't heard the news.

"Yep, he's dead and in the ground. We've kept the fact quiet, even used it to flush Windy out as the traitor he is. Too bad we didn't get Alonzo, too." Justin managed a smile. "Whatever you do here, you're not getting paid. You understand that, right?"

"You just stand down, Boden. Call off your family and let me ride away. You'll never see me again. I'm ready to be shut of this country."

Justin shook his head, not lowering his gun by so much as a fraction of an inch. Watts wasn't a man to be trusted, plain and simple.

"You've been a thorn in my flesh since the day I took this job," Watts spat out.

"Me, a thorn in your flesh?" Justin said. "I'm the one who's been shot at. I've seen my father nearly killed, my brother-in-law take a bullet, my brother almost killed too, my sister fighting for her life against Dantalion—which she won, by the way—and a woman I care about get kidnapped. *I've* been a thorn in *your* flesh?"

"That's right." Watts's eyes went killing cold.

Justin could see he was getting ready to pull the trigger.

A rope came flying toward Watts from his left and hit his arm. It wasn't a rope—it was a rope tied to a rock. The rock whipped around Watts's arm and jerked it sideways as he fired his gun. The shot went wild, but after a second of off-balance shooting, he brought his arm back up just as a dull thud made his eyes go wide and glaze over.

He dropped the gun and collapsed in front of Justin. As his body sank slowly to the ground, Cole appeared, an inch at a time, standing behind Watts. Cole held a gun by the muzzle, and it appeared the gun butt had just been applied with some force to the back of Watts's head.

Justin heaved a sigh of relief. Cole nodded his head. And Justin knew the owner of that rope. He turned as Angie came dashing out of the woods into sight.

Sadie and Heath came next. All five of them stood and grinned at each other. Justin said, "I think we'd better get them tied up and slung over their horses before they wake up."

Heath pointed. "Their horses are over there. Only two of them, though."

"What about Alonzo?" Sadie looked around, sharp-eyed and wary.

"I know where his horse is." Angie raised her hand shoulder-high and wiggled her fingers a bit.

Justin turned to Angie. "Angie snuck up and knocked him cold. She led me to him, and I left him trussed up like a spring calf. We'll go fetch him and load him up."

Sadie shook her head. "So Angie got two of them?"

"I helped with Watts," Cole said, but with no real upset in his voice.

"And I've been keeping an eye on Windy," Heath added. "I took over right after Justin conked him over the head and knocked him out." Heath didn't look like he cared much who got the credit.

"We'll round up their horses and haul 'em to Skull Gulch, and then so long as we're in town, Angie and I are getting married." He strode to Angie's side and caught both her hands. "Right?"

She smiled without one second's hesitation. "Right."

Sadie laughed, and the whole family started clapping. When they quieted again, Sadie said, "I haven't even told you about the wanted poster we found on top of Skull Mesa."

Angie whispered to Justin, "I climbed Skull Mesa yesterday. Sadie told me I'm supposed to taunt you with that fact."

Narrowing his eyes, Justin looked at his sister. "What wanted poster?"

"It's a picture of Dantalion, but with a different name, wanted back east for murder. We thought if we could find out what he'd done, we might find friends of his who would give us more to investigate."

"We'll ask the sheriff to check it out," Cole said. "We know Dantalion was paid to attack the Bodens. We know someone higher than him is involved. But whoever it is no longer has anyone working for him. Let's hope having all his hirelings arrested puts an end to this."

"Angie and I will go find Alonzo's horse and get him packed up. We'll meet the rest of you on the trail." Justin held on to Angie's hand and started hauling her toward Alonzo. He needed to hurry up with the arresting, then get on to the more important part of this day.

Once they'd left the woods and crossed the trail, Justin looked at Angie and smiled. "Taunt me, huh?"

She nodded. "But being nice to you is much more fun. Is it over, then? Are these three the last of the men conspiring against you?"

"Yep. Cole still needs to figure out all those chicken scratches in that notebook, just so we can be sure and find who started everything, and we'll track down Dantalion and his old crimes, but I think our troubles are finally over."

A chill rushed down Justin's back, and he wished he hadn't been so bold. It was like he was daring someone else to shoot at his family.

34

Chance's troubles came in a hail of bullets.

The man held two six-shooters and fired them from where he stood in the hallway straight at the bed. Chance couldn't get his gun aimed true without stepping out from cover. He held back from returning fire, bracing himself for the first break in the rain of bullets so he could make a move. He wished the man would be reckless enough to empty his guns.

A snarl from the man broke off his firing. Then a hard smack surprised Chance, then another and another. Pillows exploded feathers into the air, and the smell of cordite filled the room.

Ronnie had slammed the door into their assailant with strength that must have been powered by fury. After the third hard smack in the head, the man stumbled against the doorframe, and one gun went flying.

Quick as a striking snake, Chance reached him and snatched the other gun out of his hand while plowing a fist into the fool's face.

Ronnie, a woman raised amongst cowhands, grabbed a rope off a table where they'd stacked a few things in the event of trouble. With moves so fast Chance could hardly see them, she snagged the gunman's hands and whipped the ropes around his wrists. Hog-tied him like a calf ready to be branded. The man began fighting Ronnie, but she'd already jumped away like any good cowpoke would.

The man then lurched to his feet, and it was with grim satisfaction that Chance punched the varmint once more, this time so hard he might've broken his jaw.

He might also have broken a couple of fingers. Good thing there was a doctor nearby who knew his way around a fracture.

Finally, the man slumped to the floor and lay motionless. Ronnie hurried around him, struck a match, and lit a lantern so light flared into the room. Chance moved to grab the other gun, just to keep count of both weapons. The man was beyond using them now.

"Do you recognize him?" Ronnie, breathing hard, came to Chance's side. She stooped to pick up his crutch, which he'd dropped, and tucked it under his arm.

"Never seen him before in my life." Chance crouched awkwardly and searched the man, finding little in his pockets. But he did have a name on a letter he was carrying. If the letter was to him, they'd have his name. Chance quickly unfolded the letter, but it was near impossible to read. The name Dantalion popped out at him—if he was reading it right. The man whose name had figured prominently in John's letters could have been close to the front of his thoughts.

"Help me up, Ronnie." Chance was growing mighty tired of being slow moving. "We took him down, didn't we?" He smiled at her as he tucked the letter inside his shirt pocket.

"We've been a fine team for a long while, Chance." She leaned close, and together they managed to stand up without too much trouble.

A loud crash coming from the front of the house had them ready for the next fight, guns in hand.

"What's going on in here? I heard gunfire. Come out with your hands in the air."

Chance looked at Ronnie. "It's the sheriff."

Ronnie sniffed. "Our landlord. A lot of help he was."

"We're fine, Sheriff." Chance raised his voice but stayed where he was. He'd probably trip over their prisoner. "A man broke into our house and tried to kill us."

"We're armed, Sheriff," Ronnie called out. A woman's voice was a good idea when it came to calming a nervous, armed lawman. "We've got an unconscious man, who broke into our house and did a lot of shooting. My husband has his leg in a cast and finds it hard to walk, so he can't come out. You come on back, but slowly."

"I'm obliged for the warning, ma'am. All right—I'm coming back."

Soon he entered the room, a tall, bulky man with his gun drawn. "You said trouble was on your trail. Well, it looks like you were exactly right."

Chance didn't waste time answering. He and Ronnie would both be dead if it wasn't for John's steady letters, keeping them up on what was going on at home.

"Who do you think wants you dead?"

"A mighty good question, Sheriff. One I mean to get an answer to."

"The trouble followed us from New Mexico Territory." Ronnie glanced at Chance. "I think it's high time we went back and got to the bottom of it."

"Back *home*." Chance felt his spirits lift.

"I want you here until I find out who this man is, and what he's up to."

Chance nodded. "I'd like to know that myself." But the minute he thought it was time to go, he'd be on his way home.

It was nearer to morning than Chance thought. He felt like he hadn't been sleeping long when their intruder arrived, but it was almost dawn now. The sheriff gave them time to dress, then helped Chance onto a buckboard. Ronnie sat beside him, their prisoner tied up in the back, wearing the sheriff's shackles on his wrists and ankles, still unconscious.

"We need to send a telegram to the children. I've mostly been sending letters, except when I gave them the address of the house we moved into. But I want them to get this message quick." Ronnie rested a hand on Chance's arm. "I wish we knew this man's name and could send that along."

Chance's arm twitched under her touch. He glanced at her quickly and knew she understood him. Right now he was mighty thankful for being able to send a wire. He was also thankful his children had written, even though they sugarcoated everything, while John told his news straight out. Chance wouldn't know much at all if it wasn't for John.

"It might change things for them back at the CR," Chance said. "Sheriff, after you've talked with us however long you need to, I have to send a telegram. Is there an office close to the jail?"

"Yep, and close enough to walk there on crutches."

All Chance needed was a few minutes alone with Ronnie. He wanted to read the letter he had and get any information he could glean from it, then send the telegram and afterward maybe give the sheriff the letter.

It was possible the sheriff would have something to say about that, but Chance didn't much care. Even if he was a fine sheriff, no Denver lawman was apt to get real stirred up about trouble hundreds of miles away in New Mexico Territory. Chance wasn't going to withhold this letter from the law here, yet he couldn't risk it being taken away from him and leaving him without whatever information was in it.

He'd face whatever trouble that caused when he had to.

The sheriff had a good-sized staff of deputies, who helped carry the man into a cell. Since the outlaw didn't stir, and the sheriff couldn't find anything in his pockets, Chance and Ronnie told their story and things went quickly.

"Can we leave to send our telegram now?" Ronnie asked with a smile. Just like a concerned mother, which she was.

The Denver jail was a big building with a lot of men working. Right now every available man sifted through a mountain of wanted posters. They were busy trying to identify the man they'd just locked up.

The sheriff nodded without looking up. "Come on back, if you will. We'd appreciate the help searching for this outlaw."

"We won't be long." Ronnie was doing all the talking.

Just as well, because Chance was afraid he wouldn't be able to conceal his anxious desire to get out of there.

She asked, "Would it be all right if we stopped for breakfast on our way?"

"Yep, no hurry. There's a diner a few doors down on this side of the street. The telegraph office is right across from it."

Leaning on the crutch, thinking of how soon he planned to defy the doctor and head for home, Chance tried to be gentle with his leg. They headed for a sign that said *Harvey's Diner.*

"Let's read that letter."

Chance smiled at her. "After you, wife."

They both stepped inside the diner. It was early enough still that not many folks had shown up yet for their morning meal. Chance led Ronnie to a table around the corner from the door. He had the letter out before his backside had barely hit the chair.

It was one page long. "The address says Bert Collins." He looked up at Ronnie. "We can't be sure if this is a letter sent to the man we caught, so we can't say it's Bert Collins in that cell."

A young woman came up and set a cup of coffee in front of each of them.

Ronnie said, "We'd like flapjacks and fried ham, please."
She looked across the table at Chance. "Is that enough or are
you extra hungry?"

"Fry me up three eggs besides the flapjacks and give me a
double serving of ham. That's enough, to start."

"And miss, can you bring me a paper and a pencil? We'd be
glad to pay for it, but we need to make a list for our shopping."

The waitress smiled sweetly. "I'm sure I can find that in the
back. I'll ask the owner if he wants to be paid." She hurried away.

Chance said, "We're taking notes?"

"We have to hand over that letter, and I'm not trusting one
word of this to my memory."

Chance groaned as he looked again at the chicken scratches
on the letter. "I think we're going to need more time. I can't
make this out."

Ronnie took the letter from him, leaned closer and squinted
her eyes. "The signature at the bottom says . . . it could be . . .
Dantalion. But I'd never have said that if John hadn't written
that name to us."

By the time she finished studying it, the waitress was back
with their meals, along with paper and pencil. "My boss said
you're welcome to the paper at no cost, but he'd like the pencil
back."

"That will be fine, thank you." Ronnie set it all aside and
dug into her breakfast.

After they'd finished eating, both of them poured a fresh
cup of coffee, Ronnie went back to her deciphering. Moments
later, seeing her struggle, Chance finally said, "We have to take
the note home. Whatever the trouble from that man who attacked us, the one possibly named Bert Collins, the fact that
our bedroom got shot up is enough to keep him in jail for a
while. Our problem is back in New Mexico Territory at the
CR. We need this evidence more than the Denver sheriff does."

"He would be furious if he knew we were taking it. Maybe if I found a magnifying glass and spent more time studying it, I could—"

"We don't have more time, Ronnie."

"We don't?"

"The train leaves in less than an hour, and it'll take us most of the time we have left to get there."

"I know you're itching to get home, Chance, but the doctor wants at least another week in this smaller cast before you leave." She reached up and rested her hand on his cheek. "I want us to stay for as long as Dr. Radcliffe says we should—I want you to heal straight and strong."

"And I want to get back to Skull Gulch and help fight for our children and for our home. We've been a long time gone."

"Our children are smart and tough because we raised them right. They'll be okay."

Chance knew this wasn't a battle of wills because they both wanted the same thing and almost equally as bad: Chance not to cripple himself with his need to rush home. Besides, he wouldn't be much help in a fight if he ruined his leg permanently.

Chance blew out a breath. "That land is the legacy I've wanted for our children, Ronnie. Now that they're fighting for it, it hurts I'm not there for them."

"I know, but we need to stay right here in Denver. Now let's go send that telegram. We can tell the children about Dantalion's name, and add Bert Collins so that Sheriff Joe can look for someone with that name. I'll explain about the trouble with the cramped handwriting."

Chance nearly smiled to hear Cole, Justin, and Sadie referred to as "the children."

"I'll tell them I'm studying it and that I'll write them a letter with more details just as soon as we have any."

He nodded, then looked down at his broken leg. "I suppose

the fact I can walk at all is a near miracle. I could have died. I could have lost my leg. I could have kept the leg, but been maimed to the point I couldn't use it. I need to be grateful." He raised his chin and looked his pretty wife in the eye. "I agree, Ronnie—I should wait for the doc's okay before I head home."

"And I'm doing my best to trust my children with this trouble." Ronnie stood and offered a hand to Chance. He caught hold and stood. "We're going to have to strike out on our own, too. It's not the doctor's fault or the sheriff's that we were found. But someone knew, Chance. Someone followed one of them. The only way to be safe is to tell no one where we're staying."

"But I'm mighty noticeable with this crutch."

She paused for a moment, lost in thought. Then she looked up at him, and a smile bloomed on her face. "I've got an idea."

"I don't have to ride in a casket again, do I?"

She shuddered, but never lost that beautiful smile. "Nope, I've thought of a better way. C'mon. Let's go send that telegram."

35

The afternoon was wearing down as they approached Skull Gulch. Justin hoped this was their last spell of fighting.

"Angie," Justin said as he swung down and went to her. With his hands securely on her waist, he lifted her out of the saddle and smiled as he lowered her to the ground. Her eyes were so pretty and blue that he forgot what he was going to say.

"What were you going to say, Justin?" She didn't even look confused as she stood there grinning at him. Which reminded him.

"Let's get married. We can go find Parson Gregory while these criminals get locked up." He looked over her shoulder to see his family watching him. They seemed to be overly entertained.

"Don't let him say the vows until we get there." Sadie sounded as stern as Ma. "Promise me, Angie. I don't trust him to remember his name."

Angie exchanged a very female sort of look with Sadie. "We'll wait, but don't linger. I'm as eager as he is." After a moment's hesitation, she added, "Can you tell Aunt Margaret to come? I'd love to have her at my wedding."

"I'll see to it." Sadie gave Angie a hug. "Welcome to the family."

Angie smiled and hugged Sadie back, then looked at Justin and reached out. He took her hand and hooked it to his elbow. Together they walked away from all the troubles.

Parson Gregory wasn't at the church, but he had a small house next door where he lived with his plump wife and three half-grown children.

"You want to get married right now?" The parson didn't seem upset. Surprised but not upset. He must be used to sudden weddings.

"Yep. Can you come to the church?" Justin smelled food cooking, and Mrs. Gregory had a wrinkled brow—probably annoyed by the interruption, if Justin had to guess, but probably also used to them. "It'll be a real short ceremony, ma'am," he told her. "You and the youngsters are welcome to come too, if you'd like."

Parson exchanged a look with his wife, who shook her head. He said, "I'll be over after I put my parson's collar on. Unless you're in need of a witness, my wife will stay home."

He shook Justin's hand, then slapped him on the shoulder in a good-natured way while nodding to Angie. "Congratulations to you both. I'll be glad to bless your marriage."

"Thank you, Parson. We'll wait for you in the church. My family will come shortly, and I've sent someone for Sister Margaret."

On their way to the church, Hank from the telegraph office came running up to them. He thrust a slip of paper into Justin's hand. "From your ma and pa."

"Thanks." Justin handed Hank a coin, looked at the folded paper for a long moment, then shoved it into his shirt pocket, unread. He took Angie's hand and walked on toward the church.

"Aren't you going to read it?" she asked.

Justin touched his pocket and felt the paper crinkle. "No, I don't think I will. I'm not telling Sadie and Cole about it neither, not until we've spoken our vows."

Once they were inside and alone, he turned to Angie and pulled her into a tight hug. "I don't want anything to stop us from getting married."

"And you think your parents' wire might?"

Justin shrugged. "It's been one thing after another ever since I proposed. I think I'll marry you first, just in case Pa orders me to come to Denver or tells me about someone else who wants to kill me."

Angie flinched.

Justin tugged her down into a pew and sat beside her. He put his arm across her shoulders and kissed her gently at first, but it got fierce by the end.

He broke off the kiss. "I'm sorry I ever said you weren't ready for the life I could offer you. You are a brave, wise woman. I'll be the luckiest man alive to have you for my wife, Angie. I can't believe I've convinced such a fine and beautiful woman to marry me."

"I wasn't that hard to convince."

Justin disagreed, but he didn't say so. Instead, he kissed her until the church door swung open. His family was here. Behind them came Sister Margaret, who rushed for Angie so quickly that Justin had to jump out of the way to keep from getting run over.

Sister Margaret hugged Angie with enthusiasm, so Justin felt good about his chances of getting her blessing. Justin wondered if Margaret even knew Angie had spent yesterday in terrible danger.

Sadie added a hug for Angie when she finally got a turn. Cole and Heath shook Justin's hand.

Parson Gregory came in and greeted the group. He'd been the parson in Skull Gulch for quite a while and knew them all well. "This is the second Boden wedding we've had in a short time." The parson looked from Sadie to Heath. "I regret your parents aren't here. How are they doing?"

Justin remembered the telegram in his pocket from his ma and pa. In fact, it seemed to heat up and make him itch. Usually a telegram contained important news, especially since Ma had been writing regularly, and even Pa a few times. He had a strong need at that second to pull out the wire and read it. He fought back the urge. He had to marry Angie before anything else stopped him.

He took her arm and said, "I think we're ready for the service, Parson." Justin smiled down at Angie. He nearly dragged her up front to where they'd speak their vows to each other.

Yet she seemed as ready as he was, so there wasn't a lot of dragging.

"Sadie and Aunt Margaret, will you stand beside me while we have the ceremony?" Angie asked, and both ladies hurried forward.

Well, that forced Justin to ask Cole and Heath. Not that he didn't want them. He just hadn't thought of such a thing. He figured they'd be fine sitting in the front row.

With a nod, Parson Gregory said, "It's nice to see you here, Sister Margaret."

He began the vows. As he spoke the age-old words, Justin took a minute to ask God for forgiveness, for protection for his family, and finally protection for himself just in case he should've shown Cole the telegram earlier.

"I now pronounce you man and wife."

He was married. Finally.

He kissed his bride, who kissed him right back and then hugged his arm where she held him tight.

When they got outside, Sister Margaret gave Angie one last hug before heading back to the orphanage. The parson skedaddled home. He was probably only a few minutes late for supper.

It was only family now, so Justin said, "Everybody, wait." He was sorely tempted to put it off, but instead he pulled the telegram out of his pocket. "I got this wire right before the wedding. I ain't read it yet."

Cole, being his usual rude self, snatched it. "It's from Ma." Cole looked up, alarmed. "Someone tried to kill them last night."

The group of Bodens—Justin counted Heath as a Boden now, even if he had the wrong last name—gasped and stepped closer to Cole.

"Ma says they found a letter on the attacker before they locked him up. She thinks the name Dantalion is there, but she's not sure because the writing is so small and cramped it's hard to read."

Cole turned to Justin. "Sounds like the same sort of writing we found on Dantalion."

"Which means your parents' attack is connected to what's going on here." Heath slid an arm around Sadie and pulled her close.

"Ma says she'll send us a letter with more details. It should arrive in a few days. She's convinced Pa to stay in Denver another week, although the doctor is pushing for longer than that." Cole thrust the telegram back in Justin's hand. "The telegraph office is closed now. We should've sent a reply earlier. This wouldn't have slowed up the wedding much, Justin—why didn't you show it to me?"

"Because I've been trying to get this woman to marry me for a while now and something keeps preventing it."

"It's really just been two days," Angie reminded her new husband.

"Well, it's been a mighty *long* two days, and I was afraid if anything held us up, you'd get kidnapped again or one of us would get shot at or someone would start a revolution right over our heads."

"Who sent a man to kill Pa?" Cole wanted to know. "This so-called revolution could be someone just trying to confuse things. I see no evidence of it myself."

"Locking up Alonzo, Watts, and Windy, plus the man in Denver might put an end to it all then?" Justin hated to be optimistic.

"We know someone was paying Dantalion, who in turn was paying Watts. That first night we caught him, he was angry when we told him how much Dantalion had been paid, who then offered Watts so little. But we still don't know who hired Dantalion."

"We do know that the main outlaws involved are all locked up," Heath said. "Let's go home, give Justin and Angie a nice evening and some time alone before we go to war again. Cole, you can come to town in the morning and wire your ma. Then you need to get to studying that notebook and all the other writing we found on Dantalion."

"I'm trying. I haven't been able to make out some of the words, and the ones I can read don't tell me nuthin'."

"I'll get a letter written by then, too." Sadie headed for her horse. "I'll tell her we caught those men and that she missed another wedding. That way she can have more news besides the telegram you're sending."

Justin barely heard them. All he could think of was Angie and their nice evening together. He felt dizzy just thinking about it, which didn't stop him from striding for his horse. And it sure didn't stop him from keeping hold of his wife.

The bright side was that Cole hadn't even come close to punching him. It probably meant he was still a little slowed down from being shot.

"Let's go." Justin and Angie were riding home whether the rest of the group came along or not. "Tomorrow we start again with our investigating and questioning. Someone had to hire that man in Denver, and someone had to pay Dantalion to begin with. But tonight we celebrate our wedding."

Epilogue

Rosita had supper ready for them when they arrived home. Angie just now realized the Bodens hadn't picked Rosita up on their way to town because they cut an hour off the trip by not riding past the CR.

Which meant the sweet lady hadn't been invited to the wedding. Angie apologized to her.

Rosita sniffed in response. "I wouldn't have come anyway. I'm not leaving this house undefended ever again." Rosita then smiled as she pulled Angie into her arms. "Welcome to the family, little one," she whispered. "You are a fine match for my Justin. I'm so glad you aren't hurt. I've prayed for you all, but none more than you in the clutches of those desperados."

"Thank you, Rosita." Touched by the kind words, Angie returned the hug. "I needed God with me today, and of course He is always there. Yet the prayers from all of you had to help because I never gave in to panic. Somehow my thoughts were clear, and I never stopped listening to His guidance."

"I've made a fine supper. I knew you were on the trail most of the day, so I planned on having a hungry crowd. I believe it is good enough for a wedding celebration."

Rosita had fried chicken and mashed potatoes with gravy full of crunchy browned coating from the chicken. She'd made a cake too, for no reason except, she claimed, a deep need to keep her hands busy while her thoughts followed the day's troubles.

The meal was a celebration of the wedding but also of having those villainous men finally locked up.

Justin didn't let the celebrating go on for too long, however. He rose from the table, and with Angie's hand firmly in his, he said, "My new wife and I want to spend some time alone together this evening, so good night. This has been a time a man remembers the blessing of family. I love all of you."

They all said good-night, though Angie barely heard them. She was too busy keeping up with her fast-moving husband.

When they reached his room, Angie blinked to see her few things had been moved in there. Rosita must have done it before they sat down to eat. She'd gone in and out of the kitchen a couple of times.

Justin closed the door and locked it, then pulled her into his arms. She expected him to kiss her, but instead he held her so tight it nearly hurt. But she gripped him just the same and didn't want to let go.

Finally his grip eased until he gently rocked her. "Angie, having you here, alive and well, is a blessing. I can't even put into words how worried I was when those men took you."

Smiling against his chest, she said, "I was every bit as worried as you."

"I imagine you were." Justin managed a rough laugh. "Have I told you yet how much I love you?"

"Not in so many words, but I was very hopeful that you did and you'd say it soon."

He raised his head enough to look her in the eyes. "I knew I cared about you. I knew I was desperate to protect you. I knew everything was better when you were near me, but I didn't call it 'love.' Cole had to punch me, and then he said I was in love with you."

The light in Angie's eyes dimmed a bit. "Someone had to beat you to make you realize you loved me?"

"Yep, I'm glad that chore didn't end up being yours."

"As am I, Justin." She kissed him, resigned to the fact that in some important ways, she was married to a half-wit. "And I love you, too."

His eyes went wide. "You do?"

With a sigh she said, "So you don't recognize love when you feel it, nor when you see it—am I understanding this correctly?"

Justin shrugged. "The first recognition might be slow coming, but I see it now and feel it with everything in me. Marrying you has made me the happiest man alive. The time for a man to marry, it seemed for me, was a long time gone. I'd decided there was no woman for me and I'd spend my life ranching. And then a sweet, fragile miracle fell into my arms and nothing's been the same since."

Those weren't the words of a half-wit. They were more like fine poetry. When he drew her close for another kiss, she said against his lips, "My chance for love was also a long time gone, and now here you are, filling up my whole life with love and family."

His kiss deepened then. The time for talking was past. Something much sweeter was on their minds.

About the Author

Mary Connealy writes romantic comedies about cowboys. She's the author of THE KINCAID BRIDES, TROUBLE IN TEXAS, and WILD AT HEART series, as well as several other acclaimed series. Mary has been nominated for a Christy Award, was a finalist for a RITA Award, and is a two-time winner of the Carol Award. She lives on a ranch in eastern Nebraska with her very own romantic cowboy hero. They have four grown daughters—Joslyn, married to Matt; Wendy; Shelly, married to Aaron; and Katy, married to Max—and four precious grandchildren. Learn more about Mary and her books at:

maryconnealy.com
facebook.com/maryconnealy
seekerville.blogspot.com
petticoatsandpistols.com

Sign Up for Mary's Newsletter!

Keep up to date with
Mary's news on book releases,
signings, and other events
by signing up for
her email list at
maryconnealy.com.

More From
Mary Connealy

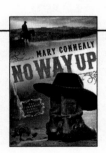

After Chance Boden is wounded in an avalanche, he
demands that the conditions of his will go into effect:
His children must either live and work at home for one
year or forfeit the ranch. He trusts Heath Kincaid to see
it done. But when Heath begins to suspect the
accident was due to foul play, he finds his desire to
protect Chance's daughter goes way beyond duty.

No Way Up
THE CIMARRON LEGACY #1

◊ BETHANYHOUSE

You May Also Enjoy . . .

After serving in the Civil War disguised as boys, the three Wilde sisters are homesteading out west with the special exemptions they earned during the war. But if anyone discovers their secret, they could lose their land . . . or worse! Will they be able to overcome the obstacles ahead—and possibly, find love?

WILD AT HEART: *Tried and True, Now and Forever, Fire and Ice* by Mary Connealy

Miss Permilia Griswold, the wallflower behind *The Quill* gossip column, knows everything that goes on in the ballrooms of New York. When she overhears a threat against the estimable Mr. Asher Rutherford, she's determined to warn him. Away from society's spotlight, Asher and Permilia discover there's more going on behind the scenes than they anticipated.

Behind the Scenes by Jen Turano
APART FROM THE CROWD
jenturano.com

◈ BETHANYHOUSE

Stay up to date on your favorite books and authors with our free e-newsletters. Sign up today at bethanyhouse.com.

Find us on Facebook. facebook.com/bethanyhousepublishers

Free exclusive resources for your book group! bethanyhouse.com/anopenbook

More Historical Fiction

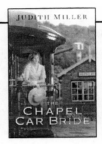

Hope Irvine always sees the best in people. While traveling on the rails with her missionary father, she attracts the attention of a miner named Luke and a young mine manager. When Luke begins to suspect the manager is using Hope's missions of mercy as a cover for illegal activities, can he discover the truth without putting her in danger?

The Chapel Car Bride by Judith Miller
judithmccoymiller.com

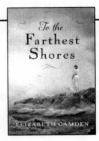

Naval officer Ryan Gallagher broke Jenny Bennett's heart six years ago when he abruptly disappeared. Now he's returned but refuses to discuss what happened. Furious, Jenny has no notion of the impossible situation Ryan is in. With lives still at risk, he can't tell Jenny the truth about his overseas mission—but he can't bear to lose her again either.

To the Farthest Shores by Elizabeth Camden
elizabethcamden.com

After being unjustly imprisoned, Julianne Chevalier trades her life sentence for exile to the French colony of Louisiana in 1720. She marries a fellow convict in order to sail, but when tragedy strikes—and a mystery unfolds—Julianne must find her own way in this dangerous new land while bearing the brand of a criminal.

The Mark of the King by Jocelyn Green
jocelyngreen.com

◆ BETHANYHOUSE

CPSIA information can be obtained
at www.ICGtesting.com
Printed in the USA
LVOW08*1446170217

524629LV00009B/105/P